Pan's Revenge

GENRE: YA/FANTASY

This book is a work of fiction. Names, places, characters and incidents are either the product of the author's imagination or are used fictitiously. Any resemblance to actual people, living or dead, businesses, organizations, events or locales is entirely coincidental.

PAN'S REVENGE

ANNA KATMORE

ALSO BY ANNA KATMORE

play with me

Some time before I started writing Neverland, I asked my readers to lend me their names for some of the characters. It was totally amazing how many of them answered to that post. Unfortunately, there aren't as many characters in this book as I got beautiful names and the choice was incredibly hard.

Here's who made it into the book...

Angelina McFarland
(Angel, the heroine)

Brittney Renae Goff
(The fairy bug, one of the twins)

Paulina
(The honey bunny, one of the twins)

Tameeka Taylor
(Tami, the pixie)

Remona Karim and Karima Olayshia Bre'Shun
(The fairy sisters)

There's a place in my mind that I call *Neverland*.
It's where I go to when I turn off reality and meet those
many special friends of mine, whose stories I try to bring
to life for you in every new book.

I'm forever thankful that I'm holding the key to that place.

Pan's Revenge

A novel by

ANNA KATMORE

ANNA KATMORE

Goodbye

FOR AN ENDLESS moment we just look into each other's eyes. Bile rises in my throat. Probably in hers, too, because she swallows hard and her lips start to tremble. I reach out and caress her cheek. "No tears. Not tonight," I whisper. "Let me remember you with a smile, Angelina McFarland."

She sniffs and the corners of her mouth tilt up, yet it's forced. Finding a hold on the net behind the crosspiece, she takes a cautious step toward me then flings her arms around my neck. I can't let go of the net, or we'd both tumble to the ground. It doesn't matter. I wrap my free arm around her waist and crush her to my chest. "I'll miss you," I breathe into her ear.

"Just don't forget me, Jamie."

"How could I ever?"

Against the skin on my neck I feel her tears. They break me. I reach for her chin and tilt her face up, brushing the wet trail on her cheek away with my thumb. Then I kiss her one last time. Only our lips touch for a long tender moment.

As she pulls away from me, I take off my hat and put it on her head. Now I get what I want—Angel's honest smile.

Peter leads her to the very edge of the crosspiece where she turns around to face me. Her mien is brave, though her eyes are filled with sadness. Slowly closing them, she takes a deep breath. I swallow against the pain in my throat. Then she tips backward and falls.

Gripping the net to my right, I rush forward and desperately cry out her name. But it's too late. Angel drops toward the sea beneath her. Her arms are stretched out at her sides and the skirt of her blue dress is flapping in the wind like it's waving goodbye. The pirate hat flies off her head. Swaying sadly, it follows in the wake of her fall.

A moment later, the love of my endless life submerges in the ocean.

I pray that she gets where she longs to be.

Peter Pan

THE WAVES CRASH together over Angel. There was a smile on her lips right before she dove backward into the ocean. I wonder if James saw it, too.

Against a coal-black night sky with only a few stars shining, he stands on the edge of the crosspiece, gazing down. The wind ruffles his fair hair about his face. Horror and sadness battle in his eyes. My brother—devastated? This is new. Not only to me, I realize, but also to the rest of his filthy crew. Their heads tilted, they watch him standing there and mumble to each other. Smee's brows, coppery like his shaggy hair, are knitted together as though he cares more than the others. I never thought him to be more than a mindless wingman to Hook. Now I find myself wondering if my brother actually has a real friend aboard the Jolly Roger.

Something comes to the surface of the sea and catches my attention. Light blue fabric. I draw in a sharp breath. *By the rainbows of Neverland, it can't be Angel's body floating on the waves?* Without another thought, I jump overboard and glide down to the dark water.

It's not her body. It's merely the dress she was wearing minutes ago. Our last plan seems to have worked. If Angel is gone and left the dress behind, chances are she made it back to her world.

I fish the gown out of the water and look up at James. His expression is hard. Unreadable. He turns and walks back to the mast in the middle of the crosspiece then starts descending. During our many battles in the past, I've seen him slide down on a rope, take a reckless jump, and slice through the sail with his dagger to drop to the deck. Tonight, he's climbing down the net, taking one step at a time.

After grabbing the black pirate hat with the big feather that bobs sadly on the water, I return to the ship and wait at the bottom of the mast. The captain's boots clack desolately on the floorboards as he steps down and turns to me. When I offer him the drenched dress and the hat, he slowly shakes his head.

I miss Angel. She was fun, she was different. She was pretty, and she smelled good. Still, when I look at Hook's face now, I know my grief is nothing compared to his broken heart. His throat twitches as he swallows and unshed tears glisten in his eyes.

This is probably not the best time to mention that

ANNA KATMORE

only little girls cry. When James dismisses us all with silence and walks to his quarters, quietly closing the door behind him, I hand the wet clothes to Smee and fly home.

Chapter 1

WITH A GASP, I break through the surface of the cold sea. Shaking the water out of my hair, I pedal and twist in the water, the usual disappointment coming over me fast. A few feet away, the Jolly Roger sways gently on the waves in the fading afternoon light. Again, I didn't make it. I couldn't follow Angel to London. Neverland won't let me go.

Smee throws a rope ladder down the ship's side. As I climb over the railing, he only has a smirk to cheer me up. "How many times are you going to try this, James? Have thirty-eight jumps not been enough?"

They weren't jumps, they were falls. The first time, I tried to do everything exactly how Angel had, and then thirty-seven variations of that stunt. I dropped backward, forward, head-first, stiff like a stick...I closed my eyes, grabbed a happy thought, grabbed a bad thought, a mean thought, no thought at all, but heck, the ocean keeps

ANNA KATMORE

spitting me out right where I dive in each time. And after five weeks of dropping forty feet and smacking hard on the water, my bones ache like I've had an encounter with the ship's bow. I need a break.

"You're right," I agree with Jack and slip into my boots, not caring about the wet leather pants or the drenched white linen shirt I wear. "Enough trial and error. Bring her back to shore."

Always skeptical, Smee cuts me a sidelong glance from his place by the lowest mast. "What are you going to do?"

"Have a chat with the fairies."

He saunters over and gives me my hat before tucking his hands into the pockets of his black pants. "Cap'n, why did you let the girl go, if you can't be without her?"

Yeah, why again? I shrug, my lips compressed. However, the truth is I'd rather be without Angel than see her crying for her family for the rest of her life and know that I'm the only one who could have changed that. "Sending her back was the right thing to do."

"And you do the right thing since when?" the familiar voice of a boy mocks me from behind. I spin around and face Peter Pan. Legs spread in a wide stance that is so characteristic of the fifteen-year-old, he has his fists placed on his hips and flashes a white-toothed grin from under a triangle leather hat that clashes with his grasshopper-green shirt.

"Did you come to play pirate, little brother?" I snarl, snatching the hat from his head and tossing it over to Fin Flannigan, its rightful owner who's scrubbing the decks with Scowlin' Scabb and Whalefluke.

I haven't seen Peter since the night he helped me send Angel back, and I don't complain about it. We worked together for a good cause. It didn't make us friends or bring us any closer than we were before. The only difference—I decided he deserves a break for helping Angel and I'm not trying to kill him...for now, anyway.

Peter drags a hand through his light brown hair, setting it back to its usual windblown look. "I came to ask if you're still right in your mind."

"Oh." Surprise overrides my annoyance. "And what brings on that question?"

He reaches into his shirt pocket and pulls out my father's pocket watch.

Instantly, my interest in having Peter aboard returns. "You opened the chest?" I drawl.

He imitates my innocence. "It seems so." Then his features turn hard. "Now tell me what this shit is and why you've been after it."

For a stunned minute, I stare at his face. "You really have no idea, do you?"

Peter jerks his hand away before I can reach for the watch. I catch a glimpse of the long scar marring his upper right arm. An old wound that was my doing. Regret is a nasty sting in my chest that I don't care for, so I shove the memory away. Peter flies a few meters backward and stands on the railing across the deck. I know better than to chase him. Instead, I head for the bridge and climb the stairs, feigning nonchalance. "Did you open it?"

"The watch? Yes."

"And what does it say on the inside of the lid?"

"J.B.H." His voice is nearer. My plan worked. Peter is following me.

I glance over my shoulder and see him hovering behind. "Right. J.B.H. James. Bartholomew. Hook."

Flying over my head, Peter lands in front of me, blocking my way to the helm. "This is *yours*?"

Although my mother named me after my father, she spared me his middle name. I roll my eyes at Peter's lack of noticing the obvious and drawl, "Yes, Peter. It's mine."

If nothing else, my wry look and heavy sarcasm get him on the right track. "It's father's pocket watch," he says, the spirit gone from his voice.

"Look who's a genius." At my push, he steps aside. Wrapping my fingers around the wheel's handles, I steer the Jolly Roger toward Neverland. Only the sun's top curve still peeks above the horizon, its light blinding me. I squint and glance over my shoulder at Peter. "Can I have it now?"

"What for?"

"Souvenir."

He quirks his brows. "I don't think so."

"I don't care what you think. Give me the watch."

As I spin around, Peter jumps back to safety. "Nuh-uh!" He waggles his finger at me, gliding out of my reach.

Yeah, it would have been too easy. I heave a sigh and pinch the bridge of my nose. "Listen, Peter. Since you're only a pain in my ass again, why don't you just flitter back to the jungle?" Without looking at him, I wave my hand dismissively in the air. "Stick with those guys who can actually stand you." *And stay out of my sight, for God's sake.* I have more pressing matters than breaking that stupid spell anyway. I must find a way out of Neverland and follow Angel.

During the past few days one thing has become clearer and clearer to me: I can't be without her. I didn't even take the time to retrieve my treasure from the cave in the rocks north of Mermaid Lagoon. The good thing is Peter doesn't know that I know where it is, so for now it's safe out there.

"Ah, the girl's gone and you're back in your eternally miserable mood," Peter says. "How could I ever, even for a minute, think that something had actually changed?"

Pressing my lips together, I give him a tight smile and shrug.

"However, I can't do that," he tells me then.

"You can't do what?"

"Go back to the jungle."

ANNA KATMORE

"Why the hell can't you?"

Peter lands on the railing, sits down cross-legged, and props his elbows on his knees, resting his chin in his cupped hands. "It's boring there."

"What the f—" A sudden realization strikes and I rock with laughter. "You damn little bastard. You miss her!"

"Who?" he snaps. *Yeah right.* The way he tenses and his cheeks turn pink proves he knows exactly who I mean, and that I was right.

"You only came here because you wanted to see if I found a way to bring Angel back." My laughing ebbs off. "You knew I was trying."

"You're delusional."

"Am I?" I step toward him and give him a push he didn't expect. Knocked backward off the railing of my ship, he drops a few feet but steadies himself in the air quickly and shoots back up. I brace my hands on the railing so we're eye to eye. "Then tell me why you suddenly prefer to hang out with me of *all* people, when you could surround yourself with your crazy bear-friends and the sparkling pixie instead."

Peter holds my challenging stare for a couple of seconds then flies around me and stands behind the wheel, turning it gently and correcting our course toward the island. "Do I need a reason?"

He doesn't look at me. So much trust is tempting. I

could skewer him from the back. Or behead him. My fingers close around the handle of the sword attached to my belt. It would only take a swipe of my arm—

The devil knows why I don't do it. My teeth clenched, I loosen my grip on the sword and shove Peter away from the helm to take over, keeping the Jolly Roger close and parallel to the shore a little outside the port. Brant Skyler drops anchor and, together with Fin Flannigan, he extends the gangplank.

My glance skates across the decks in search of my first mate. Jack sits across from Gurglin' Doug, a barrel placed between them, their elbows propped on top of the barrel and their faces red like cooked crabs as they arm wrestle. The crew is surrounding them and the men bark their support.

"Smee!" I shout across the length of the ship, dragging his attention away from Gurglin' Doug who, in that moment, wins the battle. At my beckoning, Smee rises from the low stool and meets me by the gangplank.

"Because of you, I lost my dinner to Doug in a wager," he snarls at my face. "So this better be important."

"It is. I need your help with something."

"Not the fairies!" He lifts his hands, palms out, and takes a defensive step backward.

The way those wood women turn my men into whining wimps makes me chuckle. "No. It's not them. Not yet. I need to get something first."

I can't go to the fairies empty-handed. It was a full moon last night and I still owe them the bathwater of a toddler for the answers they gave me last time—the ones we needed to send Angel home. What the hell are they brewing with bathwater? Their list of ingredients for their crazy potions gets weirder by the day.

"Fine." Appeased, Smee lets go of a sigh through one side of his mouth. "But just so you know, I'm eating your ration of food tonight."

I roll my eyes, not contradicting him.

"Where are you going?" Peter asks, still gliding above my head like a freaking seagull as I fetch my cape from where it hangs over the railing.

"Running an errand," I growl. "And since I can't seem to get rid of you, you may as well come with us. Be useful, for once."

Smee's footsteps sound behind me on the gangplank as we walk down to land. Peter, of course, prefers to fly. As we near the evening buzz on Main Street, I stop and tilt my head up. "By Davie Jones' locker, would you get your feet down on the ground, Peter Pan! I'm not walking to town with you hovering above us like a fuckin' bird!"

Scowling, he sinks to the street and falls in step with us as we head on. "So what exactly is it you need?" he wants to know. "A new frock for the vain captain?"

Ignoring his taunt, I tell them about the bathwater for the fairies and my plan to get some. "Women tend to bathe their children in the evening, right? It's almost dark so it's the best chance we have. One of us distracts the mother, the others get the water."

Smee casts me a wry look. "And how are we to take the water away? Cup it with our hands and carry it all the way through the forest?"

"Good question." I stop and pivot, searching for a jar. Down by the pub, several men dressed in tatters laugh and sing. Loaded to the gunwales, they are leaning against each other for support. One of them carries an almost empty rum bottle. That's all I need.

Heading toward them with my first mate and Peter following, I slow down and join in the drunk men's laughter. I lean my arm on one booze buddy's shoulder and say in equally slurred speech, "What ye got goin', man?"

"Jus' a li'l celebratin' with me friends," the man answers. "Me wife kick' me out like a mangy dog las' nigh'!" His breath is foul and thick with rum, his shirt torn and stained with the remains of a greasy meal. Any good woman would kick him out at first chance.

When he squeezes his blood-shot eyes closed and lifts the rum bottle in salute, I take it from him and slip it under my cape. He doesn't even notice, so I suppose there's no need for excuses and head on with Jack and Peter who are waiting a few steps away.

As we turn into an alley a little later, we all peek

ANNA KATMORE

through the windows lining the street. Some of them have drawn curtains and it's impossible to tell what's going on behind. They aren't the kind of house we're going to enter.

Peter is the first to call, "Here's what we need!"

Smee and I join him by a two-story house with crumbling yellow plaster. It has a Venetian balcony on the second floor, and the door stands ajar. In a rundown kitchen on the ground floor, there's a slim woman with braided black hair and wrapped in a simple gray dress. She's bathing a toddler in a small metal tub that stands on the kitchen table.

"All right. Here's what we do," I begin. "Peter, you fly up to the balcony. Get inside and make some noise to draw the woman's attention. Smee, you and I will climb through the kitchen window and scoop up some water once she's gone."

"Aye," Smee replies and Peter nods. While he flies upward, I take the cork of the rum bottle between my teeth and pull. It comes out with a squeak. Spitting it to the side, I wash down the mouthful of rum that was still left. "You couldn't have shared that bit?" Smee scoffs.

Sharing isn't in me. I answer with the parody of a smile and down the last drop. My first mate rolls his eyes. Then we hear the sound of glass breaking inside the house.

"Melina?" the woman shouts over her shoulder.

"That wasn't me, mother!" a girl's voice replies. "It

came from upstairs!"

"Come in here and watch your brother while I take a look."

When a girl, seven years old or less, walks into the kitchen, the woman dries her hands on her apron and hurries out of the room. That wasn't part of my plan. Well, there shouldn't be any trouble in dealing with a child. The moment she turns her back on the window, I crack it open and cautiously slide it up until Smee and I can duck through. We're standing right behind her when the little boy's attention focuses on us and, of course, the girl notices. She spins around. Her face turns pale like the stone floor.

Damn. Holding her stare, I place my forefinger over my lips. "Shh."

Yeah, like she really would... The child sucks in a lungful of air then screams as if I'd used my sword to threaten her. On second thought, it might have been the better way to go about this. It only takes a couple of seconds for the mother to rush back downstairs and into the kitchen, making the room uncomfortably crowded.

It's my hat she seems to focus on first, then her gaze lands on Jack next to me. Horror flashes in her eyes. "Melina! Run! Get help!"

The kid turns on the spot and dashes out of the room.

Smee steps in front of me, placating the woman with

ANNA KATMORE

his palms out. "Please, be quiet, lass! We only need a little of the water."

Now her jaw drops, but she recovers in the blink of an eye. "The hell you do! Get out of my house!" She grabs a vase from the counter and throws it at Smee who dodges it, putting me in the line of fire. Luckily, I catch the vase, fumbling with it before placing it on the end of the counter.

"Listen," I start. That's all I get out before she fetches a broom out of nowhere and smacks Jack hard on the head. His yelp echoes in the room as he protects his head from a second hit. Jumping out of the wench's reach, I circle the table and dip the empty rum bottle into the tub. The boy starts crying.

No more than an inch of water flows through the bottle's mouth before I feel the hard knock of the broom across my back. Whirling about with the bottle in my hand, I curse. "Damn, lady! That hurts!"

"I'll show you what hurts, you drunken bastards!" She comes after us with her broom once more, chasing us around the kitchen. My hat tears off my head as I run, and there's no time to find it.

Ducking her blows, Smee and I fight our way to the window and jump outside. Peter hovers in the street, eyes wide. "What the hell did you two do?"

"Move!" I shout at him as I drop from the windowsill and land on Smee. Getting to my feet, I try to run, but my cape nearly chokes me. The mad woman holds a fistful of the fabric in her bony hand.

She leans out of the window, her black braid dangling from her nape. "Take that, you bloody bastard!" Pain explodes in my head as the broom comes down on me again. Fighting against the dizziness, I pull at the strings of my cape until they come loose and I can flee, leaving the cloak behind.

An odd adrenaline rush makes me laugh as Smee grabs my sleeve and hauls me down the street with him. I cut a glance over my shoulder just as a potted plant comes flying at us. I duck and it crashes in the alley, pieces of the shattered clay exploding all around us.

The window is forcefully pulled down and behind it the curtains rush together. At the corner, we stop and I stoop over, bracing my hands on my knees, panting, the bottle still in one hand. "Sink me, that was more of an adventure than I thought we'd get."

Still gliding above our heads, Peter laughs. "You two want to be pirates? You don't even stand a chance against a woman with a broom!"

Smee grimaces. "He does have a point."

I don't know what comes over me when I grab Peter's ankle, pull him down to my side, wrap my arm around his neck, and rub my knuckles on his scalp. "We wouldn't have had to fight a wench with a broom if you'd done a better job of distracting her in the first place, little brother." This is the first time in our lives that Peter and I actually share a laugh. It's weird. A comfortable kind of weird.

"Let go, Hook! You smell like a codfish!" he yells at me between hiccups of laughter. Yet when I ease my hold on him, he accepts my arm on his shoulders for another brotherly moment.

Out of Peter's view, Smee lifts an amused brow at me. I let go of my brother and adjust my collar. A moment later, noise behind us draws my attention as a door opens. It comes from the house with the crumbled yellow plaster. The slim lady's unholy curses drift to us as my hat and cape soar out and land on the cobblestoned alley. The door bangs shut.

We wait another minute at the corner until we're sure the coast is clear, then I hurry to pick up my things.

"So, are you going to bring that to the fairies tonight?" Peter asks.

"No, it can wait until the morning. Who knows what they'd turn me into if I knocked at their door after midnight?" I shudder at the thought.

"And you think they'll tell you how to find Angel if you bring them the bathwater?"

"The bathwater is for an old debt. They probably won't tell me shit. Not until I bring them a damn rainbow."

Peter stops and stares at me. "A rainbow? From

Neverland's volcano?"

"That's what Bre'Shun said she wants, yes."

After a stunned second, a hearty laugh bursts from Pan's chest. "Now, good luck with that one, brother." With the fake salute of a sailor, he lifts in the air and zooms away across the star-dotted night sky.

It doesn't escape me that he called me brother. A first.

Angelina

IT'S ALMOST MIDNIGHT and I still can't sleep. My fingers keep finding the red glass heart I'm wearing on a necklace. A secret gift from Paulina, my five-year-old sister. Although she swears she didn't slip the chain around my neck when it appeared a few weeks ago, after she came crawling into my bed to escape nightmares one night, I'm sure it's a piece of the treasure she keeps hidden in a small chest under her bed. Every free gift from her many Disney Princess magazines goes in there—if it's not stamped, tattooed, clipped or hung on me, that is.

There's really nothing special about the glass heart. And still, it has me thinking far too much, far too late into the night. Paulina and her twin Brittney Renae told me I fell off the balcony that night in late February—the evening before I found the heart around my neck. I must have hit my head pretty hard, because I don't remember anything of that night. It's a miracle I didn't end up with any broken bones. The snow down in the garden and the sodden ground beneath must have cushioned my fall.

Restless, I push back my covers and swing my legs out of bed, turning on the light atop my nightstand. The floor is cold. A shiver races through me. Smoothing my nightdress, I pad barefoot to the mirror on my door. Do I look different since my fall? My hair is still raven-black and the tips tickle my jaw when I tilt my head. My eyes, too big and round for my face, flash the same hazel color as always. My appetite is usually meager, so my collarbones still stand out just enough to show I don't care much for the exquisite meals served in this huge house. It's been five weeks since the alleged fall. Nothing obvious has changed about me.

Still, I can feel it all the same.

Something is different.

Deep within me anchors a longing I can't place. Like I'm somewhere far away and feeling homesick. That's complete rubbish, because I'm in my room, in my house in London. I *am* home. Yet the longing gets worse each time I look at the heart pendant. Like right now.

My throat tightens. This is so weird. My lips start to tremble. I can't stop it. My vision turns misty. I blink. And a lonely tear trails down my cheek.

Maybe it's time to take off this necklace. I sniff and wipe my nose with the back of my hand, then reach behind my neck and open the clasp. The moment the glass

ANNA KATMORE

heart comes off, it feels like a very heavy burden drops off my chest. Breathing doesn't hurt any longer and I let go of a deep sigh.

Right then, a cold breeze wafts through the unlatched French door leading to my Victorian balcony and blows some sheets of paper from my desk. I spin around. The curtains, which have been drowsily hanging in their usual place all night, now dance in the wind.

This is all too crazy, and I blame it on my lack of sleep. I've never done well without enough rest. And rest is what I haven't gotten these past few nights. Swallowing hard, I cross to the window and close it, banning the cold and the wind from my room. When I climb back into bed, something hard presses into my palm.

The red glass heart. I'm still holding it tight.

Shaking my head at myself, I scurry to my desk, pull out a drawer, and place the necklace in the far back. Then I pick up the papers from the floor, adjust them to a nice pile, and drop them on top of the heart. Out of sight, out of mind. *Right?*

I bang the drawer shut and go back to bed. Sleep comes fast this time.

Chapter 2

A SHOCKWAVE rocks the Jolly Roger on the water, pulling me out of my sleep. In the blink of an eye, I sit upright in my bed, staring into darkness. The echo of a low thud sounds outside, one so loud it makes me think a part of Neverland has split off and dropped into the sea.

What the hell—

Getting out of bed, I forgo donning my shirt and boots and walk out on deck dressed only in my rough leather pants. Everything is quiet. We're still anchored close to the seaport. The sails are curled in, and the crew is asleep in their quarters. Nobody so much as peeks outside. I couldn't possibly be the only one who heard the noise. *Could I?*

My gaze skates out to the quiet sea. No wind, no waves, no sound whatsoever. Everything is too quiet. The thought that it only happened in my dreams takes up room in my mind. But how is that possible, when it felt so real? So final. I still bear the goosebumps from it.

Rubbing the chill from my arms, I walk back into my cabin and light a candle. It's twenty minutes past midnight. That means I went to bed less than an hour ago. *Ah no...* Dragging my hands over my face, I sit on the edge of my bed, then slump backward and stare at the ceiling. *Not another sleepless night.* Recently, I've really had too many of them. As expected, however, the night wears on and sleep stays away.

In the morning, my eyes burn like someone washed them out with rum, my head aches, and I'm in no mood to join my crew, who started working and shouting on deck with the first sunrays sparkling on the ocean's surface.

With a stretch that helps my stiff limbs a little, I walk to the small table by the wall and pick up the white shirt hanging over the back of the chair. I could wear it today. Or...I could do what I've done every morning these past few weeks: breathe in what's left of Angelina McFarland's soft scent. She wore this shirt on her last night in Neverland, and I just can't find it in my heart to let go of this final keepsake. No, I'm not going to wear it and ruin the last of Angel's scent clinging to the fabric. Pressing the crumbled shirt to my lips, I squeeze my eyes shut and breathe a kiss into it. Then I drape it over the back of the chair once again and go to my closet to find another shirt to wear.

Black is the color that draws me today. The buttons of the well-worn shirt I choose slide easily through their holes. No sweet memories are connected with this garment. All the better. With my hat under my arm and the bottle of bathwater in my hand, I leave my quarters and head for the gangplank.

Smee falls in step beside me. "Off to see the fairies, Cap'n?"

I nod. "Take command until I'm back."

"Aye."

The wooden board jolts under my jogging steps as a briny wind wafts into my face. I may not be bringing a rainbow this time, but with any luck Bre'Shun will be willing to barter more answers for something else.

Bypassing the sleepy town, I take a turn for the forest behind the port. Mushrooms and tiny wild flowers litter the mossy ground left and right of the narrow path leading deeper into the woods. High up in the brittle branches of an oak tree, a raven peeks down at me with beady eyes. It pushes out a single, hoarse croak, announcing that I'm about to enter the most bewitching part of Neverland.

Daylight struggles to break through the ever-thicker trees and bushes. It's darker here than anywhere else on the island, and cold. The strange thing is, instead of that raising the feeling of discomfort in me, like one would expect when walking through a forest that seems to have eyes and ears, a homey sensation fills me. This phenomenon surprises me each time I come here. It's like the entire forest strives to bribe me into staying. And part of me wants to give in.

Another part of me, and it's actually a much bigger part, urges me to hurry, get what I need, and leave again so I can continue searching for a way to get to Angel.

"Captain Hook," a soft voice coos beside me.

I whirl about and face one of the fairy sisters with hair so fair and smooth it reminds me of silvery waterfalls. "Remona," I say and acknowledge her with a nod.

"Bre'Shun will be delighted about your visit." She purses her pale green lips and tilts her head. "Where's the rainbow?"

"Remona, where are your good manners? He hardly stepped a foot into the forest," a voice gently echoes all around us. "Welcome back to the empire of fairies, James."

I spin on the spot to find the source of the voice, but I'm still alone with Remona. Or so it seems, until a butterfly with silky purple wings lowers to Remona's open palm. Frowning at the tiny creature, I take a step closer. "Um...Bre?"

"Oh, James Hook, you silly boy." An ice-cold hand lands on my shoulder and warm laughter chimes in my ear. "I am many things. A shapeshifter is certainly none of them."

I pivot to my old friend while, from the corner of my eye, I see Remona closing her fingers around the butterfly, scrunching it in her fist. She lets the resulting dust run through her fingers. From each grain of the purple powder raining to the forest floor, another new butterfly is born, and together they flutter away through the specks of light beaming through the leaves and branches. Remona skips after them.

My jaw drops in fascination. Bre'Shun lifts my chin with one of her cold fingers and closes my mouth. Only now, my focus is truly on her and, as always, her beauty and unearthly appearance take my breath away. Her honey-golden locks are wound up to the top of her head today, with a few careless strands framing her pale face. Turquoise eyes pierce mine as she smoothes the bodice of her burgundy dress and smiles.

"I can't smell a rainbow on you," she says in a soft voice. "You didn't find the time to collect one for me then?"

Grimacing, I rub the back of my neck. "Well, no. I was—"

"Busy." She inclines her head, still friendly and in no way looking disappointed. "I understand."

If I learned one thing from the fairies, it is that time is irrelevant to them. They know where they are going and it doesn't matter in the least how long it takes them to get there. I wish I could say the same about myself.

Her gaze lowers to the rum label on the bottle in my hand. Quickly, I lift it and tell her with newfound enthusiasm, "I got your bathwater."

"I can see that." Her eyes grow bigger with joy. "Hopefully, you washed the rum out of the bottle before you filled it with water. Rum is a nasty addition to any potion. One never knows what side effects it causes."

A traitorous heat rises to my neck. It's probably best not to answer that.

Taking the bottle away from me, Bre places one of her cold-as-heck hands on my back and steers me to the right, sweeping her other arm invitingly. There's nothing in this forest that should really surprise me, and yet I take in a sharp breath when, out of thin air, her tiny white house with a straw roof and a white picket fence appears.

Together, we stroll through the front garden where daisies grow all over the place. The low wooden door forces me to stoop so as not to bang my head when walking through. From the outside, one would expect to find a room no bigger than a doghouse, but entering the home of a fairy is like walking into a palace. A pleasant scent of mint and coriander greets me in the familiar hall with a chessboard floor of black and white tiles.

Bre'Shun has me sit at the big round glass table. It's the place where bargains are made.

"May I offer you a cup of tea, James Hook?" she says, steepling her fingers in front of her smile and lowering into the iron chair opposite me.

There's no time to decide if I'm up for her mystic

brew that will make me spot another piece of furniture inside this house at each sip, just like the last time I came here, with Angel. An elegant white porcelain cup on a saucer painted with tiny flowers appears on the table in front of me. Ignoring decency and conventions, I close my eyes and down the whole cup of tea at once. Full of expectations, I open my eyes again and...still, I'm surrounded by cold stone walls and a chessboard floor. Where's the neat and cozy house of a fairy this hall should have turned into? I blink several times. Nothing changes.

"Is there something wrong with the tea?" I ask.

"Why, no. It's peppermint tea. Known for its refreshing effect. What did you expect to happen when you drank it?" Her brows quirk. There's an unmistakable edge of mockery in her voice. "That animals of the forest would storm the house and flitter about in here?" She laughs. And I feel stupid.

Fortunately, she changes the topic. "What can you do for me, James?"

"Obviously, not much. I don't have the rainbow." Leaning back in the chair, I fold my arms over my chest. "Still, I need some answers. And urgently."

"Oh, don't you say that, James. A rainbow isn't everything. You have so much more to give." She rises from her seat and sweeps her arm to the back of the hall, where a tall door appears. "Come."

Never, in all the many times I have visited, have I

ever gotten to peek into another room of this house. The iron legs of the chair scrape on the tiles as I shove back and stand. The glass table disappears the moment I circle it to follow Bre through the door that opened of its own accord.

With the first rays of warm light gracing my face, it's clear we're not walking into another room of the house, but outside again. And what's more, we seem to be entering a totally different place than where we started inside the forest. This spot opens to the sky, no treetops blocking out the sun here.

There is a tremendous vegetable patch—actually several of them—with pebbled paths leading through the greenery. Farther back in the garden, a few tall trees stand like trolls, watching over us. Behind them...it's dark. Nothing at all to see on either side of the garden. This is a spot of light in the middle of darkness. I whistle through my teeth.

Bre'Shun acknowledges my amazement with a beam of her own. She leads me to a stone fireplace beside the vegetable patch, close to the house, where a black cauldron bears some herbal-smelling soup. She stirs it several times, producing funny bubbles that explode on the surface. The color of the soup has me frowning. Because it has no color at all. It's clear. Clearer than water. Even clearer than air. Suddenly I wonder how I can even see that it's liquid. And then the bubbles... I shake my head.

"So you want to know why Neverland won't let you go," Bre'Shun states as if the question is tattooed on my forehead. Obviously, there's nothing more to say, so I lift one eyebrow. Bre mirrors that move then smiles. "Would you allow me to cut a strand of your hair?"

If that brings me in any way closer to Angel, I don't mind. "Go ahead."

She produces scissors from a pocket of her dress, which I believe is nothing other than a big pleat she uses to cover her magic from me. She cuts the strand of my blond hair that constantly falls over my left eye. "Now, isn't that better?"

I give her a disbelieving stare.

Her mouth curls up. Then she holds my hair over the soup until the ends catch fire. Letting go of the thin strand so it trickles into the potion, she says, "Neverland's gates are closed. Peter Pan sealed them when he decided he wouldn't grow up."

"Fantastic. So because of the brat he used to be, I can't get away?"

"So it seems."

Frustrated to my bones, I rub my hands over my face. "What can I do to open the gates?"

Blatantly ignoring me, Bre skims some of the soup with a wooden ladle and sniffs the potion, closing her eyes. Next, she takes a tiny sip and swishes the liquid inside her mouth. "Too feminine," she points out with knitted brows like I should have any clue as to what this means. Then she holds the ladle in front of my mouth. "Spit."

I know better than to question a fairy and do as I'm told. Bre dips the ladle into the cauldron, stirs a few more times, and then tastes the soup again, cutting a distracted glance to the sky.

"Mm-hmm. Much better." She samples another mouthful. "You know what would make this perfect?" Her tone is meaningful, almost a whisper. "The dirt of a sailor." Quickly, she reaches for my hand and twists it, inspecting my palm. Her face turns sad in an instant. "Your hands are way too clean, James Hook."

"Yeah, I actually do wash. Sorry."

Not in the least stung by my sarcasm, she slaps her fist into her open palm. "Too bad."

Too bad for me, because I won't get more answers, or too bad for her, because I failed to make this potion taste more manly?

"Is there a way to open the gates of Neverland?" I ask to bring her back to my problems and away from hers.

"Of course there is." She cocks her head, giving me an eerily long once-over. From the vegetable patch beside her, she picks a lettuce leaf and rubs it hard and fast over my forearm. My skin turns red and starts itching. However, in the expectation of help, I hold still. Bre'Shun sniffs the leaf after half a minute, then rubs it some more on my arm, and finally dumps it into the soup. "You have to get Peter to break the spell," she says matter-of-factly and tries a mouthful of the soup once more, obviously pleased with the result. "Or kill him," she adds then, with not the least bit of remorse in her voice. She turns to smile at me. "Your call."

I freeze on the spot. The fairies are a little...special...and sometimes just don't act as one would expect them to, but this is hardcore, even for Bre'Shun. "I'm not going to kill my little brother."

"Why not? You've been after his life for nearly as long as you can remember."

"Yes, but—"

"But what?" She lifts a brow at me.

"Things have changed."

"Have they? Or have you, James Hook?" Her laugh sounds like dripping water in a jungle. She skims some of the cooking potion and pours it into a watering can that's already half full with water. Picking the can up, she loops her other arm through mine and leads me away from the steaming cauldron.

On our walk through her garden, small tags tied on twigs stuck into the ground at each different patch catch my attention. *Beckon beans. Pleasure berries. Carrots of terror.* Apart from having answers to every possible question, the fairy sisters are also known for their crazy potions and wondrous fruits. So this must be where they grow it all.

ANNA KATMORE

Bre'Shun walks with me to the back of the light-suffused place, where a young tree grows in the shadows of others. It only reaches to my belly button and bears just three juicy leaves.

"This is the tree of wishes." She waters its roots from the can she brought. Instantly, the tiny tree shoots up a couple of feet, and then a few more.

"Sink me, what was that?"

Bre beams. "You have some very healthy spittle, James Hook."

"I did that?"

"Oh yes." She brushes my arm. "Trees grow best when they have a man to rule them."

I don't understand one word, and I don't want to either. What intrigues me more is what this tree can do. "Tree of wishes, you said? Is that a random name you gave it, or is there a deeper meaning?"

Putting down the watering can, Bre stems her fists to her slim waist and tilts her head. "What do you think, James? That I take a sip of creativity juice every morning and then give common plants exotic names?"

At her wry look, I gulp and shake my head.

"This little fellow here will soon carry fruit. With the potion you just helped me hone, it might happen within the next month...instead of the usual ten years we have to wait on a new tree." She turns and starts to walk back toward the house. "Bring the can," she tells me over her shoulder. I hurry to follow her and hear more about the tree. "Once the fruits are ripe and a person eats one, they can make a wish. But beware, wishes are tricky. Remona ate a fruit a hundred and ten years ago. She wished she wouldn't have to work around the house or help me in the garden for a decade."

"Did she get that wish fulfilled?"

"Oh yes, she did." Bre's face scrunches up. "She caught a nasty disease that bound her to bed for ten years. Good thing she didn't wish for a century..."

This is totally weird and yet so fascinating. I'm thinking about the wish I would make if given the chance. I sure would word it right, avoiding all possible side effects.

"It won't help you find Angel," Bre states dryly, dashing all my hopes in a millisecond. "I told you what you have to do first. And then bring me a rainbow. You shall be able to find her then."

Taking off my hat, I run my hand through my hair. "This is impossible. How can I ever catch a rainbow?"

"Nothing is impossible, James Hook. You only have to *do* it." Bre'Shun leads me through the high hall in the tiny house back to the front door. Before we exit together, I glimpse a fluffy brown rabbit with hanging ears and a trembling little tail sitting in the corner. A fox is lying on the stony windowsill. *The tea?* I'll never get used to this place.

ANNA KATMORE

By the gate in the picket fence, the fairy squeezes my hand as she says goodbye. Another ice-cold shiver zooms through my limbs, and I lick my lips, which feel cold and numb. They may have turned blue from what I can tell. Slipping my hand out of hers, I turn and start to walk away.

Bre'Shun's voice follows me. "Get him to break the spell, Jamie, and you are free to go."

If only it was that simple. I slide a glance over my shoulder. Her gaze is on me, friendly yet intense. Mystical. It raises a bad feeling inside me. "There's more, isn't there?" I say in a low voice as I stop walking.

Bre inclines her head and rubs her arms as if she's feeling the cold she emits for the first time herself. "Dear boy, there's always more."

Peter Pan

SNEAKING THROUGH THE underbrush of the jungle, I place my forefinger to my lips and then signal to Loney and Skippy behind me that the enemy is just in front. Loney pulls at the ears of his fox hat in return, showing he understands. Skippy wiggles his own big ears.

The others are merely steps away. If we attack at the right moment, we win this game, and Toby, Sparky, Stan and Tami have to cook us dinner tonight.

I chew a handful of clover, spit it in my hand, and form a lump of it, which I shove into the reed blow tube— the only weapon allowed in this game. I glide up a tree and land, hunkering on a massive branch. If I can surprise them from above, victory is under our belt. Without a sound, I crawl forward on the branch then reach out to flatten a nest of leaves in my way.

Bad mistake.

Behind the leaves, I find a sneering pixie with

ANNA KATMORE

sparkling green eyes and pointy ears sticking out of her golden locks. She has a blowpipe at her mouth and, fluttering excitedly with her gossamer wings, she spits a lump of slimy greens at the dead center of my forehead.

"Oh no! Shot through the skull!" Dropping my weapon, I fake death and plummet ten feet to the ground, where a tangle of ivy breaks my fall. Tameeka and the guys come out of their hiding spots and start howling and dancing around me like Indians around a bonfire. My team stands aside, making disappointed faces.

Great. Now I have to catch a boar to skin and roast over the fire tonight. The glowing orange sun stands low already. Better hurry.

Wrestling free from the ivy tendrils, I glide up and shout back to the Lost Boys, "Start the fire! I'll be back in an hour."

Neverland is silent beneath me. There's no rustling, no cries, nothing that gives away the hideout of our dinner. My stomach rumbles. Hunting hungry is no fun. Sinking until only a couple of meters are between the tops of the trees and me, I glide to the border of the jungle. Wild boars are known to come out at twilight and gather at the bottom of the volcano.

The only boar I find there now is Hook. And his first, second, and third mates.

With a grin on my face, I land next to them, stealing my brother's hat as I keep pace with him. "Where are we going?"

James pulls the hat off my head and shoves me hard against my shoulder, growling. I tip sideways. "Nice seeing you too," I reply.

"If you want to hang out with pirates, get your own hat. Ever touch mine again and I'll cut off your hand." Now he turns to me and smiles. "We're going to the volcano."

"Yeah, I figured that from your determined stride. What's up? Have you talked to the fairies today?"

"Yes, to one of them."

"And what did she say?"

"She said, bring me a fuckin' rainbow."

"Oh." I scratch my head. "That's bitter."

"You wouldn't know where by any luck..." Giving me a sidelong glance he shakes his head and mumbles, "No, you wouldn't."

"Know how to catch a rainbow?" I ask. He's right. I have no freaking idea. "What does she need one for anyway?"

James shrugs and starts to climb the steeper part of the volcano side. The men and I follow him. "She didn't say. Just wants me to bring her one or, it seems, I won't see Angel again."

A feeling of pity creeps over me. Considering the torn look on his face, there must be a tough battle going on inside him. Not bothered with climbing, I fly to the top and wait for the pirates to join me there. James wears a strange expression when he faces me again, and Smee's is even stranger. I wonder what they've been talking about on the climb. I get the feeling I missed something important. Should this worry me? I grin at Hook's face. *Nah...*

"Great. You made it, Captain," I cheer for him and the crew. "Only took you half an hour."

"Shut up and help me find a way to capture one of those bloody rainbows."

Neverland is tinted in sunset gold, our shadows expanded to a foreboding length. Obviously, Hook missed that little fact. I frown at him. "Not that I would know exactly how to do that, but aren't you forgetting something?"

"Like what?"

I shrug and roll my eyes. "I don't know. Maybe that the show of rainbows won't start until midnight? Which means you still have to wait—let me see..." To mock him I pull our father's watch from my breast pocket and push the tiny button that makes it snap open. "Yep. We can powwow for five more hours."

James' eyes start to glint. I've seen this look of his before. Slowly pushing the watch closed, I lower my chin and take a deliberate step back. "What are you up to?"

His expression changes fast. A smile appears. Not one that looks inviting, just the sudden glint of greed is gone. "Don't be stupid, Peter. I'm not going to steal that watch from you."

"No?" I relax a little. "That's good then."

"I want you to throw it into the volcano."

"What?" I don't know what happened to him in the fairy forest today, but it certainly tampered with his mind. "Why should I do that?"

James heaves a long sigh and drags his hands over his face. "Because it's the only way to open the gates of Neverland."

"Is that what the fairy told you?"

"Yes. So would you please just do it?"

"No!" It belonged to my father. I'm not going to toss it into the liquid core of the island. "Are you crazy?"

"One would think so, for even giving you an option," he mumbles.

I don't understand. The eerie way his second and third mates come to flank me all of a sudden gives me the creeps and I decide it's time to leave Hook alone in his fight for a rainbow. There's a boar that needs to be slain and skinned before it gets dark anyway.

Turning away, I lift into the air. After only a couple feet, though, something wound around my ankle pulls me back to the ground hard. I land on my knees. Smee, that rat's ass, must have slung a rope around my leg when I wasn't paying attention. The other end is tightly wrapped around his fist.

ANNA KATMORE

An instant later, the pirate with mermaid tattoos on both his forearms, who's called Fin Flannigan by the other filthy pirates, grabs my shoulders and holds me in place.

"Peter. Please," Hook says with insistence. "It's essential that you throw the watch into the volcano."

"So? And what if I refuse?" I wrest myself free from Fin and shove him away. As I turn around, I hear the click of a trigger and look into the mouth of James Hook's pistol. My throat goes dry.

"I don't want to hurt you, Peter," he pleads behind his outstretched arm. Then his gaze turns cold under his black hat and he growls, "But I will. You hold the key to Neverland's doors. I want to leave and find Angel, yet I can't until you destroy the watch. Now throw that piece of shit into the volcano or I swear I'm going to toss your dead body over the edge with it."

There's no chance he's joking about this, and I wonder how much more time he will give me before he shoots. Five seconds? Maybe ten? Reluctantly, I lift my hand with the pocket watch and stare at it for a tense moment. My teeth clenched and my muscles taut, I toss it to the side, into the hole in the earth that is Neverland's middle.

Golden sparks shoot out of the volcano, just enough to assure me the watch is lost forever.

When I look up, Hook has lowered the gun. "I'm sorry, Peter," he whispers. It sounds like he's not *just* referring to threatening me with the pistol. There's more. I'll be damned if I stay to question him about it. I'm done with my brother. And after the strangely good time we had together recently, I want to slap myself. Because deep inside, this betrayal hurts.

Pulling my knife from under my belt, I bend low and slice through the rope around my ankle. No one stops me. As I straighten again, James takes a step toward me.

"Go to hell, Hook," I tell him in a low voice.

I never thought I'd again see the hurt look on his face that he wore when Angel left Neverland, but how he looks at me now comes close. I don't care. Spitting at the ground before his feet, I glide up and fly away.

Zooming over the lowlands and afterward over the jungle, I break out in a sweat of rage and wrath. My molars grind against one another as the sweat grows thicker and my vision blurs. *What the heck?* This has nothing to do with the angry storm brewing inside me. I slow down, rub my thumb and forefinger across my eyes and knead the spot between them. When I try to focus again, there are black dots in my vision, and they're growing wider.

My throat is tight and dry and begins to hurt. The pain spreads deeper. My limbs feel numb all of a sudden, my back hurts, and breathing troubles me like I'm gasping for air under water.

Everything feels wrong and rubbery. Twisting in the

ANNA KATMORE

sky, I try to make out where the tree house is. I need to get home. And fast.

My chest stings as I cough in the middle of a careful descent. I have no idea where I am. Gliding too low over the treetops, I feel twigs and leaves brush against my stomach. Nausea rises from my gut, bringing with it a bitter taste of bile.

"Tami?" I call in a slight panic. She's the only one who can find me up here. Wherever I am, though, I must be too far away from home, because there's no reply.

Dismissing my usual carefree speed, I almost crawl through the air now. The smells of the jungle sting my nose. They bite their way up my nostrils, and my teeth ache like I took a punch to the jaw.

What the hell is happening to me? "Tameeka? Loney! Stan!" My voice breaks. Sinking lower, I can finally make out the highest tree in the area. *Home.* It's just a few hundred feet away. Fighting for air as much as for each meter, I try to yell for the Lost Boys again. All that comes out is a terrible croak.

Just a little farther. Almost there.

Then I fall, like there's a gap in the air. My belly smacks hard on a branch that juts out, slapping all remaining air out of my lungs. I cling onto that limb with the feeble strength left in me...but it's not enough. My body slides downward on one side and finally even my fingers give out. I have to let go.

As I plummet to the ground, I knock into more branches, each impact splitting my bones. The final smack on the jungle floor breaks my back. The pain is excruciating. I cry out.

Everything goes dark.

Chapter 3

A MILKY WHITE moon reflects on the silent surface of the sea. Standing on the main deck of the Jolly Roger, I bend forward, fold my arms on the railing, and bury my face in them. A deep sigh escapes me and turns into a moan before it's over. What the hell was I thinking pointing a gun at my brother's face? Sure, it wasn't the first time, but so much has happened the past few weeks. It doesn't feel right any longer. Quite the contrary, an uncomfortable pressure rests on my nape.

"Cap'n? The crew wants to know where we're headed."

Smee's stern voice fails to make me straighten from my bent position. "Mermaid Lagoon," I growl into the fabric of my sleeves. "And then farther north."

"You think we'll finally find London there?"

"No. The gold." As if my betrayal isn't yet complete I'm also going to steal back my treasure before setting sail to find London.

I wonder if Peter knows what's coming at him. Not just the treasure. From tonight on, he'll age again. How must that feel for a boy who never wanted to grow up? How will I feel? And the people in town? They all will take a step forward in their existence... I wonder if they'll even notice any of it. Do the pirates feel it already?

Does Smee?

I push myself up and brace my hands on the railing, glancing over my shoulder at my first mate. There's no visible change about him. Then again, it's only been a few hours since Peter tossed the pocket watch into the volcano.

Expecting a little too much, James Hook. Behind closed lids, I roll my eyes at myself.

"So it's time to take back what's ours?" Smee says delightedly. I can't begrudge him this. We've all been waiting so long for this day to come. It really should make me a great deal happier.

And here it doesn't.

"Yes. The tide is out. This is our only chance to get it. We'll have to take the dinghies to the rocks and then empty the cave. Have the crew prepared. I want this over before morning breaks."

"Aye." Anticipation is written all over Smee's face. He doesn't have to know that we're not going to spend one doubloon of the treasure on celebrating like we planned all these goddamn years. As soon as the cargo hold is loaded, we're heading farther north. It's as good a direction to start looking for Angel as any other.

Or maybe I misjudged Jack and he knows it already? He strides away with a happy tune on his lips, making up a fancy rhyme with the word *London*.

A little later we pass Mermaid Lagoon and soon the rocky peaks Angel once mentioned in her sleep appear on the horizon. They protrude from the dark water like the rotten teeth in Barnacle Breath's mouth. With this part of the sea being rockier than any other side of Neverland, there's no chance we can sail the ship all the way to the cave. The crew drops anchor while we're still in deep waters and prepares the only two dinghies we have.

In the light of burning torches, the boats take off toward the rocks. Smee is in one of them together with Fin and Walefluke. Brant Skyler, Cheatin' Wade Dawkins and Bull's Eye Ravi row the other. From the distance, I watch them land at the rocky circle and climb the first peak. When the tiny yellow spot that is the torch in Smee's hand moves up and then moments later down, I know there's no cave there.

They try three more peaks before one of the torches finally moves in a circle in the air. The signal. My heart steps up. They found the treasure's den.

Soon the little fire dots at the horizon disappear into the cave. My mouth as dry as Potato Ralph's cake, all I can do is wait for them to come back to the ship with the first load of treasure. It takes almost an hour for the men to return.

Donning my hat and cape, I await them on the main deck. When Smee climbs up the rope ladder and leaps on board, he's grinning like a drunken sailor in the arms of a lass. "Got you something," he says and gives me a shiny gold doubloon.

Slowly, I close my fingers around it, press it to my chest, and squeeze my eyes shut. "It's been a while, little treasure," I murmur under my breath. Then I pocket the coin and join in as everyone helps emptying the boats and carrying the gold and gems into the bilge. On the next ride back to the cave, I join Smee's boat and help him row, so we get there faster.

Climbing the rocks is bothersome. As soon as I slide down the rope the men dropped through the trap door to get into the cave and breathe in the delicious scent of horded silver and gold, my exhaustion is forgotten. I hunker down on top of the highest heap of treasure and run my fingers through the cool coins. Sink me, I've missed that! A smile creeps to my lips.

Puddles of seawater cover the floor. Soft splashing sounds echo in the cave as I walk about, inspecting each little piece of the booty. A long-forgotten feeling of possession overtakes me. Then my gaze lands on an open, empty little chest on the damp stone ground. My hand inches up to the spot over my sternum where the key to this chest rested for decades, hidden only by the linen of my shirt.

A sting in my heart makes me clench my teeth. Thoughts of Peter violently shove back into my mind, and it has only been a freaking half hour since I was able to kick them out of there in the first place. Picking up the chest and stroking the lid, I silently pray that my brother is all right.

In huge gunnysacks, the men pull the treasure up through the trap door and carry it down to the boats. I stay in the cave when they cart it back to the Jolly Roger. While I'm alone in the damp grotto, I sit down on a chest full of diamonds and other colorful gems and let my gaze wander about. Soon all this will be gone from here, down to the last little heap of gold. It'll be back where it belongs—in my possession.

This moment should mean everything to me. But it fails to fully cheer me up. It's not only my betrayal of Peter that quenches my joy. Also the uncertainty about Angel adds up to my misery. The spell is over, the gate to leave Neverland should be open. Will we finally be able to sail to London? Bre'Shun wants a rainbow. How could I ever bring her one? Whatever it is she needs it for, a foreboding racks me that if I ignore the fairy's request I might fail on this journey.

Still, I have to try.

The gold doubloon Smee gave me earlier is still in

my pocket. I pull it out and spin it through my fingers, murmuring, "Heads, I'll find her. Tails, I won't." I flip the coin into the air. It twists a few times, glinting in the light of the burning torch, until it lands in my palm again. The clap echoes in the cave as I smack that hand onto the back of my other. Grinding my teeth, I frown and will it to be heads.

Slowly lifting my hand, I tilt my head and peek underneath. "Goddammit!"

The coin runs through my fingers again. Then I repeat the flipping. "Be heads!" Quickly, I lift my hand to see what I got.

By Davie Jones' locker, this can't be true! A low growl erupts from my throat.

I go for a third try, this time with altered rules. Heads means I won't find Angelina McFarland, tails says I will. My lip threatens to pop between my teeth as the coin spins in the air. I catch it and smack it on the back of my other hand. "Be. Tails." I move my hand away. "Damn little bastard!"

I fling the coin against the rock face and it rebounds, landing in a puddle of water. Kneading the spot between my eyes, I squint and decide to go on this journey nevertheless.

Voices drift to me. The crew returned to move the next load of gold. I buck up. Together, we refill the gunnysacks until not another single coin will fit in them.

Some hours later, the entire treasure is gone from this place. The only thing that stays behind is the empty chest. It waits in the corner for Peter to find when he next comes here.

Grabbing the last torch from the clamp in the wall, I wind the rope around my other hand and let the crew pull me out of the cavern. The men close the trap door and place the stones back on it before we leave.

Under the additional weight, the Jolly Roger has sunken a few inches deeper into the water. She looks like a lazy old lady, pleased to be loaded with a fine meal. I stroke my hand over the railing once we've returned, feeling the cold of the dawn creeping up the back of my neck.

When I turn to walk into my quarters, I run into a creature with hair as pale as her skin and mystic, turquoise eyes that pierce mine. The cold I felt wasn't the breaking morning after all. It was her fingers tapping my neck. "Hello, James," she coos.

"Remona." It's a surprise to find her on my ship—if not a plain shock. "How did you get here?"

"I'm a fairy. How do you think?" She smiles and shrugs. "I swam."

I lift one brow at her, about to call her out on her lie since her milky white dress, her skin, and her hair are perfectly dry. At that moment, however, a flush of water swishes out of her...body. It splashes on deck, leaving her drenched from the top of her head to her bare feet.

"See?" Remona grins like a sprightly child, although she's alleged to be older than the mountains of Neverland.

"Fine. You swam here." I still don't believe her. "Why did you come?"

"Bre sent me. Said to give you these." She holds out her hand. In her open palm are three beans.

My brows knit together. "What's that?"

"They are called *beckon beans*."

The vision of a tag with that name on it in the fairies' garden surfaces in my mind. My lips stay closed as I tilt my head, prompting her to tell me more.

"If you eat one, it'll lead you in the right direction."

"What direction?"

"No idea. Left, right, north-north-west..." A smirk appears on her face.

I wonder why Bre sent her sister. She must know how this woman loves to play games and be cryptic— excessively so, even for a fairy. Is it to torture me even more? "I meant in the right direction to *where*?" I drawl.

"Oh. Why didn't you say so? They will lead you to Angelina McFarland, of course."

Of course.

"It's our gift to you for releasing Neverland from an annoying charm. Beckon beans work like a magnet. You think it, they lead you there. Oh, here's a little warning too: when you eat one, think about Angelina and not about a one-eyed troll with bad breath." Her face crumples into a knowing grimace. "You'll know which way to go then."

I take the beans from her hand and close my fingers around them so tightly, my palm begins to sweat. "You mean, if I eat them, I'll just know which course to take, right?"

"Right. It's enough to eat one at a time, though. The effect will wear off after a day."

"Then why did Bre send me three?"

"Prevision." She snaps the word like it's the most obvious thing in the world and like, in her eyes, I'm an idiot. Then her voice takes on a tired edge. "Don't forget about the rainbow, Captain." After that, she brushes past me and clumsily climbs onto the railing. With an excited squeal, she takes a dauntless jump and drops butt-first.

As I hurry forward to look down at the sea, there's no sign of the crazy woman anywhere. She just disappeared, before any splash was heard. I shake my head.

The three beans are still in my palm. I examine the tiny white things for a minute, then pick one and pop it in my mouth. It's time to put the fairy's present to the test. I'm ready to set a new course, and this little bean might just show me which to take.

Eyes closed, I hold my breath until Angel's image comes up bright and clear in my mind. In that vision, my fingers slide through her silky black hair. I kiss her tender heart-shaped mouth. Then I swallow.

The bean, tiny as it is, seems to swell to a size that gets stuck in my throat, choking me. I cough violently, dislodging it from my throat and spit it into my hand, where it lays, as tiny as before.

"Maybe you have to chew it first."

I look up and find Smee standing a couple feet away, leaning back on the railing and rolling up the sleeves of his black shirt. Too absorbed with the fairy's visit, I hadn't noticed him standing there all along. "Maybe you're right."

With a new surge of hope swamping me, I put the bean between my teeth and bite down, thinking of Angel. Immediately, a sour apple taste explodes in my mouth. I have the feeling that, if I open my lips, a gush of green saliva might come out. Tiny bubbles burst everywhere—on my tongue, against the roof of my mouth, at the top of my throat. It's hard to swallow the tingling mash.

When it goes down, I wait for something to happen. For me to miraculously know the right course to set to reach a city called London in a different world. But the only feeling that overcomes me is a quenching thirst.

Hurrying to the rum storage under deck, I gulp down half a bottle. The thirst stays, so maybe rum wasn't the right liquid. I try a jar of water next. The burning feeling in my throat doesn't go away. Instead it spreads to

ANNA KATMORE

my chest and upper gut, the strange heat of it making me double over.

Breaking out in a sweat, I return to deck and peel my shirt off in the light of the rising sun. The crew stares as if a curse has come over me. Maybe that's exactly what happened. I need something to cool me down. Water. Or wind. Yes, wind should do fine. Glancing wildly around, one thing stands out to me. The crow's nest.

Swift and practiced steps up the net take me to the very top of the main mast. My lungs expand with a deep breath. I'm still not where I long to be. Lifting my gaze to the sky, I make out the fading moon, opposite the sunrise. Naturally, it's impossible to fly to the moon—for a pirate anyway. The brewing storm inside my chest urges me to let go of the net and just try anyway. My fingers ease off the rope.

"James!"

Smee's sharp voice sucks my attention out of the sky and down to the main deck. His face is horrorstruck. Hands cupped around his mouth, he shouts, "What in the world are you doing, Cap'n?"

My gaze switches back and forth between him and the waning moon that so eerily pulls me in. My grip tightens around the ropes once more. *Blow me down, what led me to believe I could fly like Pan?*

Warily, I make my way back down the mast. Jack Smee puts his hands on my shoulders the moment my feet are back on the floorboards. "Scuttle me bones, James. What the hell was that?"

I have no answer for him, only a shake of my head and a shrug.

"Did the bean do that to you?"

It's possible. Likely, even. "I've never felt an urge so strong before." Fishing the remaining two beans out of my pocket, I open my palm and stare at them. "That's devil's work, for sure."

"Did it give you an idea where to go? Do you know the right course now?"

I lift my head and lock determined eyes with my first mate. "Hoist anchor, Smee. Set sails. We follow the moon."

Angelina

HUNCHED OVER MY essay on Shakespeare's *King Lear* for literature, I get distracted by the noises coming from the room next door. Paulina and Brittney Renae are fighting over yet another hairclip from a new princess magazine I bought them on the way home from school. It's hard to concentrate when listening to one five-year-old twin calling the other an ugly toad. A couple more years may have to pass before either of them understands just how such an insult backfires when you're a twin. Biting the backend of my pen, I chuckle then focus on the last paragraph of my paper and try to continue.

A drop falls onto the paper. Onto the words *his heart* in particular. The blue ink blurs.

Confused, I lift my gaze to the ceiling to see if water is dripping from there somehow. No sign of a leak. It would have been strange in this noble house anyway. With a tissue, I dab the damp spot on the sheet and write on.

Only seconds later, another drop lands on the paper. What the heck?

I wipe my hand over my cheek. There's a wet trail. Surprise makes me drop my pen. Why in the world am I crying? I'm feeling all right.

Gazing out through the window above my desk, I enjoy the warm caress of sunlight on my face. It's almost the end of March. Trees are starting to bloom, birds are chirping in the twigs, and the bewitching scent of lilac drifts through my open balcony door. There's no reason at all to be sad, or worse, to cry.

Maybe it's just a dust particle causing those tears. I squeeze my eyes shut and rub my thumb and forefinger across them toward the bridge of my nose. No more tears fall after that. But something strange freaks me out just a second later.

The faint *beat, beat, pause* of somebody's heart echoes in my ears. The sound repeats over and over. And it's not my own heart, I can tell, because it beats in slight disharmony.

Jerking up from my chair, I move a few steps backward, away from my desk. My gaze is focused on the small drawer at the bottom right side. I know what's in there. But it can't be. A glass heart doesn't just suddenly start to beat. Does it?

I press the heels of my palms to my eyes for a second. Obviously, I've been sitting over this homework

ANNA KATMORE

one hour too many. A break, that's what I need. But the subsequent *beat, beat, pause* draws me in like a beacon, slinging its noose around my neck and pulling me forward. My fingers trembling slightly, I open the drawer. At the back lies the red glass heart. Of course it's not beating. In fact, the sound stopped the moment I squatted in front of my desk, ready to take a look.

Very. Very. Creepy.

Slamming the drawer shut, I rise and walk out into the wide carpeted hall on the first floor of our mansion. Brittney Renae runs squealing out of her room toward me. I catch her, scoop her up, twist her around, and press her to my chest. "What's going on, fairy bug?"

"The toad wants to steal my hairclip." Pouting, she holds her tiny hand out to me, showing me the clip with a Snow White image on it.

Only seconds later, Paulina joins us in front of my room, folds her arms over her chest, and taps her foot. "Put her down, Angel. She has my hairclip. I want it back."

My laughter spills out at how much determination comes from that five-year-old. I set Brittney Renae on her feet and take each girl by a hand. "Come on, get your coats. We're going out and I'll get you another magazine, with another hairclip."

Both their faces light up like birthday cakes. They hurry to slip into their identical *Alice in Wonderland* shoes and red coats. With a quick shout to Miss Lynda, our housekeeper, I usher the girls out the front door.

Peter Pan

EVERYTHING HURTS. I moan as I turn around in a place that feels a lot like my bed in the tree. My eyes open reluctantly. Colors swim in front of them, light fading in and out of my vision.

"Loney! Quick, get the others! He's waking up!"

"Tami?" I croak through a sore throat, identifying the voice as that of the pixie.

A cold, damp cloth is pressed to my forehead. "*Oh Peter!* Yes, it's me. How are you feeling?"

"Like a dragon had me for lunch and spit me out again." Trying to focus without real success, I slowly drag my hands down my face. Something on my cheek scratches my palms. *By the rainbows of Neverland, what is that?*

"And you look exactly like that happened to you. Peter, what's going on?"

"Don't ask me!" A biting pain in my back makes me

yelp as I sit up. It's gone quickly, only the aftermath leaves me breathless. I hunch forward, resting my arms and forehead on my bent knees. "Why am I hurting so badly? And how did I get here?" The last thing I remember is looking into the mouth of Hook's gun and then tossing our father's watch into the volcano. Anything after that is a blurred image of colors and sounds. And loads of pain.

Goddammit! Did he shoot me?

"You didn't come back from the boar hunt, so after some time, the boys and I went looking for you. Toby found you close to the tree house. You were unconscious and had so many bruises. We didn't know if we should even touch you, but we couldn't let you lie there either, so the boys carried you home."

My vision comes back. I tilt my head and look at Tameeka's worried elfin face. "How long have I been asleep? What time is it?"

"It's almost noon." She gulps and the new look on her face scares me. "Peter, you've been knocked out cold for thirty-three days."

The air freezes in my lungs. "And I'm still alive?" This seems impossible.

"At the beginning, we tried to feed you berry mash and pour water down your throat. You choked on it and we almost lost you then. We didn't try to feed you after that." Her soft hand strokes over my forehead and down my cheek. "Peter, we were out of our minds. No one knew

ANNA KATMORE

when or if you would wake up again. The Lost Boys and I took turns keeping watch over you. They're out on the hunt now—" Her eyes take on a more gleeful shine. "Oh, everyone will be so happy to see that you finally came around!"

"What's that on my face?" I ask her, rubbing my palm across my chin.

There's a long pause before Tami answers. "Stubble."

"What?"

"It started a couple of days ago."

In her look I can read that there's more. "What else?"

The pixie's wings sink behind her back. "You grew. About six inches."

This is impossible. Complete bullshit. Throwing back the covers, I get out of bed, ignoring the pain that comes with the movement. I jump from my sleeping booth to land on wobbly legs at the bottom of the tree trunk. The moment I look down at myself and see how the hem of my shirt has ridden up my belly, I know Tami was right. I grew. And I sprouted a beard too. What the hell—

The pixie glides down beside me. Her hands are clasped in front of her chest as my frightened gaze finds hers. "You're aging, Peter," she whispers.

"No!" The word is a painful croak. "This can't be."

"It's happening. I just don't know what brought it about."

"I do." My voice has gone deathly cold. "Hook."

Whatever it was that started this plight, it has something to do with the pocket watch he forced me to destroy in the volcano. "He found a way to end the standstill." Pulling the too-tight shirt over my head, I fling it aside and clench my teeth. "But I'm the Pan!" Hands fisted, I fly through the hollow tree toward the hole at the top. "I won't grow up! Never!"

The warm wind of a race through the sky slaps me in the face. At least flying still works. Beneath me, the jungle is a blurred sea of green. Headed north, I pass Mermaid Lagoon and fly out over the ocean three quarters of a mile. In front of me rise the peaks of the treasure's den, the waves splashing against their rocky sides.

I land on the one with the hidden trap door and start moving stones aside. Lifting the second one, my finger gets crushed between two rocks. "Ouch!" I stick the finger in my mouth and suck until the pulsing pain ceases. Then I pull it out and stretch all fingers as I twist my hand in front of my face to examine it.

My hands are bigger now, and so are my feet. Coordinating my movements takes some adjusting. I stumble a few times and have bruised knuckles before all the stones are carried out of the way. *By God, I swear Hook will pay for this.* He'll pay dearly.

When the entrance is free, I pull on the leather strap attached to the wood and the door flaps open. The familiar scent of rusty silver and gold that usually wafts at my face is missing. I peek inside and my heart stops for a couple of seconds. A small jet of daylight lands on the ground of the cave. It's empty.

With a racing heart obviously trying to make good on the missed beats, I glide down and stand in a shallow puddle. All around me there's only rock face. The floor is wet and deserted. Nothing of the treasure is left. Nothing other than the small chest that carried the pocket watch for so many years.

The ultimate betrayal.

James gave me the key to the watch so I could free it and deliver it right into his hands. I don't know how he found out about this hiding place, but I sure can put one and one together. *Angel.* She told him before she left Neverland. Now my brother has it all. The treasure—and the satisfaction of seeing me grow older.

Every muscle inside me tenses to an aching point. I start to shake, the blood draining from my head and limbs. Falling to my knees in the puddle, I lift my chin. A soul-tearing cry bursts out of my lungs.

"Hook, you bloody bastard! I'm going to run a sword through your heart for this!"

Chapter 4

AN ENTIRE MONTH lost! Dammit.

Gazing at the ever-growing island outside the windows of my study as we sail toward its shores, I fist my hands, my nails digging deeply into my palms. Twenty-one times we've tried to sail to London. Twenty-one times we've found Neverland. It's just like back when we set off with Angel still on board and tried to help her leave this place. There is nothing out on this goddamn sea. In all these waters only one island exists.

Heck, did the fairies lie to me? Are the gates of Neverland closed after all?

I spin on my heel and stride out on deck, into the burning afternoon sun. Smee tilts his head when he notices me and stops playing cards with Potato Ralph. Passing them, I see it was a wise decision by my first mate. He held a poor hand and would have lost the couple of doubloons.

ANNA KATMORE

He follows me down to the main deck. "The plan, Cap'n? Shall we round the isle and set off again?"

I face him and snap, "We've covered all possible routes at ten-degree intervals. Do you honestly think it will make any difference if we do the same routes in reverse order?"

Smee lifts his hands in a baffled surrender. "Man, you're in a mood today..." He laughs a throaty sound. I want to put an end to it by showing him where the ship's plank extends out over the water. But it's not his fault we're stuck here.

I tamp down on my frustration, shoving my hands into my pockets. As always, whenever I've done this the past thirty days, my fingers close around the two remaining beckon beans and I'm tempted to eat another. Maybe this time it'll work.

Fishing them out, I stare at them for a long time. "*Think of Angel and eat one*, she said. *It'll lead you in the right direction.*" I bite my bottom lip and fling the beans across the deck. "To hell with them!"

Smee ducks. "Maybe you're forgetting something essential?" he suggests when he straightens again.

"And what would that be?"

"Well, she also said, *don't forget about the rainbow*, didn't she?"

"Yeah, so what?"

"So maybe we should start spending our days trying

to catch one instead of looking for an island where there is none."

He does have a point. "Drop anchor as soon as we reach the shore. And find me some gunnysacks." I rub my temples. "I've no idea how to catch a blasted rainbow."

Smee's eyes suddenly grow wide as they focus on a spot over my right shoulder and the constant murmur and whistling on deck stops abruptly. I whirl about to see what put them all in shock. A young man stands in front of me. The first thing I'm aware of is that he doesn't look or stink like a pirate. He's none of my crew. "How the heck did you get on my—" Realization strikes hard and fast. "Peter?" I whisper.

"Good afternoon, Hook," he says through gritted teeth. A heartbeat later, his fist crashes into my jaw.

Pain explodes in the left side of my face. Hauled several feet backward across the floorboards, I'm knocked into a stack of boxes. My lip split from the punch, and blood gathers in the corner of my mouth. I spit it out and wipe the rest away with the back of my hand. Hunched over a box for support, I glare sideways at Peter. "Good afternoon to you, too."

I push back to my feet and brace myself for a fight when Peter stalks forward, hands fisted. Smee and Skyler rush to his side, holding him back by his arms. Peter wrestles to get free. Only wearing pants, there's a display of twitching abs and pecs under his skin—muscles that weren't there when we last met. Stubble shadows his cheeks and chin now and his hair has grown enough to notice. More, he made good on the few inches I always had on him. My little brother has become a man.

"Let him go," I tell my men calmly.

Reluctantly, they release his arms.

"What? Do I look like I can't handle a fistfight?" I scowl at them until they step away, their gazes remaining on us. So be it. I ignore them and focus on Peter. "What happened to you?"

"Why don't *you* tell me, bilge rat?" Free of the pirates, he comes at me again, fists lashing. "How did you make me age so fast?"

This time, I'm prepared for his attack. I dodge another hit aimed at my jaw and block a sucker punch to my stomach with my right forearm. Grabbing his, I twist it to his back, step into the hollow of his knee and shove him forward. He lands on all fours.

"I didn't know this would happen! I thought time would start where it stopped when you cursed Neverland." And it's the truth. Seeing my younger brother at the same age as me, when really only a month has passed, is a shock to the bones. "The destruction of the watch should have set things back to normal—not turn you into a man in an instant," I add in a lower voice as Peter rises to his feet again, facing me.

"But it did!" he barks. "And I'll make you pay for it!"

His kick to my chest comes too fast and I fly backward against the mast. Pain spreads in my lower back. I twist around and grab the mast for balance, recovering quickly. From the corner of my eye, I see how Peter starts his next attack. Another kick. This time, I react faster and his bare foot only hits the mast. If it hurt, he doesn't show it.

Taking the opportunity, I knee him in the guts and head-butt him. Briefly dazzled, he stumbles backward, finding support at the railing. He shakes his head to clear his dizziness. I could end this battle in a minute, if I pulled my sword and skewered him through the heart or sliced his throat. But I don't. In fact, I've done enough to him. For a moment I wonder if any treasure in this world was worth hurting my brother.

Then I see Angel's face in my mind, and I know I would do it again.

"Peter, I'm sorry." Panting, I brace myself on my knees. "I didn't mean to put this fate on you. It was...the only chance I had."

His face glistening from sweat, he slowly lifts his gaze to mine. Blood drips from his nose. "You damn asshole," he says slowly. "I was a fool to believe you and I could ever be brothers. You haven't changed a bit—never cared about anyone but yourself."

It's not true. I care about him. Only, I care about Angel *more*.

ANNA KATMORE

"Next time we meet," he continues, "I *will* kill you. I swear, James Hook, I'll find the sword that's forged only for piercing your black heart."

Understanding his wrath, I don't doubt him for a minute. But he's mistaken if he thinks I won't be prepared. I straighten, the gap hewn into our newly discovered brotherhood widening fast.

Suddenly a fire of a wholly new kind blazes in his eyes. "Or maybe killing you isn't enough... What would be the worst thing that could happen to you?" He bends forward and picks something small up from the deck. One of the beckon beans.

Shit!

"I bet it's something to do with Angel." A sneer crawls to his beaten face. "What did you say before? Think of her and eat the bean? It'll lead the way...right?"

Before I can rush to him, Peter flies up and puts the bean into his mouth. From his appalled look I know when he's chewed it. Then he swallows hard and coughs. "Wicked stuff." Looking up, he gazes at the sun for a second, then he turns his head and focuses on a spot in the sky in the opposite direction. As he looks down at me next, he laughs scornfully. "You really tried to *sail* there? Major fail, *brother.*" Spitting the last word, he zooms off.

Without hesitation I pull my gun, aim at Peter, and shoot. The bullet misses its target.

"Follow him!" I yell to the crew, fighting against the

fear in my chest that he might hurt Angel just to get back at me if he finds her.

Smee steps in my way. "Cap'n, he's flying. We're on a two-thousand-ton ship. How would that work?"

"Right." I twist and tilt my head, cupping my mouth, and shout up to the crow's nest, "Bull's Eye! Where's Pan going?"

The short, bald man with dark skin lifts the spyglass to his eye and looks through. "Up, Cap'n!" he shouts after a moment. "East and up."

"What do you mean *up*?"

"Pan is flying higher than I've ever seen him fly before. And he's still going up."

I remember the urge to climb the mast when I ate the first beckon bean and how I almost tried to jump. Maybe I was misled all along. In the past, Bre'Shun had sent me a stellar map. It was supposed to help me find London. *Is Angel really on a different star?*

The headache from Peter's punch to my jaw is getting worse. I rake my hands over my skull and lace my fingers at the back of my neck, tilting my head back. A tortured sigh escapes me.

"What we do now, James?"

I look at Smee. "I don't see any other choice than to get the fairies what they want. Get us back to shore. Tonight we hunt rainbows."

Peter Pan

LIKE A VORTEX, the sky pulls me up with incredible strength. I don't know where I'm going or what it really is that leads me straight up and on. My fighting against this power is in vain. After some time, I relax and simply go with the warm flow.

Far away from Neverland, the sky starts to darken. Stars are shining so bright all around me that it feels like I only have to reach out to pluck them from the canopy. It's beautiful beyond words.

In this place, a person completely loses track of time. I could have been here for minutes or traveling for hours. There's nothing else than light spots against darkness and a bluish white crescent to my right. Flying through a shower of falling stars and finally a loop around the moon, I feel how the flow starts to drag me downward. New lights appear beneath me. They're not stars, they are lights of a town.

London.

The houses there look like nothing people would build on Neverland. Some of them are as tall as mountains, scraping the night sky it seems. Ships float on a broad, serpent-like river, and in the distance a clock strikes ten. I follow the sound to a high, angular tower tinted in yellow light. There's a huge white watch with black hands built into it.

An awful lot of bustling activity is going on in the streets beneath. Weird for this time of night. Coaches zoom past, except they aren't pulled by horses. And crowds of people are still out and about. Staying in the air high above them all seems to be the safest way.

I'm gliding across a wide green area, when the pull suddenly increases again. Following the impulse, I soon realize I'm headed to London's outskirts. The activity is fading behind me. Hardly any man is seen in the streets and alleys now, and there are more trees and bushes here. Some windows in the lower, fancy-looking houses are illuminated, but most are dark.

I'm wondering how far I'll be sucked on this powerful current, when the pull stops abruptly and I drop. Moments before I crash into the roof of a mansion, I catch myself in the air and come down gently.

The dark shingles are cold and rough against my bare feet. And now that the warm flow has stopped completely, goosebumps rise on my arms and back. I

ANNA KATMORE

ignore the chill as soon as I hear the familiar voice of a girl.

"Yes, I will. Good night, mother."

I sneak toward the edge of the roof and peek down. There are two balconies attached to this side of the house, both semicircular and facing a wide garden. Light falls through the open door to the one right beneath me. Behind the drawn net curtains, a person moves back and forth several times, casting a shadow below me, then walks out onto the balcony. It's a young woman. Somebody I know. Her short black hair reveals a slender, pale neck and her fragile body is wrapped in a light pink dressing gown.

When I lean farther over the edge to get a better glimpse, a shingle comes loose and drops. It misses the balcony by a few inches, falls down into the garden, and breaks in two.

Her hands braced on the balustrade, Angel glances down, then slides a look up toward me. Quickly, I duck back. It's not a good idea for her to see me up here...and the way I've changed. She wouldn't recognize me.

After a few calming breaths, I lean out once more. She's disappeared from the balcony and the light in her room is out. Temptation rides me hard to fly down and sneak inside, but what would she say if she found a half naked stranger in her room?

Right, I have to find some clothes first.

Several windows on this street are open, mostly on the second floors. I try those that are dark, hoping that whoever lives in those houses have gone to sleep by now. The first two windows I fly through lead into beautifully decorated nurseries. Babies are sleeping peacefully in their cribs. I try a couple more houses farther down the street. In the last one, I get lucky. A young man is snoring in a wide bed, the covers draped up to his hips. From what I can see in the dark, we're both the same build. There's a closet opposite the window with a selection of clothes that might fit me.

Carefully skimming through the many shirts on hangers, I try to make no sound. Suddenly, the man stirs in his sleep, rolls onto his back, and his left arm flops sideways over the edge of the bed. Startled, I retreat to the shadows. He doesn't wake up, so I quickly grab a few items from his closet and rush out through the open window.

There's no one out here to see me, so it should be all right to change on the roof. My booty is a dark red t-shirt with long sleeves, a leather jacket, and pants that look like the ones Angel wore when she came to Neverland—a funny light blue material. Everything fits fine.

The only problem is that my feet are still naked and cold. Raiding another house, I grab a laced pair of black shoes that, after holding them against my soles, seem to be my size. Back on the roof of Angel's house, I sit down and

ANNA KATMORE

put them on, then I rock back and forth on the balls of my feet a few times. The shoes feel comfortable, perfectly made for running.

Now that I'm dressed, hopefully I'll fit into this strange world. I silently glide down to Angel's balcony. A double-wing door leads inside. One part is closed, the other stands wide open, with silky white curtains drawn together.

As soon as I slip inside, a whiff of her familiar scent envelopes me. Angel is fast asleep in the four-poster bed on the other end of the room. Her deep breaths sound peaceful in the silent darkness. I tiptoe over to her side and gaze down at her face.

Her soft hair and rosy lips tempt me to touch them. Much more than the last time I saw her. Or maybe they looked the same back then and I just didn't notice? I'd love to skim my fingers across the tender skin on her cheek, but I don't want to wake her. Instead, I tug gently at the duvet until her bare shoulder is freed. She's wearing some strappy silk top or dress the color of eggshells. It almost blends in with her pale skin.

Pulling the duvet down a little more, I realize there's no chain around her neck. She's not wearing the ruby heart she got from James. The one I gave her first. It's not on her nightstand, or anywhere on the desk next to the balcony doors. Damn. I would have loved to take it back to Neverland and dangle it in front of Hook's nose. The rat's ass would freak out, thinking I hurt his lovely girlfriend. Phase one of my plan to take vengeance on my brother.

There are several shelves and a chest of drawers on the other side of the room, which I could search for the gem. However, I have a better idea. I'll come back tomorrow and just ask Angel about it.

Suppressing a snicker, I slip out through the curtains and glide up into the sky. Finding home is easy. I don't need any more beans to show me the way now that it's been etched into my memory by the weird flight here.

Dawn is breaking when I reach Neverland. I'm starved and dead tired, but when I return to the tree house there's no chance for me to crawl into bed. Five worried Lost Boys and an anxious pixie are awaiting me. Tami flings her arms around my neck even before my feet touch the ground.

"Oh, Peter!" she cries. "Thank the fairy light, you're alive!"

I hug her to my chest then put her down on her feet. "Of course, I'm alive. What did you think?"

"You were gone half a day and the entire night," Toby says and claps a hand on my shoulder. He has to reach up now to do so. It surprises me, how little my aged appearance seems to unsettle them. Then again, they had thirty-three days to get used to it, while I got the full transformation slammed at my face in a second.

ANNA KATMORE

"After what happened to you"—Toby grimaces and his gaze moves up and down my front—"we just didn't know if we'd ever see you again. Where have you been? What happened to you?" He frowns as if the next thing he's going to say is the most important question of all. "And where did you get these weird clothes from?"

I almost blurt out that I visited London. Just in time, I hold off. No one needs to know yet. Not before I get a chance to talk to Angel. Jaw set, I tell them in a cold voice, "Hook did this to me. Somehow he found out how to make me age again. I got these things from town." Swallowing hard after a short pause, I say through gritted teeth, "And he took the gold."

Appearing the most appalled of all, Skippy sucks in a breath. "Hook found the treasure?"

I nod. "It's all gone."

Everybody looks as stricken as I felt when I found the cave empty. Everybody but one little pixie. Her eyes closed, she lets go of a relieved sigh.

Stan turns to her, quirking his brows in a reproachful frown. "What the hell was that?"

Tami searches his face for a long time, then her gaze skates over the rest of us. "Now come on, you all." She flutters a few feet up and puts her fists to her hips. "For once in *forever*, we don't have to worry about pirates ambushing us or Hook coming to slice all our throats because of this darn treasure."

When I suck in a lungful of air to reply, she cuts me off with a raised finger that she points at my nose. "No, you won't, Peter! Maybe you and Hook had your peaceful moments. But after what he did to you—making you grow up and all—it's obvious things haven't changed. He'd be chasing us until he got what he wanted. And it was his from the beginning."

She glides down until her bare feet are planted firmly on the ground again, then she stalks up to me and stands on her tiptoes, gaze lifted to mine. The top of her head is level with my navel right now, and still she manages to make me back off. "It's time to stop this stupid game and give us all a break!"

After a long pause, I say in a low voice, "I didn't know you felt like this."

"Maybe because you never asked, Peter Pan."

She's right. I never did. All these years, I simply assumed everyone was having fun and liked things the way they were. The pixie, too. Big mistake, obviously. Arms folded over my chest, I look at the Lost Boys, one by one. "Do you feel the same way?"

Sparky digs a hole in the dirt with his toe. His face turns an evil red from the base of his throat up to the hairline of his buzz cut. "I think I'm actually with Tami on this."

All the boys gasp, turning to him. They might have been prepared for Tameeka to back out. Sparky's retreat is a surprise to everyone, though. He lowers his gaze to his toes—or he would if his round tummy wasn't in the way.

"Fine. Anyone else?" I snap. This really isn't my week.

Toby pulls his black hair back and ties it in a ponytail at the back of his head, showing his undercut. He always does this when he's in battle mood. "I say we leave the kids home and the rest of us go and bring the treasure back!"

Tami growls at him for this comment. Then she takes Sparky's hand and pulls him away from us, while Skippy, Loney, and Stan howl in agreement with Toby. They drum their fists on their chests and dance around me like Indians.

"What's the plan?" Toby asks.

Looking after the pixie and stout Sparky, I feel a rift cracking between us. Is this because I'm older now? And why am I the only one aging so fast? The other boys are still the same as they were yesterday, last month, ten years ago.

Toby tugs on my jacket. "Peter...?"

Pulled out of my thoughts, I turn to him. I do have a plan. It's just too early to tell them about it. First, I have to see Angel again. "All in good time. Let me just sleep a couple hours"—I stretch my neck and yawn—"and later today I have to run an errand." I want to time my next visit to London so that Angel is awake. "We'll talk about everything tomorrow."

Running the zipper of his bear vest up and down, Stan asks in a skeptical voice, "Since when do you have to run errands without us?"

"Since I grew a beard," I snap back. Then I start laughing. Just because I look older now, doesn't mean I have to act or actually feel older, right? Grabbing a wooden sword from the rack by the mattress mountain, I challenge him. "And don't you ever question me again. I'm still the best sword fighter out of all of you."

Never one to miss out on a good fight, Stan draws his own sword and we battle across the ground level of the tree until one of us is lying flat on his back, begging for mercy. Today, it's me, and only because the pixie got in my way and I tripped backward over her.

"Die, Peter Pan!" Stan barks and pushes his sword at me, which I catch between my arm and my ribcage, moaning and coughing like I was drawing my last breath.

The Lost Boys cheer for my opponent. Tami, who's still trapped under my left leg, scowls at me and curses in a language not made for young girls. I lift my leg and set her free, then accept Toby's and Loney's hands to pull me up.

They let me get to bed eventually. Exhausted and fully dressed, I slump face-first onto my pillow. Thank God, sleep comes over me before I can start mulling over the doom Hook pushed me into.

ANNA KATMORE

All is quiet when I wake again. The Lost Boys must have gone out to play *Catch the Indian* or hunt dinner. My stomach rolls in protest at the thought of missing another fabulous meal roasted over a campfire. I haven't eaten in...weeks! Raiding the pantry, where we always keep fruits, nuts and sometimes even veggies, I grab a handful of berries, a carrot, and two apples and plow through them in record time.

Next to the kitchen sink, there's a catapult for garbage. I place the apple cores into the leather strap and shoot them out through the hatch into the jungle, one at a time. Usually, the boys and I fight over who gets to operate this little self-made piece of ingenuity. Today, however, it's boring.

When all the garbage is discarded and I'm ready to leave, I slide a glance over to Tami's door. It's closed. This normally means the pixie is in her room. She should have heard me being up and about. I'm wondering why she hasn't come out. Oh boy, she must be pretty mad.

I don't like it when the pixie is in a bad mood, or any of the others for that matter. I grimace and sigh. Finally I walk to the door and knock. "Tami? Can I come in?"

There's no answer. After another knock, my hand drops to the brass doorknob. A slight twist, and the door cracks open. Used to simply walking inside, I'm not prepared for the consequences of my new height. A moan escapes me as my head knocks hard against the top of the doorway. Stars dot my vision. Damn, is this the kind of trouble I have to deal with from now on? Rubbing my aching forehead, I stoop to fit through the door.

It takes a couple of seconds to recover and for my eyes to focus again. Tami's room is empty. Her bed, the shape of a pink seashell, is neatly made. I turn and head out, but then I stop and cast a glance over my shoulder. A music box stands on the chest of drawers that the Lost Boys and I carved for the pixie ages ago. Even though I've never told anybody, the tune was always one of my favorites.

Since there's no one else but me in here, I sneak over and spin the key. The porcelain princess begins to twirl on the small round platform. A smile tugs on my lips as the sweet song starts. When I hum along, my voice is deeper than usual and strangely raspy. My happiness slips away.

I sink to the floor, lean against the tower of drawers, and tilt my head back. How can everything change in the blink of an eye? I don't want to be old. I don't want to look and sound like an adult. My nails dig into my palms until I feel the warm drops of blood in my fists. I hate that the Lost Boys have to lift their chins now if they want to look into my face. I hate that tossing garbage out of the tree with the catapult isn't fun anymore. And I hate Tami being angry at me. She never was before.

Why, Hook, did you have to change my life when all

ANNA KATMORE

was perfect?

Breathing deeply a few times through my nose, I press my lips together and grind my molars. The pixie might be happy there's no reason for another battle with the pirates. For me, on the other hand, the real fight has just begun. I'm not done with Captain James Hook yet. I swear I won't rest until his dead body lies at my feet.

Pushing up from the floor, I rush back to the main room and zoom out through the hole in the treetop. It's time to start phase one of my plan to destroy my father's greatest mistake.

After last night, finding my way back to London is easy enough. East and up, then straight on toward a set of three stars in a triangle. Through a shower of falling stars, a loop around the moon, and descend behind it. Finally, a hard left curve at the clock tower.

I follow the river for a mile and a half. Reaching the outskirts, I aim for the street with Angel's house. According to the bright sun high in the sky, it must be around three in the afternoon. The perfect time to arrive in London.

Best would be to return to the roof and then sneak down to her balcony to meet her. I've barely landed when Angel's voice drifts up to me. She's calling for Paulina and Brittney Renae. If I remember it right, they're her little sisters. Stepping closer to the edge of the roof at the front of the house, I spot her, and two strawberry-red-haired girls squeal as they come out the door and run toward her.

Angel is wearing a black coat that's shaped like a dress and barely covers her knees, her feet stuffed in painful-looking high-heeled shoes. Amazing, how easily she can walk in those. The girls flank her, taking her hands, and together they head down the street.

Never letting them out of sight, I follow, sneaking along the roofs. Less than a mile away from their home is a park. Since the line of houses stops quite a bit before the entrance, I glide down from the last roof, using a massive chestnut tree for cover.

As soon as the three girls enter the park, the twins let go of their older sister's hands and scuttle away, their pink dresses fluttering in the steady breeze. Angel strolls on.

Hands in the pockets of my new leather jacket, I amble a safe distance behind her. After another couple hundred feet, she lowers onto a bench at the side of the pebbled walkway and fishes a book out of her tote bag. She's alone, reading—there might not be a better time to meet her. I pick up my pace.

"Peter Pan!"

Baffled, I whirl around to the voice of a young girl. "Yes?"

"Stop or I'll skewer you from the back!" one of Angel's sisters shouts after the other, wielding a twig like a sword.

"You can try, Captain Hook, but you have to catch

ANNA KATMORE

me first!" the other yells back over her shoulder. Laughing, both children scurry in their neat strappy shoes across the lawn, not cutting so much as a glance at me.

What the heck?

With my brows pulled down to a frown, I tear my gaze away from them—and instead look into the shiny brown eyes of a smiling Angel. She lowered her book and is staring at me from across the path, her expression intrigued.

The moment drags on, because I'm not sure what to do or say now. There's only this funny warmth spreading in my chest when I look at her. Eventually, she breaks the awkward silence and asks, "Your name is Peter, isn't it?"

By the rainbows of Neverland, she recognizes me! I nod, a smile tugging on the corners of my mouth.

"I thought so. You turned and said *yes* when Paulina shouted that name. They're my sisters."

My smile slips. "Oh." Then again, it doesn't matter. She'll know who I am in a minute. "So you told them all about Neverland?"

Angel laughs like this is a joke. I don't get it. "It's actually their favorite story. I think in the past three years I've read the book to them a thousand times."

"The book?" I frown as I sit down beside her. More importantly, how could she tell the story over three years? It's only been two months since she left Neverland. She doesn't look older to me, so more time can't have passed here than in my world.

"Peter Pan?" she answers with a slight edge to her voice. Then her face relaxes again. "You probably only know the movie, right?"

Whatever is a movie?

I shrug, leaning forward to prop my elbows on my knees, and mumble, "Yeah."

"That's all right. Disney did a great take on the classic."

My head starts to hurt. What in the world are we talking about? I need to put an end to this and get down to the point before she confuses the hell out of me. Slowly, I tilt my head toward her. "Do you ever miss Neverland?"

Now she makes big eyes at me. "Miss it? Well, that's a big word, isn't it?" She chuckles, and it sounds a little uncertain. "Of course I'd love to go there somehow, but to miss it means I'd have to have been there before. Right?"

"Right." *Which you have.* I guess it's only logical that she'd hold back with a stranger. "You have no idea who I am, Angel, do you?"

She sucks in a breath, her eyes turning sharp. "Why did you call me that?"

"Because it's your name."

"My name is Angelina. Only the twins call me Angel. And I don't remember telling you either."

Now it's my turn to chuckle about her defensiveness. "Well, I might have been a little younger when we last met. I'm Peter."

"Yeah, I know. You said so before."

"Peter...Pan."

"From Neverland?" Her tone is flat, like she's mocking me.

I straighten and lock gazes with her. "Yes. James found a way to make me age."

"James...as in Captain Hook?"

I nod.

"And he did something that made you look twenty instead of just fifteen?"

"Yes." Finally, we get there. A surge of relief swamps through me and I smile.

A moment later, Angel starts to shake with laughter, shocking the hell out of me. "Oh, now I get it! It's a joke! You were at that one fancy dress party my dad threw for my thirteenth birthday, right? Are our fathers business partners?"

"My father is dead."

Immediately, she stops laughing, her expression turning grave and her cheeks glowing pink. "I'm sorry. I didn't know."

Why did she say that? James certainly told her all about the tragedy of our past. Unless...she doesn't remember. An odd thought comes to mind. When Angel came to Neverland, she started to forget things about her home, about London. What if she forgot Neverland after she returned to her world?

On the other hand, she and her sisters knew my name, and they know about Hook, too. What, by the rainbows of Neverland, is going on here?

I need time to think this through. Abruptly rising to my feet, I obviously startle her, but I can't worry about that now. "I have to go," I tell her curtly and spin on my heel to walk away. Only when I look over my shoulder and find that Angel and everyone else is safely out of sight, I fly up and back to her house.

I'm stunned out of my mind when I discover the pixie sitting on the chimney, her arms folded and legs crossed.

"Tami! How did you get here?" I hiss.

"I followed you when you left the tree house. But I can't walk in the street like you." She beats her wings a few times to demonstrate what exactly made her stay hidden. "I don't think there are many pixies in this world."

I agree with her on that. "Why did you follow me?"

"I was worried about you, Peter. And obviously with good reason! What exactly are you doing here?"

Oh man, I hate it when Tami acts like a grown up. It so doesn't fit her appearance of an eight-year-old girl.

"I'm here to take revenge," I tell her in a voice gone frosty. "My plan was to kidnap Angel back to Neverland and blackmail Hook. Then something came up which I didn't consider, and it might present a whole new option for revenge."

"What is it?"

"Angel doesn't remember Neverland. At least that's what I believe after talking to her today, even though she said some queer things about a book with me and Hook in it. I'll try to figure it all out later, at night, when she's back and I can slip into her room again."

"Again?" Tami's pointy ears wiggle with surprise. "Does this mean you've sneaked into her room before?"

"Yes. Last night while she slept." Heck, why do I feel the need to justify myself to a pixie? "Go home, Tameeka. And don't tell the Lost Boys where I am. I'll talk to them tomorrow, when I come up with the perfect strategy to get back at Hook using Angel."

Tami gets to her feet on the chimney, locking gazes with me as we stand nose to nose and smacking me on the chest with her tiny fist. "Shame on you, Peter Pan! Angel is a nice girl. I liked her when she came to Neverland. And so did you and all the Lost Boys. How dare you drag her into your plans of vengeance!"

"She told Hook about the treasure. Is that reason enough for you?"

"No!" She leans back and crosses her arms over her chest once again. "You know what I think about the treasure. Let things rest...at least for a while." Then her face turns thoughtful. Not a good sign. I wish I could clap my hands over my ears before she goes on, but that would only end in me getting pinched on the nose by her.

"Have you ever thought of offering to show Hook the way here in exchange for the treasure? He's still trying to find Angel, isn't he? It probably won't work until he learns to fly, so you could help him there."

"Shut up, Tami!"

The pixie gasps.

"Look at what the bloody codfish did to me!" I lift my arms to get her attention on the horrible, aged body I'm stuck in now. "And you want me to be nice to him? No way. If you're not on my side in this, you better leave me alone. I don't need you to spoil this for me." I stomp my foot on the roof and pout. Hell yeah! I haven't felt this *myself* since I woke up from my crazy long sleep.

Tami's chest expands with a hurt intake of air. "You just send me away?" Her angry face starts to glow red like a strawberry. "You—you ugly old man!" Beating her wings faster than a butterfly, she takes off to the sky and disappears in the beams of the sun.

I want to call after her, make her wait. But it's not a good idea to shout up here, where people might hear me. Also, if the pixie wants to be stubborn, fine with me. I don't need her, goddammit. Or any of the Lost Boys. I can do this on my own.

Hunched against the chimney, I wait until Angel and her sisters return from the park. It's a lot louder inside the

ANNA KATMORE

house after they're back. As soon as dark falls and the streets empty of those funny coaches and people walking, I take a flight around the neighborhood to stretch my spine and get some blood back into my limbs. On my return, all windows of the house are dark and no sound is to be heard inside. Angel closed her balcony door tonight but she left the window open. Lucky me.

Hovering a few inches above the floor prevents my feet from making any sound that might wake her. Up on the roof, I had a lot of time to think about her story—this book about Neverland. It's the one thing I'm after right now. There's nothing on her desk, and the chest of drawers only holds framed photos and some boring books without pictures.

Sneaking over to her bed, I'm once again tempted to touch Angel's soft face while she sleeps. This unfamiliar longing starts to get on my nerves. I want to shake it off, but it stays, so I decide to ignore it and tear my gaze away from her. With quite some surprise, I catch a glimpse of a book on her nightstand then. There's a smiling boy portrayed on the front cover, his eyes big and ears pointed like those of a pixie. He's flying with a bunch of kids following him. At the bottom of the cover are two words.

Peter Pan.

A sneer creeps to my face as I lift the book and skim through the pages. Many pictures of pirates, a girl in a blue dress, mermaids, and even Tami is in there. Amazing!

I slide the book under my jacket and fly out through the window again. Back on top of the roof, I settle down and start to read.

It's a story about a Peter Pan visiting a girl named Wendy. Funnily enough, she lives in London. He takes her and her brothers to Neverland for a big adventure. They meet the Lost Boys—man, they do look a lot like the guys in my tree—Tinker Bell, who seems to be a replica of Tami, only with a jealous nature that is totally unlike the pixie I know, and of course, Hook. He's a hilarious character. Totally describes my brother, minus the hook on his hand.

In the middle of the book, I happen across a name I haven't heard in a very long time. Tootles. In this story, he's one of the Lost Boys, and marbles seem to play a special role for him.

I remember how I saved a boy called Tootles from Hook's plank once. He never became one of us, though. Actually, I always thought he headed off to the port to live there. Now I'm forced to rethink that easy assumption. After everything that's happened lately, here and in Neverland, is it really so far-fetched to believe Tootles could have returned to this world? Maybe *he* was the one writing this story. Just why in the world would he invent lies about me and this Wendy girl?

I scratch my head. Things are turning weirder by the minute. Snapping the book closed, I put it aside and study

ANNA KATMORE

the stars. Angel knows about Neverland, but she doesn't remember that she's been there. She knows who Peter Pan is, but she doesn't know who *I* am. For all it's worth, she might not remember that not so long ago, she fell in love with Hook.

Oh, the possibilities that come with that!

If only I can convince Angel that we've met before. That she was in love—a nasty shudder surges through my body—with *me* and not with Hook. It would kill him. And the pain would be worse than a sword through his chest. My mouth curves up and I snicker.

Hook will never find the way to London. Even if he does, it'll be too late. By that time, I'll have planted the idea in Angel's mind that he's the ruthless pirate from this very book. Everything will be perfect.

I fly back into Angel's room and return the book to its former place. Then I think about what I could take with me to tease Hook when I see him next time. Maybe a piece of her clothes to prove I really found her? No...I have a better idea. A lock of her hair.

Cautiously rummaging through the drawers in her desk, one by one, I search for scissors to cut a strand from Angel's head while she sleeps. In the last drawer, I touch something that makes me stiffen.

A gem in the shape of a heart.

Chapter 5

"PULL IT IN!" Smee shouts to the crew, but I already know the net will be empty. Trying to catch a rainbow with a fishnet as it lands on the ocean's surface was a waste of time. Just like running after them to capture one with a bucket or a gunnysack, which was our brilliant plan last night.

The men haul the net on board, just to prove my hypothesis. There's nothing in there. Not even the ropes bear a single stain of rainbow colors. "Dammit!" It's incredibly frustrating to know what could get me to Angel but not being able to collect it. Restlessly, I pull at my hair.

"Keep your head on, Cap'n," Jack placates me as he winds up the net with Walefluke Walter. "It was only our second attempt. We'll think of something new before the next volcano eruption."

Which will be twenty-four hours from now...minus

fifteen minutes.

Grunting, I leave the men to finish the work on the fishnet and return to my quarters. The candle on the table flickers calmly. About to blow it out and go to bed, the sound of an exaggerated sigh drifts to me. Who would be so stupid as to enter without permission? I tolerate very few rules to be broken aboard the Jolly Roger. Intruding in my study is not one of them.

Grabbing the candle, I cross the room to my study with the broken door. After only a few steps, I stop dead and pull the gun from my belt. I point it straight at Peter Pan's heart. "How did you get in here?"

"Easy. You guys were all busy chasing a rainbow." Hands laced behind his head, he sneers at me from my chair, his feet stacked on the wide desk. "Any luck with that?"

Gun still aimed at him, I step forward and put the candle down. Warily, Peter straightens in the chair, but his sneer remains.

"Not yet," I snap coldly. "But we're getting closer. We might be lucky tomorrow night. You, on the other hand, seem to have run out of luck. Say goodbye, Peter Pan."

He chuckles. "You're going to shoot me?"

I have every intention of doing so, simply for threatening the girl I love.

"But then you'll never hear what Angel said."

This, however, makes my finger freeze on the trigger. What Angel *said*? Does this mean he found her? He *talked* to her? My heart beats faster. Even though I'm scared to hear that he might have done harm to Angel, I must know what happened. The past couple of days I've started to doubt there really is a chance to reach this town called London. Now, hope returns.

"Ah, did I capture your interest, *Captain*?" Peter drawls in a snide tone.

I lower the pistol. An annoying shakiness creeps into my voice. "How is she?"

"Oh, she's doing really well." Rising from my chair, he turns and steps to the window, clasping his hands behind his back, then he casts a glance at me over his shoulder. "Today, I met them, Angel and her sisters. Lovely little girls," he adds with an exaggeratedly wide grin. "Guess what they were playing?"

No idea. I keep staring at him.

"They were playing Peter Pan and Captain Hook. Isn't it funny?"

I'm not so sure about that. Regarding his cynical look, it's probably not.

"Only, in their version, I'm the lovable boy and you're actually the bad guy." He moves his gaze back to the window. "Ruthless. Ugly as hell. Stinking like a codfish, you know."

I can hear the sneer in his voice. "Why would Angel

ANNA KATMORE

tell them such lies?" I counter.

"Memory." Peter shrugs and pivots to me. "You know what a strange thing that is. One day you have it, the other day...it's just gone. Seems like your *Miss London* doesn't remember ever being to Neverland. But people do know of us there."

Severe confusion knits my brows to a frown. "What—"

"Yeah, yeah. I know; it's odd." He lifts his hands to cut me off. "I'm still trying to figure that one out myself. Apparently someone visited Neverland before Angel. And by *visited*, I mean he left again. Wrote a funny book about us afterward—even though I don't understand why he's telling those terrible lies about me and some weird Wendy girl." Peter shakes his head. "He calls himself Walt Disney or something."

"So you're trying to tell me that Angel knows about us from a book, but she doesn't remember staying here with us for almost a week?"

"You got that right, Cap'n." Peter nods and waves a cynical finger at me. "And wanna know the best part of it all?"

I don't, but that won't stop him from telling me anyway.

"Now I can tell Angel a...let's say"—he grimaces, as though searching for the right word—"*edited* version of her vacation with us. I'll tell her that you tried to kill her and I saved her life. You know how it is with girls, right?" The sucker winks at me. "I'll be her hero then."

Tampering with her memory? Peter would jam a fatal wedge between Angel and me. What's the use in trying to get to her, if she'll fear and hate me in the end? At least, if this all was true... "How do I know that you were really there? You could be making this up just to get back at me."

He chuckles again. Damn, I'm tempted to shoot him just to stop that sound. "I knew you would say that," he answers. "That's why I brought you a little something." His expression turns bitter, his eyes never leaving mine as he reaches into the pocket of his strange new jacket. My mouth dries out.

Slowly, Peter pulls his hand out and lifts it. A pendant drops a few inches. It's attached to a silver chain looped around his middle finger. I suck in a breath through my teeth as I recognize the ruby heart. "Where did you get that?"

"I found it in her room." His face lights up with new malice. "Oh, did I forget to tell you that I actually sneaked into her room last night? She does look like an *angel* when she sleeps. So many things that one could do to her then—"

Enough! I dash forward and knock Peter backward over the desk, wrapping my hands around his throat as we land on the floor. Knees bent, he kicks me hard in the gut,

ANNA KATMORE

tossing me across the room. He's back on his feet before me, and out of the study too. I follow him although, with his irritating ability to fly, he's always one step ahead.

Standing on the very top of the main mast, he wiggles his fingers. "Good bye, Captain. I have to return to London and bring this little treasure back to my new friend!" His snide laugh drifts down to me before he zigzags away through the starry sky.

And here I thought I'd been the cruel brother.

Adjusting my collar, I walk back into my cabin. Time is pressing on me. Each day I have to stay here while Peter is up to mischief in London, the risk of my losing Angel gets a little greater.

I flop onto the bed on my stomach, feet dangling over the edge, and bury my face in the crook of my elbow. Tonight feels like the end of doomsday. Rainbows are shooting out of the middle of the island every day at midnight and I have no idea where to start to catch one. My long-lost treasure is back on the Jolly Roger, yet it won't help me to buy a ride out of Neverland, while the fool, Peter Pan, has a natural talent for flying and can see the girl I love whenever he wants. He's probably brainwashing her by the minute.

All he wants is vengeance. And I, of all people, can understand why. I didn't want him to grow up so fast...I really didn't. It all should have gone differently. What went wrong? Bre'Shun said he had to destroy the watch. I made him. Everything should be different now. Peter should age slowly like any other person. And I should be the one meeting Angel again.

Tilting my head, I gaze out through the window, counting the stars surrounding the moon. They sparkle like Angel's eyes did when she laughed. A sigh escapes me. The last time I heard that sound, she lay in my arms, right in this bed. The memory of it warms my heart...only to leave it cold and empty a moment later.

Reaching for my pillow, I pull it to my side, wrap an arm around it, and close my eyes. Moments later, sleep pulls me under and I return to Mermaid Lagoon, where not too long ago I sat through a chilly night with the loveliest girl in my arms.

Peter Pan

FEW CANDLES ARE burning when I arrive at the tree house and glide down the hollow trunk. It's so silent, I assume everyone is asleep, except the Lost Boys' booths are empty, the beds still made. Stan is sitting alone on a stool down by the wooden table.

I land in front of him. "Where is everybody?"

Chin resting in his hands, he looks up. "Gone."

"Why?"

"You really have to ask that, Peter?"

Walking slowly around the table, I study him sideways. "Tami came back?" It wasn't really a question. I take an apple out of the larder and rub it against the sleeve of my jacket.

"Yes, she did. And I can't believe what she told us." His voice grows louder, angrier with each word. "Peter, we all understand how hard a shock this...this *growing up* thing was for you. But dragging Angel into your plans of revenge is just *wrong*. She's a nice girl. You liked her. *We all* liked her."

My fingers close around the apple, my nails piercing the peel. "She told Hook the location of the treasure! Was that actually nice of her?"

"You can't know if she did." Stan rises from his seat. It seems to take an endless amount of time. Then he scowls at me with fox-like eyes. "Tami and the boys left. They want nothing to do with you until you get back to your senses."

I lower my gaze to the fruit in my hand. Hunger has taken leave. "And you?" I ask in a low voice.

"I told them I wouldn't leave you without trying to change your mind. You're my friend, Peter. Let's put our heads together and find a different way to steal the treasure back."

"You don't understand. This isn't a game anymore!" I grit my teeth. "Hook forced this doom on me. He has to pay for it. And I'll get him where it hurts. Angel is his weakness. His *only* weak spot. I'll destroy him, no matter what it takes."

Stan gazes at me for an extended moment. Eventually, he sighs. "Then you'll have to do it alone." Grabbing his bear vest from the hook on the wall, he pushes his arms through then walks to the secret tunnel that leads outside. Before he ducks in, he looks back at me. "Take care, Peter Pan."

ANNA KATMORE

My lips stay sealed.

Traitors! All of them! So many years we've been family. I thought I could count on them. But at the first sign of trouble, they leave me like rats leave a sinking ship. To hell with them all!

I toss the apple against the wall, where it bursts in a juicy mash, then I grab my dagger from the table and zoom out of the tree. My way leads me east and up with one destination in my mind. Since my friends all took leave of me, there's no reason to stay in Neverland any longer.

Angel is still asleep when I get back to her room. Seeing her lying peacefully in her bed brings an unexpected calmness over me. She's rolled close to the wall. The empty spot beside her tempts me to sit down and just look at her. *Yeah, that's not a good idea.* Instead, I return the ruby heart to the drawer and sneak back out through the window.

It's windy on the roof. Perched against the chimney, I pull my legs to my chest and wrap my arms around them. Resting my forehead on my knees, I close my eyes. Not the most comfortable of positions for falling asleep, but it'll do until the morning.

Or...maybe not. My butt starts to hurt on the hard shingles after a while, and a tremendous iron bird flies over the place every once in a while, high up in the sky. The roar of it raps me out of my nap each time.

Tired and annoyed, I fly from the roof and glide in a slow circle over the neighborhood. Two gardens down, there's a huge house with boards nailed over some of the windows on the second floor. Maybe it's vacated. Sinking, I inspect the perimeter. Everything seems old. The swing in the garden is rusty and squeaks when I push it. There are holes in the floor of the porch, and cobwebs decorate the corners of the windows. A grin stretches my lips.

I might have just found a new home.

Ripping away the boards from one of the windows, I break the glass with my elbow and slip inside. The house is empty and dark, but the former owners left some furniture behind. Not many pieces, just a couple of shelves and an empty wardrobe in the great room downstairs. A dusty wing chair stands in front of an open fireplace. It's the perfect bed for the night. I curl up in it and drift off to a dreamless sleep.

*

Something tickles me in my face. I squint and rub my nose. The tickling continues until I sneeze and open my eyes. Dust mites dance in the slim jets of light shooting through the gaps in the boards that cover the windows. With a good stretch, I get up and walk to the back door. It's locked. Two hard kicks against the doorknob crack it open. Daylight blinds me. Boy, it must already be afternoon.

Standing on the porch, I enjoy the view of the wild

ANNA KATMORE

garden and wonder what it would be like to live here. The house is vacated. No one would be bothered if I moved in for a little while. Upon further inspection through the inside, it turns out that all the faucets function. Even though they say *hot* on one side and *cold* on the other, there's only ice-cold water. That's fine with me.

I wash my face and drink from my cupped hands until there's a gurgling sound in my stomach when I walk. Then it's time to get some work done on my new home.

Outside, I start to tear the brittle boards from the windows, one by one, break them over my knee, and toss them aside.

"Hi there!"

At the sound of Angel's shy call behind me, a smile curves my lips before I turn around. She's standing on the sidewalk near the fence, wearing a short plaid skirt and a dark blue pullover. The collar and hem of a white blouse flash from beneath. She brushes her hair behind her ear, then her hand finds its way back to the strap of the bag she's wearing over her shoulders.

"Hey," I reply.

"Um, Peter, right?"

"Yep." I drop the last board I ripped from the window and casually walk down the pathway to meet her at the gate.

"I didn't know someone was moving in. Did you buy the house?"

I begin to shake my head but quickly realize my mistake and answer, "Yes."

"That's...cool. I actually live just two houses up."

"I know."

"You do?"

Damn. What just got into me? "Um...yes." Then I remember what she said yesterday in the park. "The party? At your house? I've been there, remember?"

She smiles a little. "Right."

It's better to have her believe we know each other from this party than to tell her stories about Neverland again. That will have to wait for a while. Until she knows me better. "You look like you're going somewhere." I nod at her bag. "With all that baggage. Vacation?"

Now she laughs. "No. School. And I'm not going, I'm coming home."

"Of course." I roll my eyes like it was a stupid thing of me to say when, in fact, I'm dying to know what *school* is. When she starts bouncing on the balls of her feet, obviously ready to walk on, I quickly think of a way to meet her again. "Will you go to the park with your sisters later?"

Angel tilts her head, shielding her eyes from the sun with her hand. I follow her gaze southward. A sinister front of dark clouds is gathering at the horizon. "Not today," she says then. "Looks like it's going to rain in a bit." Her eyes find mine again, and her mouth curls up in

ANNA KATMORE

a friendly smile. "Maybe tomorrow?"

Irritated by the lack of a chance to talk to her again today, I force a smile in return and nod. "See you then."

Lifting her hand, she wiggles her fingers in a feeble goodbye and walks up the street. With my hands braced on the gate, I lean out and stare after her until she turns into their front garden and disappears out of my view.

Great. Now I have to slay time until I can see her again. And flying into her room when she's asleep at night just seems like a rotten thing to do. That really shouldn't become a habit.

I rip the boards from the last window and carry them inside just in time, before the rain starts to fall. There's already a pile of wood in the open fireplace. Rubbing a twig on one of the boards until smoke rises, I blow gently then put some dry weeds on the blaze and wait until the flame is big enough to light the rest of the wood. Soon a cozy warmth spreads in the room. For a long time, I stand in front of the window and look out at the darkened sky. Flashes zoom down to earth while hard rain washes several years of dirt from the windows of my new home.

I haven't seen rain in over a hundred years. It never rains in Neverland. My throat constricts and I sigh. I miss home. Or maybe I just miss Tami, Stan, Toby, and all the others. Being alone, especially when there's a gloomy storm outside, isn't fun.

Hands tucked in my pockets, I hang my head as I

turn and walk to the fireplace. At least the flames give me some comfort. They remind me of the bonfires we used to gather around most evenings. Unfortunately, they also remind me of my hunger. I decide to wait until after dark and then fly to the little wood not too far from here. Maybe I can catch some pheasant or a rabbit. Boy, even a squirrel sounds good at this point.

*

I wake up in front of the mantelpiece. No fire burns in it anymore. There isn't even smoke rising from the embers. Heck, how long was I sleeping?

I roll on my back and stretch on the floor, yawning loudly. The quilt I found in one of the upper rooms after dinner last night made for a nice camp. It's far better than sleeping curled up in a wing chair where most of my limbs went stiff during the night.

A glance out the window proves the rain has stopped and the dark clouds made room for a bright blue sky once again. Warm sunrays flood the house. Rubbing the sleep from my eyes, I sit up. *Damn, head rush.* My brain seems to twist in my skull like a carousel. It's nauseating. Moaning, I rise from the floor and, with squinted eyes, feel my way to the bathroom using the wall. Drinking some water from cupped hands helps a little. The sick feeling disappears.

As I look up and glance at my reflection in the mirror, I draw in a horrified breath. The stubble on my face has grown over night, and not just a millimeter. What was only a dark shadow on my cheeks last night is now a half-inch layer of fur on the lower third of my face. *What the hell!* My heart clips like a racehorse.

I need to get rid of this beard—and fast. Angel can't see me like this when we meet in the park later.

After cleaning my dagger, which I used for killing the pheasant last night, I shave. It's a good thing the slim blade is sharp enough to cut the beard, even if it leaves my skin red and burning. Cold water splashed on it eases the pain.

In the front garden of my new home is an apple tree. I pluck a dainty red fruit on the way out and eat it while I head down to the park. Time to meet Angel again.

Angelina

PAULINA LIFTS THE Polaroid camera my parents gave me last month for my eighteenth birthday in front of her face and pushes the release button. A black square picture comes out, which I take and shake until the colors come to life on it. It's me who smiles from that photo—again. Seems like she's found her favorite object to shoot.

"Why don't you take some pictures of the ducks in the pond?" I suggest.

Squealing, she runs off with Brittney Renae fast on her heels. I lean back on the bench and reach for my book, but a shadow falling over my face makes me look up instead. Against the blinding sun stands the silhouette of a young man, hands tucked into the pockets of his leather jacket, head tilted. "Hi," he says.

"Peter!" I'm surprised about the joy I feel at seeing him again. Scooting to one end of the bench, I invite him to sit down with me. "Where have you been the past couple of weeks?"

He eyes me sideways as he lowers. "Couple of weeks?"

"Yeah. I was afraid you'd changed your mind and hadn't moved into the house after all." Why in the world did I just use the term *I was afraid*? It's not like it would make any difference to me if he lived on our street or not. Or so I'd want him to believe. He doesn't need to know that I actually went down to his house one afternoon last week and rang the bell to see if he was home.

Placing one leg up on the bench, I face him—and gasp. Gosh, hopefully he didn't notice that. Just, what's with his face? He looks...older. Not much, only enough to notice a change. Or is it maybe just because he shaved unlike the last time when he sported an enticing dusting of stubble? Then again, shaving usually makes men look younger. Peter, on the contrary, looks to be in his mid-twenties all of a sudden.

My staring obviously makes him uncomfortable. He runs a hand through his hair and clears his throat. Ashamed, I quickly lower my gaze to the book I'm clasping. "So um, where have you been?"

Peter takes a surprisingly long time to answer. "Home. I was with friends. Sorry I missed you here last time."

"Nah, it's okay." I wave a dismissive hand. I'd only waited two hours for him to show up. However, I don't say that out loud. It's been a long time since I felt attracted to any guy, but Peter captured my interest the first time we met. Even though he's dressed like a normal young man, he somehow seems not from this world whenever I look into his sky-blue eyes. And the way he often studies me before he answers one of my questions makes him even more mysterious. *Let's see if I can uncover some of his secrets.*

"Do you have a job in London?" He suddenly seems too old to be a college student. "The house you moved into is pretty big and probably quite expensive too."

Peter places his ankle on his other thigh and grabs his shin with both hands. "My father was rich. He sort of horded a treasure before he died."

That reminds me, in a terrible way, of how I put my foot in my mouth the last time we sat on the very same bench. To avoid going down that road again, I change topics. "How do you like your new home?"

"The house is big. Way too big for me alone." He shrugs. "But I like the neighbors."

"You already got to meet some of them?"

He gives me a lopsided smile. "One."

I smile back. "Now, that's not really a lot, is it?"

"Enough for me." Peter winks, and there it is—the first moment that he looks like a totally ordinary young man. My cheeks grow a little warmer.

When he tilts his head a bit more, a strand of his

ANNA KATMORE

tousled brown hair falls forward into his eyes. I want to reach out and brush it away. My fingers actually itch to do it. Luckily, Brittney Renae's call from down by the little round pond breaks this awkward moment between us.

"Angel! Paulina won't give me the camera! I want to take pictures now! Tell her she should give it to me!"

While my baby sister obviously has no trouble with screaming the birds away from the park, I refuse to do the same. Rising to my feet, I look back at Peter. I don't want to leave him just yet, and from his boyish pout I suppose he doesn't want me to go either. Words evade me, though, so I nod over my shoulder in the direction of the pond, sweep my arm in a come-along gesture, and finally I shrug—not to forget my silly grimace.

Peter laughs, gets up and comes with me.

Hands tucked into the pockets of my coat, which I wear over my long-sleeved shirt and light blue pair of jeans, I amble next to Peter and try to distinguish that funny scent on him. Considering it's rude to tell him he smells like he slept in a coal cellar last night, I'd rather not mention it.

Ducks chatter in the water and it doesn't take long for us to make out Paulina squatting in front of them, taking more pictures. Brittney Renae stands behind her, tapping her tiny foot on the pebbled ground. Her face takes on a hopeful shine when she sees me nearing.

"Come on, Paulina. Give your sister the camera."

"Why?" the honey bunny protests, rising. "She'll only take more pictures of grass."

"That's not true. I was going to take pictures of Angel."

Again, I think and suppress a sigh. At my stern look and outstretched hand, Paulina hands over the camera.

"What's that?" Peter asks me then. Obviously, he's never seen one like this before. Our generation takes pictures with their phones or maybe even a digital camera. I'm probably the only girl my age who wanted a relic like this for her birthday.

"It's a Polaroid," I tell him. "An old-fashioned camera."

He just keeps staring at me as though I've switched to a different language.

"To take pictures?" I continue. "Wait, I'll show you." Lifting the camera so that I can look through the lens, I take a photo of him, which then comes out at the bottom of the camera. After shaking it, I show him his dazed portrait and laugh at his even funnier expression when he studies it.

"Wicked," he breathes.

A smile pulls at the corners of my lips. Sometimes he's just sweet.

"Now let me take one," Brittney Renae urges and tugs on my coat. I hand her the Polaroid and she targets me.

I glance over my shoulder to Peter. "Want to be in the picture, too?"

He shrugs. "Sure."

I feel how he stands behind me, the warmth of his body seeping through my clothes at my back. "Ready?"

"On three," Brittney Renae exclaims. "One..."

On two, Peter startles me as he scoops me up in his arms and cuddles me against his chest. On three, I already have my arms wrapped around his neck and laugh out loud. There's a click, then the Polaroid spits out the picture and Brittney holds it out to me before she scurries away with Paulina.

When Peter seems reluctant to let go of me, I say cheerfully, "Put me down?"

"If you insist," he answers and smiles. Then he sets me on my feet. Maybe I shouldn't have insisted after all.

I take a shy step away from him. Together we wait until the black disappears from the photo. The image that shows after a few seconds is lovely. Showing teeth, I laugh happily while an adoring half-smile plays around the corners of Peter's mouth. His eyes are warm and on my face in that picture.

Peter smirks as he looks at it. "Can I keep this?"

"Um...sure." Hopefully my disappointment doesn't show through. At least, I still have the picture I took of him before.

Somewhere in the distance, a clock chimes half past

five. I wave the twins back to me then face Peter. "It's time for us to walk home. Our housekeeper always prepares dinner at six."

He nods yet he doesn't look too happy. I like that. "See you again tomorrow?" he asks.

"On Wednesdays and Thursdays I have school until five. Maybe we'll be here Friday afternoon again." I give him a hopeful smile, but even before he can agree or refuse, my smile slips. "No wait. There's a school dance Friday night." It's the spring formal in the middle of May. "I won't have time to take the girls to the park that day."

"Pity," is all he says. But he looks as though not meeting the next three days bothers him as much as it—strangely enough—bothers me.

Brittney Renae and Paulina come running and grab my hands. They twist around me in a cheerful dance that makes me twirl with them. Catching a glimpse over my shoulder, I see Peter lick his bottom lip and briefly suck it between his teeth.

"Maybe Saturday?" I suggest when I stand still again.

Peter nods. Once again he looks like a boy from a different world. Smiling to myself, I shake my head and walk home with the girls.

ANNA KATMORE

Chapter 6

NOON HAS PASSED when I wake up in my quarters. My boots are kicked to the corner, and my clothes dropped in a bundle on the floor along with my hat on top. Chasing after rainbows is starting to wear me out.

I roll onto my back and place one arm behind my head. For a long time, I just stare out the window, the sheets draped halfway up my chest. The sun sneers through the glass from a bright blue sky. It's another glorious day in Neverland. I can't remember the last time I felt happy to wake up in the morning. Not any day recently—or today, either.

With a deep sigh, I rub my hand over my face. I should get up and make plans for tonight—come up with a new idea on how to capture a rainbow. But honestly, I think we've tried every possible way there is. And still, we've caught none.

Peter's visit fourteen days ago gave me a new boost

of ideas. But failing time and time again, night after night, has trampled my hopes. At this point I wonder if I'll ever see Angel again.

Most likely not.

I don't even want to get out of bed anymore.

About to drag the sheets over my head and drown in gloom, something nailed to the door catches my notice and I roll to the other side. My attention on the wooden panel, I roll off the bed. Absently, I pick up my pants and put them on, eyes focused on the dagger that's fixing a picture and a note on the door.

Holding the picture flat against the wood, I work the dagger out. It's none of mine. With the *P.P.* engraved in the blade, it's not hard to guess to whom it belongs. "Peter Pan," I murmur. The bloody bastard. He must have sneaked into my quarters last night while we were on the volcano again. Dead tired when we returned, I barely paid attention to anything in my room, let alone the door. I just wanted to sleep.

I slip the dagger into my belt at my back and take a look at the picture. My heart stops. In the photo is the prettiest laughing girl in the arms of my filthy half-brother. I grit my teeth and my throat constricts painfully as I read the note.

Having fun with your girl.

I almost crunch the picture in my hand. Just in time, I stop. It's the only reminder I have of her. She looks lovely in that picture. Happy. Breathtakingly beautiful. A muscle in my jaw ticks. I run my thumb over her hair and try to remember how it felt. Silky and soft. A strand always fell into her face when she was angry with me.

Now Peter Pan is the one who gets to brush her hair behind her ear. I slam my fist against the door. *How is this fair, goddammit?* Close to breaking, I trudge to the bed and sink onto the mattress, staring at the picture of the two of them. My vision blurs. I blink a few times, but it's not getting better.

There's no use in ignoring the truth. I've lost her.

All the hard work with the rainbows, all the trying has been in vain. I'll never be able to go where she is. Where Peter is. He'll continue sending me reminders of how happy Angel is with him. And me? Here I'll be, forever trapped in Neverland. That's my fate. My doom. I can't take it any longer. I don't want to go on like this.

At that moment, I make a decision that allows me to breathe again. It gives me hope of getting rid of the pain inside my chest. Very soon. Feeling a little less burdened, I light a candle and hold the note from Peter over the flame. It burns and scatters into floating bits of black ash. The picture of Angel stays untouched on my desk.

Shrugging on a clean white shirt, I walk out on deck and find Smee on the bridge.

"Afternoon, Cap'n," he greets me. My lips remain closed. I just hug him to my chest briefly but hard and clap him on the back.

"Shit, what's wrong with you?" he blurts when I release him.

"Nothing. Just...you're a good friend, Jack."

If I startled him with the hug, I shocked the hell out of him with my last words.

"James—" He frowns at me. "Did you drink too much of the rum last night?"

I give him a tight smile and shake my head. Then I turn on my heel and walk to the gangplank extended to shore. Before I leave the ship, I look back over my shoulder and meet Smee's confused gaze. "Take over," I tell him.

It's an endless time until he finally nods and I know he understands and won't follow me. Tonight, I want to be alone on top of the volcano.

The sun has set when I reach the foot of the mountain. It'll be midnight by the time I get to the top. Fine with me. Why not go down in a firework of rainbows? It fits, doesn't it?

All the way up, it's Peter's scornful face I see. The way he snickered when he got his ultimate revenge. I don't want to waste the last moments of my life thinking about him, so I shove the image of my brother away and pull the sound of Angel's soft laugh from my memory instead. That's better. Thinking of her gives me peace.

Before long, I stand on the very edge of the volcano,

ANNA KATMORE

looking down into the deep black hole. Tiny sparks of gold glisten far below. I hope the jump will kill me. Neverland and I have been bonded one day too many.

Closing my eyes, I spread my arms out and list forward. My feet leave the ground. Warm wind gushes at my face. I fall.

My only thought is to hold Angel again—until a battering ram hits me straight in the chest and busts the thoughts from my mind altogether. The unexpected power catapults me back out of the volcano in a high arc. My arms and legs flail in all directions. It does me no good. An instant later, I land hard on my back, the impact pushing out what little air was left in my lungs. I try to focus on something, anything, when light spots dot my vision. Or maybe it's the starry sky above me I see. My body feels like it's broken in two. I close my eyes. Everything fades out.

*

"Good morning, James."

The soft female voice drifting from miles away brings me back from a deep black hole within me. It was cold in there. The farther I climb up to consciousness, the warmer my body feels.

"It's time to come back," the voice tells me, sounding closer this time. Most likely she's standing just across the room. Which room is this?

"Where am I?" is what I want to say, except all that

comes out of my mouth is a throaty moan. I cough—and immediately regret it. The pain in my chest is excruciating. Reaching to my sternum to ease the ache, my hand touches bare skin. Whoever is talking to me must have taken off my shirt.

"You're in my house. Tending to your wounds is easier when I have everything at hand."

Whose house? A distinct note of warm milk and blueberry muffins lingers in the air. The scent reminds me of my early childhood—I haven't had blueberry muffins in so many years. But it certainly isn't my mother talking to me. I do remember her voice. And she's dead.

A cold, wet cloth is pressed to my aching head and ice-cold fingers run from the base of my throat over my right shoulder and down my arm. A tingling chill races through me. "Bre?" I croak.

She chuckles. "Oh yes, Captain. It's good to see you didn't lose your mind."

I draw in a long, slow breath that expands my chest and hurts like hell. "Why am I still alive?" *Or am I?* According to the pain, I might as well be in hell and the person talking to me could be a deceiver.

"James Hook, you disappoint me." She clicks her tongue as she lays her hand flat on my stomach. A nauseating sensation comes and goes with that touch. "You're much stronger than you think. A rainbow won't kill you."

　　　　　　　　　　　　　　　ANNA KATMORE

"Rainbow?" My eyelids flutter open. Instantly, Bre'Shun places her hand over them, sealing them closed.

"No," she hums. Her cold touch continues to send strange vibes through my body. Right now they concentrate in my skull. She cups my face, skimming her thumbs over my cheekbones. The throbbing I've felt in my head since I came to eases and finally disappears. "Now you can," she tells me.

I open my eyes.

First, there are only blurred colors, mostly shades of brown and white. Slowly, my eyes focus. I'm lying on my back, looking at a ceiling that's made of wooden panels shaping a roof. The bed is placed in a corner, with a white wall to my left. My gaze wanders about the room. The floor is made of stone, and so is the furnace built into the wall. A cast-iron pot hangs from a bar over low flames. Steam erupts from it as Bre'Shun stirs the contents with a long wooden spoon.

"What's cooking?" I ask.

She smiles at me over her shoulder. "Medicine. I'm sorry I haven't healed you thoroughly yet. You can cope with my touch for only so long before icicles start forming on your nose."

"Yeah." I chuckle and it hurts. "There's just something *cold* about your personality, fairy."

"Back to joking, pirate? I'm glad you are." She skims off some of the brew and pours it into a cup. Expecting this to be for me, Bre startles me when she sips it herself. Her eyes focus on mine over the brim of the cup until she's downed it all. Then she puts the cup away and comes back to my bedside. "Turn over, James Hook."

It's never a good idea to question one of the fairies, but with all the pain and prospect of getting frozen by her hands again, an odd reluctance creeps over me.

"Come on," she urges me in a friendly way, like she's talking to a child. The mattress sinks as she lowers herself next to me. "You want this done while the medicine is still fresh in my veins."

Moaning from the pain, I roll on my stomach. "So you're what? The conduit for the thing you just drank?"

"One could put it that way." She pulls the covers down to my waist and places her thrillingly cold palms over my kidneys. In a slow caress they move up and run in wide circles over the back of my ribcage. "If I gave you the medicine to drink instead of letting the power flow into you through myself, you'd be forever happy, all-knowing, and unbreakable." A short pause, and she laughs. "That would be cheating on life, now wouldn't it?"

Right now, I wouldn't mind some cheating, especially concerning the unbreakable part. Yet I'm happy with whatever Bre's doing to me. The pain eases. I can breathe, cough and talk again without feeling like a swordfish is stuck in my chest.

She continues massaging the spot between my

ANNA KATMORE

shoulder blades until a sigh of pleasure escapes me. "Damn, you're doing some good magic there," I groan.

Bre laughs and stops the kneading. "That last part was just to loosen you up, James Hook. Way too much tension here." She pinches the base of my neck.

I rub that spot as I turn around again and sit up in bed. Only now I take in the rest of the room—or maybe it wasn't there moments before, like so often in the past. A heavy wooden door is built into the wall next to the bed, and across from it warm daylight flows in through a square window that begs for some cleaning. Flowerpots in various sizes stand on and beneath the windowsill, and even though the window is closed, butterflies and bees busy themselves in the jungle of colorful wild flowers inside.

The strangest thing, though, is the structure placed next to the stone fireplace. It's as tall as Bre'Shun, made completely of wood, with cogwheels that connect to a tiny replica of a ship's helm. Bre grips the handles and spins the wheel three times in one direction. Clamps on both sides of the construction hold what looks to be my shirt in the middle. Only it's not white anymore, but shimmers in all colors of—

"The rainbow," Bre finishes my thought and gives me one of her typical omniscient looks that come with her smiles. "You finally captured one."

"I did?"

The more she turns the wheel, the tighter my shirt is twisted between the clamps and something similar to sparkling liquid is wrung from it. A bucket beneath the construction collects the mysterious stuff.

"Well, it might have caught you first when you threw yourself from the edge of the volcano. That it soaked into your clothes is what counts in the end. Which reminds me...would you care to give me your pants, too? I wasn't sure if it was okay to strip you naked, so I decided to leave the leathers on you."

Lifting the covers, I peer underneath. My pants glow in shades of blue and violet from the waist down to the middle of my thighs. The rest is the dark rough leather it should be. "So, um, you want me to walk back to my ship in the nude?"

"Oh no, silly, of course not. It'll be a trade-off, like always." She winks one warm, turquoise eye at me. "Where you're going, you need different clothes."

"Where *am* I going?"

Her mouth curves up even wider. "London?"

I almost swallow my tongue. *Angel.* Her face, her laugh, her growl when she's angry—it all rushes over me, leaving me breathless. "I can see her again?"

Bre'Shun nods. "It is time, Captain." She wrings my shirt some more. "You brought me the last ingredient for my potion, now I will keep my part of the deal. I shall have the charm ready for you in a few minutes."

ANNA KATMORE

I get up, walk toward her, and dip a finger into the multicolored, glistening slime in the bucket. "So that's the stuff big wishes are made of?"

"Not everyone's wish. Only yours." She takes my hand and gently wipes my finger with the skirt of her dark red dress. "Rainbow essence is a powerful matter," she explains in her ever-patient tone. "Unless you're comfortable with turning into a unicorn overnight, I suggest you don't stick your hand in it again."

Her amused laugh while I shudder feels totally out of place. I'll certainly heed her warning. "How's that crazy stuff getting me to London?"

At that precise moment, the other fairy sister bursts through the door—not bothering to actually open it. "Did somebody say my name?"

"Crazy"? I did. Biting my tongue, I take a step back, not to give her any reason to walk through me like she tends to walk through doors.

Remona swipes her long silvery hair over her shoulder and tilts her head at me. "I heard that, Captain. You're lucky I like you." She grins and pinches my cheek. Then she hands a jar the size of a foot and filled with white sand over to her sister.

Bre unscrews the top. "Go for it," she tells Remona.

The crazy one erupts in hiccups of giggles as she scoops rainbow essence with her cupped hands into the glass jar.

I lock gazes with Bre'Shun over Remona's shoulder and mouth, "Does she know about the unicorns?"

Throwing her head back, Bre laughs. "It is, in fact, why she's been dying for you to bring the rainbow. She's going to have the best week of her life."

Remona pours some of the essence over herself, which results in multihued strands of violet and yellow appearing in her hair. "Oh, it will be so good!"

When there's no more essence left in the bucket, Bre is obviously content with the amount of rainbow slime in the jar. She seals the lid and shakes it until the sand takes on the rainbow's bright colors. When she opens the lid once again, a bluish cloud puffs out. The sand turns gold and specks of light sparkle in it. She hands me the jar.

I lift one brow. "Pixie dust?"

"Pixie dust." She nods. "A little altered. If you strew this powder on your ship, it will take you away from Neverland."

I wonder if I can—

"Yes, you can touch it," Bre cuts my thought short. "No turning into a unicorn." Then she explains, "When you've finished the dusting, eat a beckon bean." She quirks her brows. "You do have one left, don't you?"

I reach inside my pocket and fish out the last bean. The day Peter stole one of them, I had the entire crew search for the other until it was safely returned to me.

"Good," Bre'Shun says. "Eat it when you're ready to

go. The ship will follow your course then, no matter where."

Good to know, since my suspicion is that we'll have to fly into the sky to get to Angel.

"But beware, Captain." The fairy's voice loses all the friendliness the next instant. "You must only anchor in Angel's world at night. The land you're going to can be unfriendly at times. Don't expose the ship to any person's eyes. Clouds will shroud it in the dark, but you must return to the sky before daylight breaks each morning."

Okay, I'll manage that somehow.

Remona searches my face as though she can read my mind—which she probably can. "It is your ship, Captain Hook. It will only follow your lead. Don't leave it to anyone else during the day, or you won't find your way back to it."

"Fine. So I have the nights to find Angel and win her back."

"You have the nights, yes." Bre'Shun scrunches her face, sending a shiver of foreboding down my spine. "Three of them exactly."

"*What?* Only *three*?" That's far too little time with Angel!

"It's a faraway place you're headed to. One third of the bottle's contents will get you there. You have to dust the ship again as soon as you feel the Jolly Roger sinking of her own accord. One third will keep her going for one day exactly. The Jolly Roger will return to Neverland at the end of the third night, and you have to be on board." At my obvious glaring, Bre heaves a sigh. "I'm warning you, James Hook, there's no way around that condition."

"All right," I mumble after a long pause. "Guess three nights is better than nothing."

Remona pats my shoulder. "Be yourself, Captain, and it will be enough." There might be a hint buried in her dry reply. If there is, I don't get it. Then she steps up to me and runs the nail of her long cold finger from my navel to the waistband of my pants. Hooking her finger in it, she winks and pulls at it slightly. "We will get that too, won't we?"

I roll my eyes as I nod, which sends her out of the room on a happy skip.

My next question is addressed to Bre. "You said you had other clothes for me?"

"Right here." She smiles again and taps her fingers on a white wooden chest that appears next to her on the floor.

This doesn't surprise me, I keep telling myself.

"I'll leave you to yourself for a moment. Put your pants over there." She nods at the footboard of the bed. "And when you're ready, knock on the top of the chest three times. Knock like you mean it. You shall then find the right clothes inside."

"What do you mean, like—" I don't get to finish the

sentence, because Bre has already scurried out of the room and the door shuts behind her of its own accord. *Great.*

I inhale deeply. Why do I keep finding myself in this weird house?

Whacking my head over it won't get me out any faster, so I pull off my pants and drape them over the board at the bed's end. Then I knock on the chest like I was told. Seriously, how do you knock on something like you mean it? I try to picture the chest as the door to a tiny troll's house. When I'm done, I almost expect someone to shout "Enter" from inside.

Of course, there's no reply, so I lift the lid and take out a bundle of dark clothes.

The pants are made of gray fabric that reminds me of ship sails. They are wide and baggy. Without a belt they sit loosely on my hips. The top is something similar to the long-sleeved shirt Angel wore the first day we met. It's black with a hood and two pockets on the front.

A pair of gray shoes was in the chest, too. I lower on the bed and put them on. The soles are flexible and long laces are threaded crisscross through tiny metal hoops. After tying them, I stand up and test the new footwear. It feels a bit strange to have my ankles bare. At least the pants are long enough to cover them and even scrape the floor as I walk.

The weirdest item of this new clothing is, however, the dark gray hat...if one could call it that anyway. There's no feather on it, and the brim is practically non-existing. There's only this small part that shades the eyes. Raking my hair back, I put the hat on. Like the rest, it fits perfectly. It doesn't mean I'm feeling in the least comfortable in these clothes, though.

When I close the chest and turn around, Bre is standing behind me. I didn't hear her come in and gasp.

"You look good in London clothes, James Hook." She fumbles with the hood on my shoulders, weaving an aura of cold around my face. "Otherworldly."

And that's exactly how I feel. Putting on these things also brought a whiff of adventure with it. My heart speeds up at the prospect of seeing Angel again. Tonight?

Hopefully.

I decide not to think about Peter and his cruel plan right now but let the rush of anticipation sweep me away. There will be time later to figure out the rest.

I grab the jar with the pixie dust and slip the last beckon bean into my pocket. Bre shows me out through the door. It leads into the familiar front garden of her neat little cottage. "Thank you," I tell her and head along the path leading toward the low picket fence. Halfway there, I whirl on the spot and jog back.

Bre smiles as I stop in front of her again. I kiss her on the cheek. "Really, thank you, fairy," I say.

"Good luck, James Hook."

I nod and make the mistake of glancing over her

ANNA KATMORE

shoulder. Behind her, inside the house, all the furniture has disappeared once again and all that's left is a great hall with stone walls and a chessboard floor. Shaking my head, I smile to myself and head off through the forest.

Another rush of excitement makes me pick up my pace. These new shoes are perfect for a jog through the woods. Once back under an open sky, I can hardly cope with the anticipation boiling inside me and run as fast as I can.

Almost to the Jolly Roger, I hear Bull's Eye Ravi shout from the crow's nest, "Commander Smee! Someone's coming at us—crazy look, wants to enter!"

From fifty feet away, I see how Jack gapes over the railing in my direction. A couple of seconds later his voice rises above all. "Pull in the gangplank!"

I skitter to a halt just before I'd have dashed over the edge and into the ocean, with the gangway being drawn in right in front of my nose. "What the hell—Smee!"

Everybody comes to stare at me; Jack Smee does so the hardest. "Cap'n?" he shouts, grimacing.

"Yeah, well, that would be me." Pulling off the weird hat, I send him a wry look. "Now lower the gangplank, dammit!"

The board is extended. "Thanks for letting me on *my* ship, Mr. Smee," I snap at him as I enter.

"You're welcome." He flashes a bright grin, which then turns into a really clueless expression. "What in the name of God are you wearing?"

"Clothes."

"Not yours."

"The fairies gave them to me."

"You've seen the nutcases again? Why didn't you say so when you left?" He steps a little closer and lowers his voice. "I actually started to worry about you, James."

"It's all good." Smirking, I clap a hand on his shoulder. "I didn't mean to see them, but as it was, I happened to run into a rainbow. Literally."

Smee's eyes grow wide. "You caught one?"

"Aye. Now pull anchor. I've a date with my girl."

After looking at me in quite a wondrous way for half a minute, Jack swallows his bafflement and turns to the crew. "All hands on deck, ye filthy bilge rats! Draw anchor! Set sails! We're leaving Neverland!"

Excited bustling starts on the main deck. The men hum a well-known tune as they turn the wheel that lifts the anchor. In the meantime, I open the jar and start dusting the entire ship with the glimmering gold powder, careful not to use more than one third of it. Wherever the dust rains down, the boards of the ship turn a fancy golden color. Gasps erupt from around me. Oh yes, the Jolly Roger looks quite impressive when I'm done.

"Which course?" Jack demands as I join him on the bridge.

"Let that be my concern." Grinning, I pull the last

beckon bean from my pocket and pop it into my mouth. When it bursts between my teeth, the expected longing for the sky takes hold of me once again. Only this time, I know exactly what to do.

Spinning the wheel hard to the left, the Jolly Roger takes a turn that knocks everybody off their feet. "Hold on, ye mangy dogs!" I shout over my shoulder and laugh out loud as the ship's bow rises out of the water and glides into the air. The wood creaks, the sails bloat. Water drips from the ship's belly. On a slow, steady ascend, we climb to the sky.

"Wicked," Smee breathes next to me, gripping the railing with clawed fingers.

I cast him a sidelong glance and nod, then I face forward again. "You wait, Peter Pan. I'm going to get my girl back."

Chapter 7

WHATEVER I DO, whichever way I turn the wheel, it feels perfectly right. The crew latches onto the railing or ropes so as not to fall off. Fin Flannigan kneels on the main deck, his arms wrapped around the mast, teeth clattering. The rest of them don't look any happier. Except for Smee—he laughs as the ship cuts through the sky, higher and higher.

"Scuttle me bones, Cap'n! If this is what you get for catching a rainbow, we should've doubled the men's efforts from the start."

He gets a nod from me. Secretly I'm wondering if I'll ever tell him how I really happened to knock into one. Chances are slim.

The sky rapidly grows darker until we sail in the midst of a midnight blue canopy decorated with sparkling bright diamonds on all sides. At a constant, calm pace, the Jolly Roger moves through a shower of falling stars, then I

ANNA KATMORE

turn the wheel gently to the right and steer her around a breathtaking moon.

"How do you know the route?" Smee asks and leans out, extending his arm as far as possible. Still, he's not able to touch the silvery orb, if that was his aim.

"The beckon bean, I guess. I just know." Behind the moon all I have to do is think *down*, and the ship starts a lazy descent. If the feeling in my stomach can be trusted, we're getting closer. And really, it only takes a few more minutes until a new sea of lights appears beneath the ship's belly.

Evading the overcrowded area from which an overflow of sound drifts, our destination is a little outside this tremendous town which can only be London. The lower we sink, the thicker the layer of clouds gets around us, and they soon change their consistency. It's almost like we're looking through the rippling surface of water. Everything is visible underneath, if slightly blurred. This must be what the fairy talked about. Our shield, which protects us from the foreign world below.

At my command, the ship dips slightly portside after we pass an impressive clock tower, following that direction. The brighter lights fade along the ride, giving way to empty streets lined with trees and an occasional streetlamp at the corners. My stomach twists in a funny way all of a sudden, almost like someone is twirling it in a spiral. A huge house stands under the ship. It has a dark roof, two half-circle balconies extend from one side of the façade, and ample gardens stretch all around the property. Some of the windows cast a warm yellow shine into the darkness.

"I think we're here," I whisper to Jack.

"Do we drop anchor?"

"Not necessary." The ship comes to a standstill by itself. We must be hovering right above Angel's house. "Ravi," I call with a suppressed voice to the man in the crow's nest. "What can you see?"

The bald, black pirate lifts the spyglass to his good eye. "Not much, Cap'n. No one's outside. Movement on the second floor. Someone just closed a window."

My heart thuds in my chest. "I'll go down."

"What? Now?" Smee's brows shoot up. "We haven't checked out the perimeter. What if someone sees you? And how do you go down anyway? For all it's worth, you can't fly."

"I don't care. It's dark, no one's in the street. Let me down on a rope if you must."

"And then what?"

"Then I'll knock on her door."

Smee gives me a skeptical look. I don't care. From these staring contests, I always come out the winner. Captain's authority. Eventually, Smee fetches a rope and winds it around the main mast then he hands me the other end. "Jerk twice when you want back up."

ANNA KATMORE

The rope wound tight around my hands, the men let me down into the garden. The air is chillier on the ground. I sneak around the house and step up to the wide wooden door that has bits of glass in it. A button with a bell sign glows yellow in the dark. At my push, a soft melody of eight notes plays inside.

Moments later, a middle-aged woman with graying hair tied into a bun at the back of her head opens and greets me with a polite smile. She straightens her black dress over her chubby body as though she was in a hurry to get the door. "Good evening, sir. What can I do for you?"

If this is Angel's mother, there is no likeness between the two of them. "Hello. Is this the house of Angelina McFarland?"

"It is, sir."

It's hard to keep my face straight, to keep from beaming, as my heart does a double-somersault.

"But I'm afraid you're calling at an inopportune moment," the woman continues. "Miss Angelina has gone out with her parents and her sisters."

Ah, not her mother then. Probably the housekeeper. I make an effort to sound like a gentleman and less like a pirate. "You must be Miss Lynda." She smiles at my recognizing her. "Can you tell me when they'll be back?"

"Not before late tonight, I fear. Maybe it's best for you to call on the young lady again tomorrow."

"Yes, maybe." *Not.* "Good night, ma'am." I nod at her and walk down the path to the street then cast a brief look back. The door has already closed. Ducking under the trees, I sneak into the garden and signal Smee with a double jerk on the rope that they can pull me up.

"Did you see her?" Jack asks, his voice excited, as he hauls me over the railing.

"No. Just the housekeeper. Angel is out with her family. They won't be back until later." Time to come up with a plan. If she returns with her parents at night, they might not be too happy if I ring the bell again and just steal Angel out of their house. However, I don't have time to wait until tomorrow, especially when I can't meet her during the day. It has to be tonight.

"So, what's your plan?"

"There should be a way to lure her outside after they return. Secretly..." Taking off my funny hat, I toss it at Smee's chest and smirk. "That's it!" He scrunches up his face in wonder. I ignore him and call up to the crow's nest, "Ravi, keep an eye out for Angel. Let me know when she and her family return."

"What are you up to, James?" Smee demands, following me to my quarters.

"I'm going to slip her a note." Oh, the brilliance of me. "I'll ask her to come out to her balcony"—the one she fell off from when she came to Neverland for the first time—"and meet me there. No one else has to know."

ANNA KATMORE

Smee slowly wobbles his head like he's testing my plan. "Might work."

"It will!" I dash into my study and find a blank piece of paper in the top drawer. After I scribble the words *Meet me on your balcony* at the bottom, I tear the strip off and pocket it. Now all I can do is wait for Angel to come back.

As I slump over the railing and scan the street below for any movement, minutes turn into hours. So close, and still there's no way to tell when we'll be meeting again. It's gnawing at my patience, the longing for Angel uncomfortably burning in my chest. Then Ravi shouts down to me, "Cap'n! Someone's walking around the corner down the street!"

In an instant, I straighten, holding my breath, and lean farther out to see what he saw. The people strolling up the walkway are too far away. The only thing certain is that there are five of them. "Ravi, give me the spyglass."

Bull's Eye Ravi drops the metal tube from the top of the mast. Smoothly catching it, I deploy the spyglass and lift it to my eye. A wild rhythm takes over my heartbeat the moment I see Angel. She's walking a few steps behind a couple, the man carrying a child sleeping on his shoulder. Another child, an identical one, holds on to Angel's hand. There's no way to tell which of the girls is Paulina and which is Brittney Renae. And right now, I couldn't care less. My gaze is stuck on Angel. She makes me draw in the relieving breath I was waiting on for so long.

Anticipation foams over. I grip the rope and turn a bright smile at Smee. "Let me down. Quick!"

Smee knows better than to hesitate. Silently, I glide through the dark until my feet touch ground behind Angel's house. As fast as possible, I dash through the bushes and duck under the trees then jump out over the fence. A constant tingle in my limbs makes me aware of just how close I am to the girl I love. Only a few more steps and they'll reach the gate to their front garden. It's time. *It's time.* I step away from the shadows and walk toward the family.

Angel's father and mother don't pay me any attention as they sidestep me. I keep my chin dipped low, so the fancy brim of this hat covers my face. Whatever Angel's reaction is to seeing me—whether she recognizes me or believes I'm a total stranger—I want to save that for when I'm as close to her as possible. When her shadow moves into my vision, I lift my head.

Bang! All I see is her beautiful face, all I hear is the surprised intake of her breath when our eyes meet. She doesn't smile or fling her arms around my neck. I was prepared for this reaction from what Peter had told me. It doesn't mean I hadn't wished otherwise anyway.

Heck, now's not the time to whine. I only have a couple of seconds to give her the note. Passing very close to her, I slip the folded piece of paper into her hand.

ANNA KATMORE

Instinctively, her fingers close around it. Soft and warm. Heck, how I want to stop and take that delicate hand of hers into mine. Hold it, feel it, kiss it. Being so close to her makes me feel all these hard emotions that I can barely control. But I have to. For now.

Not even slowing down, I keep walking straight ahead. Only when I notice that the clacking of her sandals on the pavement has stopped, I slide a glance over my shoulder. She's staring back at me. Surprised and fascinated. One corner of my lips curves up. *Read the note*, I want to mouth at her, but it's not necessary. I know she will as soon as I'm out of sight. So I keep walking.

Three minutes should be enough for Angel to read the note, catch up with her parents, and walk into her house. It takes me this long to head down the street and round the block to finally re-enter their garden from the backside. Up in a tree with a perfect view of the two balconies, I hide out until lights come on in both rooms.

Through the sheer curtains behind the door on the right balcony, I see the mother tucking in one of the twins. Angel follows and sits on her bedside for a moment, kissing the small girl on the cheek. That's all I need to know. My aim is the other room.

Angelina

AFTER I SAY goodnight to the twins, I finally head into my own room and close the door. My parents have gone to bed as well. They won't get up until early in the morning and if they do, none of them will come to my room. They never do. Still, tonight I lock the door.

My heart races like that of a frightened rabbit, only I'm not frightened at all. Just curious. And more than a little excited. Who is this guy? Why this note? There's no chance I know him; can't recall his face from school or even recognize him as the son of any of my father's business partners. To me, he's a total stranger.

Yet he looked at me like we know each other.

I unbuckle my white sandals and kick them off so as not to make a sound on the balcony, then I smooth my dark blue dress with tiny daisies on it and move the straps perfectly into place. Thrills zip through me as I open the French doors and slip outside.

Without my coat, it takes only seconds for goosebumps to rise on my bare skin. In late May, the nights are still a little chilly. Rubbing my upper arms, I pad across the cold balcony, brace my hands on the balustrade and lean over. There's no one waiting for me beneath. On tiptoes, I try to look over the entire garden, scanning for a face in the dark. Nothing. Did I get this wrong? Maybe he didn't mean tonight. Or he meant *later* tonight. With a sigh, some of the excitement that has kept me in a stranglehold for the past fifteen minutes slips away from me.

And then something warm envelopes me from behind. The warmth of someone. Hands touch the sides of my shoulders. I gasp and jerk around.

The same guy who gave me the note in the street now stands only inches away from me. With my mouth dropped open and eyes wide like saucers, I stare at his shockingly handsome face. Deep blue eyes gaze back at me from under long, fair lashes. Without his ball cap, his blond hair falls tousled over his forehead, accentuating boyish features under a manly mask. A delighted smile pulls hard at the corners of his mouth, even though it looks like he's doing his best to keep it under control.

Reality drags me out of my daze. I swallow hard and hiss, "How did you get up here?" The frightened rabbit metaphor hits a little closer to home right now. It was romantic to think of this guy waiting for me down in the garden. To find him just outside my room is creepy.

He nods to the tree next to my balcony.

A frown pulls my brows together. "You climbed up? But why?"

He hesitates a second before he finally speaks. "Because I couldn't wait another minute to see you again, Angel." His melodic deep voice, weaved with the evening breeze, settles like a veil around me. It tries to stir something awake. A memory maybe...

"See me *again*?" I cock my head. "Do I know you?"

He reaches for my hands and strokes his thumbs over my knuckles. I jerk my hands away. "I'm sorry," he says. "It's just been so long, and you have no idea what it took to finally get here and find you."

I don't have a clue what that means. With the confusion also comes the suspicion that he's not quite right in his mind. Jeez, what if he's a stalker? Or worse, a serial killer? Sure, I never imagined serial killers to be this gorgeous, dressed in baggy pants and black hoodies, but one can never be cautious enough, right? I take a step back and promptly knock into the balustrade behind me.

He reaches out to help me then stops before he touches me this time. "Careful," he warns. "You don't want to fall off this balcony a second time."

If I do, it'll be his fault, because the sound of his voice makes my head spin in the weirdest way. Where have I heard it before? He acts like he knows me. But I certainly don't know him. "Who *are* you?"

"My name is Jamie. We met some time ago. In a different...*place*?" The last word sounds like he's probing for something. I don't know what place that should have been, so I only shake my head at a loss.

His hopeful face falls. "I know you don't remember anything from the time we spent together. Peter told me."

"Peter?" I stiffen. That's just too much of a coincidence. "Peter from next door?"

"No. Peter from Neverland."

Yeah, too funny. "Why is everyone speaking of Neverland these days?" Now I'm almost certain the two guys know each other. "Is this a prank you and Peter plotted together?" I jab my finger at the center of his rock-hard chest. "Because I don't find that funny."

Jamie backs off, hands lifted in surrender. The shadow of a smile settles on his face. What's amusing him so?

A beat passes before his expression sobers. "I haven't talked to my brother recently. And this is most definitely not a joke," he says.

"Oh, now he's your brother? Well, if this isn't getting more enthralling by the minute."

"Please, let me explain."

"Go ahead. I'm dying to hear this." Saccharin-sweet sarcasm drips from my voice.

All of a sudden, Jamie takes my hand in his,

preventing me from stabbing him with my finger once more. His grip is both firm and gentle. This time he doesn't release me when I try to tug myself free. Instead, he pulls me closer. Mere inches separate us now. The wild scent of tangerines and seawater clings to him like a tropical cologne. It calls to me. My knees go weak and I realize, to my horror, I enjoy being near him.

No, no, no! Serial killer! Serial killer! The only reasonable thing is to back off and scream. Except I can't. There's something absolutely non-frightening about him hidden under the obvious aura of danger that surrounds him. Something untouchable, yet unmistakably there.

"A few months ago, you dropped from this very balcony and landed in Neverland where Peter Pan caught you as you fell from the sky," Jamie starts to explain. And that's the exact moment when I opt out of this conversation and suck in a breath to scream for help.

I don't know what gave me away, maybe the horrified expression that must be on my face, but he claps his hand over my mouth before so much as a tiny squeak comes out. "Please, listen to me," he urges.

In my current position—pressed flush against his front with one of his arms wrapped tightly around me and the other hand still placed over my mouth—I don't have much of a choice here. Wide-eyed, I stare at his face. He tries to soothe me with a reassuring smile, pretending everything is all right. I'm tempted to fall for it.

ANNA KATMORE

"Promise not to scream when I take my hand off?"

It's easy for him to ask that, he's not the one being trapped, so I neither nod nor shake my head.

"Fine." His shoulders sink. "Maybe if I trust you first and just let you go, you will give me the chance to explain?" With a hopeful tilt of his eyebrows, he waits for my reaction I still don't move. In the end, his hand slowly lifts from my mouth.

To scream, or not to scream?

Our gazes stay locked, even after he lets me go, with only the tips of his fingers still touching my arm. It's like he's trying to but just doesn't want to fully let go. Until now, I haven't screamed. I'm still considering it, though. Maybe I should make it dependent on what he says next. Only he doesn't say anything for a really long moment.

At one point, his eyes lower to my collar and then quickly move up again. A streak of red crosses his face. His look makes me feel a little warm...edgy. I can't understand why he affects me this way. And for some reason his dejection troubles me.

"Why aren't you wearing the ruby heart necklace anymore?" he asks me then.

Now that definitely holds my interest. "How do you know about that necklace? And it's not a ruby, it's a glass heart from my sister," I add in a reprimanding tone.

"You think so?"

"Of course. What else could it be?"

"As far as I know, I put it around your neck, so yeah...I'm pretty sure it's a piece from my treasure. Back in Neverland."

"Stop!" I cry out under my breath and lift my hands to keep him at a distance. "I don't know how you found out about that necklace, but I'm not listening to this crap. And don't give me any more rubbish about Neverland. I know the story of Peter Pan. Every kid does. You and Peter next door are certainly not characters from it. So either you be serious with me, or better yet, go down the way you came up." I point a straight finger at the tree. Should I mention that I'll call the police too?

The silence that follows gives my heart time to calm, and I get lost in his gorgeous eyes. They are the color of the wild sea, and no matter what expression he wears, confused, determined, or if he smiles, there's always this devilish spark in them.

He heaves a resigned sigh as if deliberating my last words. "When your sisters were born, you sneaked into their room after everyone else went to sleep." He takes the tiniest step closer and his voice lowers a little more. "You slept on the floor between their cribs, because you couldn't stand to be away from them for even just one night."

My chin hits my chest. Where in the world did he get that information from? I've told this to nobody. But he's not done yet. "If your mother had found out, she'd have given you the shittiest lecture of all time about how well-behaved girls don't sleep on the floor." He lifts his hands, palms up, and smirks. "Your words not mine."

Motionless and full of intrigue, I stare at him. "You're on to something here."

"I certainly am. I'm trying to make you believe me. You told me that when you were about to lose your memory back in—" He coughs and rolls his eyes. "Well, you know where."

"Neverland," I say flatly.

"Yeah, you see..." He hesitates. "We never figured out how you landed in my world." Slowly, he lifts his hand and brushes the backs of his fingers along my jaw. "And believe me, it was damn difficult to find out how to send you back to London."

I can't believe that I'm listening to him and letting him touch me. About to jerk my head to the side, push him away and run, the haunted look on his face keeps me rooted to the spot.

Suddenly something he mentioned before hits me again. "You said I fell off this balcony and landed in Neverland. And that's when you gave me the necklace?"

He nods.

Boy, if this is a prank, they really did some good research. I woke up with the glass heart around my neck the morning after I fell. And the twins are the only ones who know about this mishap. We decided not to tell my parents, so they wouldn't start to worry over nothing and find a new nanny. It's all so weird. My confused gaze drops to my toes.

"Not convinced yet?" Jamie ask, as if aware of my jumbled thoughts.

I look up into his eyes. "How can I possibly be?"

After taking a deep breath through his nose, he suggests, "Let me try something."

"What do you have in mind?"

His gaze turns intense. "Let me kiss you."

"What?"

"Please. Just once. If I fail to recall your memory with that and if you feel absolutely nothing for me afterward, I'll leave and not bother you again."

"You're— *No way!*"

He gauges my reaction for a moment, then the left side of his mouth slides up. "Why not? Are you afraid I could be right and you'll feel something?"

"No!"

His frown becomes mocking. "Ah, I see. So you just don't want me to leave you alone…"

I don't know why, but his taunting, self-assured attitude makes me laugh. "You're insane, you know that, Jamie?"

The teasing expression disappears from his eyes. Hands clasped behind his back, he leans closer and whispers in my ear, "Say it again."

"What?" I croak, suddenly all too aware of how good

ANNA KATMORE

he smells.

"My name." His lips brush my skin. "You're the only one who ever called me Jamie."

"I—um..." My breaths come twice as fast as usual. No idea how he does it, but when he moves his lips across my cheekbone, there are stars in my mind instead of any real thought. I lick my lips.

His hands gently lay down on my hips. "Are you ready to be kissed?" he breathes against the corner of my mouth.

My knees start to tremble. There are butterflies in my belly now. Way too many. "I don't think this is a good idea."

"I think it's the best idea I've had in a long time." His forehead touches mine. We're eye to eye and, once again, I'm lost in the fathomless blue of the sea.

As his palm shapes against my cheek, my gaze lowers. His breath feathers against my skin. With a will of their own, my hands move to his chest. There's a steady, faster-than-normal heartbeat underneath. Heck, for all it's worth, I'm ready to make out with a complete stranger.

Eyes at half-mast, I part my lips for him. Yet he never gets the chance to go through with the kiss. Something huge flies in from the side and knocks Jamie out of my arms, right over the balcony's balustrade. Too appalled to scream, I lung forward, gripping the edge of the rail, and gape down. Jamie lies in the grass beneath.

On top of him is the guy who rammed into him. My heart stops.

The attacker gets to his feet and kicks Jamie hard in his side. He lies still on the ground from the impact of the drop. Fear crashes through me that he could be unconscious. Then a low, pained moan crawls out of his mouth.

As fast as my wobbly legs carry me, I dash back into my room and fumble with the lock at my door. My parents have to call the police. "Mother, Father," I croak, still in too much shock to get a real sound out. The door just doesn't want to come open. And then there's this frightful click behind as someone closes the balcony door. From inside.

Shaking like a leaf, my fingers keep working the key. Just when the bolt springs back, strong arms reach around me and firm hands wrap around mine. I'm being pulled away from the door, and I still can't scream.

"Shh," the person behind me whispers in my ear. He turns me around.

It takes a moment for the information—of who is holding me—to sink in. Then I fling my arms around Peter and cling to his body, sobbing against his chest.

"Hey," he says. "It's okay. He can't hurt you now. I won't let him."

He? The guy who wanted to kiss me? Or the one who knocked him off my balcony? Suddenly a realization hits me hard and I jump back, struggling to swallow through a throat that closed up in horror. "How did you get in here?"

He ignores my question. "We need to talk."

These words and the way he looks scare me even more. I take a wary step back. "Did you just push that guy off the balcony?"

Peter waits a second before he nods. His entire composure radiates doom. "I had to. He's here to kidnap you, Angel."

Both my palms press against my temples. I rake my hands over my skull. "What?"

Peter walks closer, disentangling my fingers from my hair. He leads me to my bed and has me sit down. Good thing, because my knees would have given out any second.

"Listen, and listen well, because this is important." He lowers and rests on his heels in front of me so we're on eye level. "I tried to tell you when we first met, but you didn't remember me or Hook or Neverland. You thought it was a joke. Well, it's not. Neverland is not a made-up story from a book. It's real." He pauses then speaks with more insistence. "I live there."

I blink a few times. "You live in Neverland?" My voice is flat. Detached.

"I do, indeed. And you were there a while ago."

"When I fell off my balcony."

Peter's eyes take on a hopeful shine. "You

remember?"

A crazy laugh escapes me. "That's what Jamie told me before you knocked him over." *Oh my God.* My spine goes stiff. "Did you kill him?" As I jump to my feet, Peter pushes me back down, his hands on my shoulders.

"I wish I had." He rolls his eyes. "But no."

"We must go down and help him!"

His fingers dig into my bones. "Did you hear what I said? He wants to kidnap you."

Yes, and he said weird things about Neverland, too. I just don't believe him. "He wanted to kiss me is all."

"He wanted to seduce you onto his ship. So he could steal you back to Neverland. He's a pirate, Angel. One of the worst sort. Believe me, there's nothing romantic about his intentions."

"His ship?" Things are taking a spiral tonight, from weird to worse. "Where in the world would he park a ship? This is London."

"Right above your house."

Oh God, I'm surrounded by crazy people. I stare at Peter for an immeasurable time. He seemed like such a nice guy in the park. Now I'm scared that I'm with the wrong man in my room. He's a lunatic.

Slowly, I stand up, ignoring his restraining grip, and walk to the French doors. There's not much to see through the pane. Glancing over my shoulder, I cast Peter a scrutinizing look. His chest heaves in a resigned sigh. I open the door and step out.

Down below, the garden is quiet. There's no sign of Jamie or evidence of a fight. Lifting my head—and I'm not saying that I believe Peter about the ship—I scan the sky for anything unusual. Nothing. Not the tiniest boat hovering above the roof. Not even a raft. The sky is clear, black, with a Milky Way to die for.

"His men came down to take their captain away."

At Peter's voice so near me, I jerk around. "You want me to believe that Jamie is the captain of an invisible ship above my house?"

"His name is Captain James Hook, and his ship has gone. It's not *invisible*." His brows furrow to a line. "Not to me, anyway."

"James Hook. From the story of Peter Pan," I say, casting him a wry look. Deliberately, I rub my temples. "I'm coming down with a headache."

"You're making it really hard for me to convince you, Angel." Peter pinches the bridge of his nose, then he throws me a determined look. "Now just don't freak out, okay?" All of a sudden, he bends down and scoops me up in his arms. A surprised gasp escapes me, which no one can hear because we're shooting upward into the sky.

I shriek and he winces. It doesn't make him fly slower.

Fly.

Dear Lord.

I'm going insane.

When the city lights of London zoom past beneath us, he finally starts to speak. "You have this book in your room. *Peter Pan.* I borrowed it a while ago and read it."

Okay?

"I don't know what the story about Wendy has to do with my life, but I do remember this guy called Tootles. A long time ago he was in Neverland." Tilting his head, Peter glares at me. "Like you."

I'm cold up here. In a dream you normally don't feel cold, do you?

"Somehow he returned to your world and obviously he wrote this story about what he saw in Neverland. To you it's just a fairy tale. To me...it's reality."

I swallow hard, because now even I can't deny that there's something very fictional about the man flying with me over London. "Are you saying that you're Peter Pan? The *real* Peter Pan?"

A muscle beats in his jaw. "The *only* Peter Pan."

What am I to make of all this? Everything that's happened tonight shouldn't be happening at all. My head spins. "Please take me back home," I whisper.

Peter looks me sternly in the eye. "You believe me now?"

One deep breath. Two. Three. I nod.

"Good, because there's a lot more you need to know. Let's get you back to your house first, then we can talk."

ANNA KATMORE

He flies a loop, his arms tight around me all the time, and carries me back to my house. As soon as he lands on my balcony and releases me, I pad into my room and walk straight out through the door into the hallway.

Peter closes the balcony door and follows me. "Where are you going?"

My voice flat, I don't bother about whispering. "I need a drink." My nerves are on edge. Whatever happened a few minutes ago can't be undone, so who cares if my parents hear me or not? This is bigger than secretly having a boy in my room after midnight.

Down in the kitchen, I fetch the milk from the fridge and, for once in my life, drink straight from the carton. Only when my nerves have relaxed a little, I give Peter the chance to explain it all. "Spill. What's the deal with you, this guy, the ship? Why do you flitter around in my world and not in a fantasy book? And why, *of all people*, does Captain Hook want to kidnap *me*?"

Peter hesitates a moment. "Because he knows you matter to me."

I do? That keeps me stunned, the milk carton inches from my lips.

"When you fell from the sky to Neverland last time, I caught you and saved you. You stayed with me and my friends for a while." He gives me a bashful smile, and it's so out of character for him, that a laugh rattles up my throat. "We had fun..." he adds. "You and I."

"Fun?"

He moves around the kitchen isle and takes the carton out of my hand. "Actually, more than fun."

Why did his voice soften all of a sudden? Uneasiness grows in me when he lifts his hand to my face and strokes my cheek. "Are you trying to tell me that we were..." *Yeah, what exactly?* "...together, then?"

His lips shifted sweetly to one side, he cocks his head briefly and shrugs. "I guess you could call it that."

Peter is a gorgeous man. Only two days ago in the park, I could have imagined developing a small crush on him. Then again, that was before I met Jamie. *He* was pure godliness, no matter how hard Peter tries to make me believe he's dangerous. And there was just something about him that drew me in, besides the fact that he knew things about me. Things that I never told anyone. I clear my throat. "Where does Captain Hook fit into this story?"

Peter's hand drops from my cheek. He takes a step back and leans against the isle, folding his arms over his chest. "Hook stole you from me. He brought you to his ship, hoping that he could get to me through you."

"Why would he do that?" Now I'm wondering how much of the original Peter Pan story is true. "Did he want to kill you?"

"Probably. Most of all, he wanted to get to the treasure that the Lost Boys and I keep hidden from him. He's a greedy man, that pirate. Cares about nothing and

ANNA KATMORE

no one, only about what he can steal from others."

I want to slap myself for even asking, "How did that end? Did he trade me for the treasure?"

"No. He wouldn't let you go, even if we gave him what he wanted."

"How did I get free then?"

Now Peter smirks like a teenage boy up to something. "I saved you."

"Ah." So I was the real Wendy in his tale. That would be so romantic...if it wasn't completely insane. "How did I get back to London?"

"I taught you to fly."

"How?" *No, wait! I know it, I know it!* "With a happy thought and some pixie dust?"

"Exactly." His grin turns into a frown. "That wasn't the right way to send you home, however. You had to fall again, the same way you fell into Neverland."

"Oh. Weird." I put more volume into my voice as I say, "So why are you here now?"

"I missed you, so I followed you. And Hook must have followed me. He surely thinks if he can steal you again, he'll get the treasure eventually."

"So I'm just a pawn in this battle of yours?"

"To him you are. To me"—he takes my hand and squeezes it—"you're more."

Does he think I'm his girlfriend? I can't be! I don't know him at all. Gosh, this is crazy. "So, what do you want me to do now?"

"Stay inside until I take care of Hook."

I laugh. "That's definitely not going to happen. I have school tomorrow, and then there's the dance in the evening." My friends and I have been looking forward to it for most of this year. It's my last high school dance. Nothing will stop me from going.

"It's too dangerous with Hook in this world."

I take a moment to recap the situation. Peter can fly, so he probably is the real Pan. *If* he's the real Pan, then Jamie might be the real *Hook*. And I've read the story often enough to know just how cruel Captain Hook is. Even though it doesn't apply to the gentle guy who tried to coax a kiss from me less than an hour ago. He didn't look anything like the pirate captain from the movies or book. Heck, he even had both of his hands—and I would know since they were on me when he leaned in to kiss me.

For all I know, I should be scared of Jamie—*James Hook*. And yet the fascination I hold for him runs deeper than that. I wonder what would have happened if Peter hadn't interrupted the kiss. Well, if Jamie really is the ruthless pirate, it's probably best to be thankful for Peter's help.

"How can I protect you from him if you're out there and free for him to approach you?" Peter insists.

A funny thought sneaks into my mind. "Easy. Come with me."

"To the dance?" Contemplating my offer, he purses his lips.

"So?" I prompt him.

He scratches his chin that by now holds a dusting of stubble again. "It might work."

At that moment, footsteps carry down from the stairs. Peter and I both jerk around to the door. "It's my mother," I hiss.

Lifting his arms in a helpless shrug, he grimaces, definitely devoid of a solution. Before we get caught, I dash to the window and open it for him. He just stares at me, so I gesture with my arms in sweeping moves. "Outside!" He can fly, so that won't be a problem. When he glides past me, I grab his arm and hold him back for one more second. "It's a spring dance. You can wear whatever you like. Pick me up at eight."

He nods then zooms off.

Jeez! Peter Pan just freaking flew out of my house.

Quickly closing the window after him, I pivot and grin at my mother's sleepy face as she stands in the doorway. "I heard noise. What are you doing up this late?" she demands and smothers a yawn with her hand.

I scrunch up my face, chewing the inside of my cheek. "I had a weird craving for milk." There's really nothing else I could tell her. I mean, no one will ever believe that I have a date with the notorious Peter Pan tomorrow.

Peter Pan

NOW THAT DIDN'T go too badly. Hook is gone. His ship is gone. And I have a date with his girl.

After Angel let me out through the kitchen window, I intended to fly back in through her balcony door, except clever me locked it before we went downstairs. Perched on the chimney on top of the roof once more, I scan the neighborhood. Everything is silent.

Gazing at the black-blue sky, I can't stop wondering where Smee has steered the ship. Hook himself certainly isn't in a position to command anything tonight. The impact on the ground knocked him out cold. It'll take a while until he comes around, and then with a mean headache for sure.

Seems like Angel bought the lies I told her about him, if not a hundred percent. When he tries to sneak up to her next time, she'll be a little more alert than she was tonight. I'll be damned if she lets him kiss her again. A

ANNA KATMORE

sneer creeps to my lips, though I manage to suppress the rising snicker. Phase one of my plan to take revenge on my brother is playing out perfectly so far.

I think Angel even liked it when I touched her. A couple of days ago in the park, she let me carry her. The look on her face then had been etched into my mind. It was...*enamored.* It actually hadn't been easy to leave that picture of us back in Hook's cabin. I debated half the night whether I should keep it to myself. Angel looked adorable in it. I could have stared at it for hours, but the image doesn't even come close to the original.

Tonight, when Angel clung to me, recovering from the shock of the incident outside her room, I would have given a lot to be able to keep holding her like that. She always feels so soft and fragile, and in the next moment she can be a sassy little thing. I like that. It makes me want to spend more time with her. Makes me want to make her smile.

All these new thoughts are confusing as hell. I wonder if it all came with me aging. Dammit, I must stop thinking about Angel that way. Beautiful or not, I can't afford to let her distract me so badly.

In the end, revenge is all that counts.

Chapter 8

"WATER, CAP'N?"

Struggling to open my eyes, I turn my head in the direction of Smee's worried voice. I swallow and try to move, but my head feels like it's being weighed down by an elephant's ass. When a cup touches my lips, I drink in small sips. It takes a while until I can focus on anything. "Care to tell me why I'm in my quarters and need you to tend to me?" I whine.

"Took a blow to your head."

Not only to my head, it seems. Pain surges in my side, making me wince at my attempt to sit up. "Explain."

"As far as I could see through the shield of clouds, you were about to kiss the lass. Then Pan knocked into you and the both of you dropped from the balcony."

Rubbing my forehead and temples, I moan. Slowly, everything comes back to me. I *was* about to kiss Angel. I almost had her ready to believe me. Damn Peter's bad timing. That fucking little bastard, I'm going to kill him for ruining that moment for me. "How did I get back?"

"Pan left when Wade Dawkins and I lowered on the rope to get to your aid. We brought you up. As soon as you were back on the Jolly Roger, she moved."

"Moved? Where are we?" There's not much to see through the windows in my cabin. Outside is black with some faraway dots that might be stars.

"We sailed—or flew—higher up into the sky. If you ask me, we're somewhere between Angel's world and Neverland now. You've been out cold for almost ten hours."

"What?" This can't be. It means I wasted the first night of three snoozing away in my cabin instead of winning Angel over. I throw the blanket aside and jump out of bed, which after a blow to the head is obviously punished with a dizzy spell. Ignoring the black dots taking up most of my vision, I shove Smee aside and stumble to the door, pulling it open. The crew sits on deck, playing cards and drinking the hours away. The ship stands totally still in the sky. Everything around us is a velvety black sea with diamond stars all around.

It's a wonder my wobbly legs carry me up to the sterncastle. Grasping the wheel, I spin it around. Nothing happens. There's no wind in the sails to move the ship. "Go, you damn thing!" I kick the helm hard. "Go, go, go!"

"Maybe it's because she mustn't be seen down in

Angel's world in daylight hours. You said the fairy insisted we only go down in the shelter of night."

It's true. Still—a whole night wasted and being stranded until it gets dark down there again? This isn't fair!

After some good persuading from Smee's side, he convinces me to eat a few bites of food and take the time to rest some more, since there's no chance to change things anyway. My headache ceases after a while and I start pacing the decks for what seems like forever.

Eventually, the sounds of linen catching wind draw my gaze up. The sails billow. The ship sways. Then it starts to sink.

Sink? By Davie Jones' locker, where is the fairy's magic dust? Finding the jar with the rainbow sand in my cabin, I use the second third to dust the Jolly Roger. As soon as the job is done, I dart back to the bridge and grab the wheel. This time, my mere touch is enough to move the ship. We're heading back to London, the sea of lights coming into view.

Taking the same route as last night, we soon reach the suburb and the peaceful, dark street with Angel's house. There's not a minute to waste. "Let me down on the rope, Smee!" I holler as anticipation takes complete control over my heartbeat.

He hands me one end of the rope. At the same time Bull's Eye calls out, "Cap'n! There's someone leaving the house. I think it's Angel. And she's with—"

I look up at the crow's nest, meeting Ravi's grimace. "Pan," he finishes.

Finding another spyglass on deck, I take a look myself. Dressed in a floating, dark pink dress that reveals her delectable legs from her knees down, Angel clings to Peter's arm as they move across her front yard. A black coach without a horse is waiting for them outside the garden fence. Peter lets her get in first and then stoops to follow. They slam the door and the vehicle moves down the street, slowly at first, then it gains speed, taking off in the direction of the town.

"Follow them!" I shout, making Jack wince as he's standing next to me.

Wherever Angel goes tonight, I'll go too. I don't care if I have to chase her across the globe. This is the second night I have with her, and I'm not going to waste a single minute of it.

Angelina

DURING THE PAST couple days, the gym at my high school has been successfully transformed into the hall of *Thousand and One Nights*. Kudos to our outstanding ball committee. Lanterns and colorful veils decorate the walls and ceiling, cardboard castles with flame-like tops fill the corners. The air is thick with a distinct musky scent. I'm sitting with five of my best friends at a table with a yellow cloth, a flower bouquet in the center, and then Peter Pan at my side.

Of course, no one knows who he really is. To them, he's just a friend of mine, a last-minute decision who won't take off his leather jacket in spite of the twenty-five degrees Celsius it must be in here. They all seem to like him, even though he casts an uncomfortable look at me every now and then. Of course he would—they're talking about video games and the pros and cons of a stick-shift car versus an automatic. Things that, as far as I can tell,

ANNA KATMORE

don't exist in Neverland.

"Overwhelmed?" I ask him under my breath as I lean closer to his side.

"A little," he confesses.

"Now you have an idea of how I felt last night, when you broke the news to me that you're actually a character out of my favorite fairy tale."

Peter smirks. "Ah, you can't fool me. You liked the flying. I could tell by your excited"—he waggles his brows—"screams."

Screams? Yes. Excited? Not so much. "More hysteric, I'd say." Although I have to give myself credit for handling this weird situation surprisingly well. Okay, I had half a night and an entire day to get used to the thought of Peter Pan being my date tonight. After the spinning of my mind and my questioning my sanity had lessened toward the morning, I even got a couple hours of sleep.

The hardest thing about all this was not telling my little sisters. They would freak out if they knew. With my parents *so* not living in a fantasy world, I don't want anybody to sell me out and earn me a visit with the shrink.

And then there's still Hook.

I might not have slept much last night, yet the little time I was sucked into the land of dreams was enough for his eyes and smile to haunt me all the way down. And not in a bad way. In fact, I was wondering most of today how a young man as gentle as Jamie could actually run with a pack of pirates. And worse, be their ruthless captain. Maybe it was the lack of the long, curly wig, the wide hat, and Disney's infamous red brocade coat that is deceiving me. I just can't imagine him being capable of kidnapping or murder.

Then again, what do I really know about him? Nothing. It's certainly wise to stop thinking about his lips brushing mine, and instead keep close to Peter. He's the good guy after all. Everybody knows that. Even though in my mind he always was a boy of maybe fifteen with green clothes and a funny hat with a red feather. Definitely not the grown man who sits in the chair next to me now and reads the label of the Red Bull bottle in his hand like he's never seen a more exotic juice.

He takes a swig—and grimaces. "Eew. Who drinks such nasty stuff?" he whispers in my direction.

I laugh. "Want to get an orange juice or something?" At his nod, I get up. Just as he is about to rise and follow me, Sebastian Wilton turns to him and asks him about his account name on Facebook. I know it's mean, yet I can't resist waiting, with folded arms and a smirk, for his answer.

Peter goes the safe way and slowly shakes his head. "No *Phasebook*." That gets Sebastian started on a tangent about social media and how it's unfairly damned by society when so many possibilities come with it. Peter is a patient listener.

ANNA KATMORE

Since they're just starting to warm up to each other, I don't want to drag him away with me. "I'll get you a cup of OJ," I mouth and he nods, although he makes a helpless face at me. Sebastian is a nice guy. I trust him to keep Peter in a good mood until I'm back in a few minutes.

Unfortunately, I don't get far. On my way to the bar through the crowd on the dance floor, I run into Melissa Strathford. She lived in my street through half of our school lives. A couple of years ago, her family moved to Soho. I almost don't recognize her with her new hairstyle, a pixie cut instead of the willowing blond mane she used to love so much.

Since we haven't seen each other in a while, I don't get away with a simple *hi*. I compliment her about her new hair, and she replies with compliments about my halter-neck satin dress and my strappy sandals in silvery synthetic leather. Then we catch up on each other's lives, even though I leave out the most recent events including a pirate and a flying visitor from Neverland.

Once every few minutes, I cut a glance back to our table to check if Peter is still happily entertained. Obviously, Sebastian is doing a good job. One time, Peter catches my eyes across the room and makes a quirky face, sticking his tongue out at me when no one seems to be looking. He looks years younger at that moment. Almost like the boy I imagined Peter Pan to be. The gesture makes me chuckle, and I turn back to Melissa for the umpteenth time during the past ten minutes. Except, this time, my gaze gets stuck on a striking set of eyes in the crowd.

Seawater blue.

An invisible chunk of ice slides down my spine.

"Angelina, are you all right?" Melissa touches my elbow and I shoot around to face her.

"What? Oh, yeah, sure." At the same moment, I pivot to find those haunting eyes again. They're gone. Spinning on the spot, an uncomfortable feeling nestles in my stomach. Did I just imagine it? What if this dangerous pirate who apparently wants to kidnap me has somehow found me at my school dance?

"I'm sorry, Mel," I tell my old friend, bouncing uneasily on the balls of my feet. "Can we talk about this later? I really need to get back to my friend over there." I point at the table behind me—and stiffen. Peter is no longer sitting with the others. His chair is shoved back as if he rose in a hurry, his bottle of Red Bull still standing on the table.

"Sure, see you later," I hear Melissa say, but I don't pay her any attention. I need to find Peter. If he left the table, there's no doubt about it: Captain Hook is here.

With a heartbeat matching the rhythm of the band on stage, I scan the room. Where the heck is Peter? He was supposed to take care of me. Wasn't that the whole deal with me bringing him here as my date? To have a bodyguard? And here I am, alone. With a pirate on the loose.

Don't panic, I tell myself. I'm in a gym where people are packed together like sardines in a can. No one would be so stupid as to try to kidnap someone from here. Or so I hope.

Slowly, I wander from one end to the other, sweeping the room with terrified glances. Gone is the longing feeling I had after those intense dreams of last night. It's completely sucked out of me. All that's left is a slight tremor of my bones.

Someone says my name—quite close. And so seductively, it makes the hair at the back of my neck stand on end. I whirl about. My mouth is dry and my stomach is churning, but there's no familiar face behind me. Obviously mistaken, a relieved sigh leaves me. I turn around again.

And freeze.

"Jamie." The word escapes me in a whisper.

"Angel," he replies.

As my eyes dart from left to right, searching for the best way out, he takes a step closer. Breaking into my personal space so easily, he gives me half a smile. I try to back away when he takes my hands and pulls me against him, slowly, gently.

"What do you want from me?" I croak, somewhat

short of air.

Leaning down to my ear, he drawls, "We have unfinished business." His hands slide up my arms to linger on my shoulders. The touch leaves a trail of goosebumps on my skin. "If I remember it right, you promised me a kiss last night."

Breathing in the adventurous scent of the sea mingled with tangerine brings back the horde of butterflies that bred in my stomach last night. "Things have changed," I answer, sounding not in the least as confident as I wanted to.

He inches back and lets a killer smirk loose at me. "Have they now?"

I try to hold his intense gaze, yet all I see is a face to die for. At long last, I manage a nod.

"I see. No kiss then." I almost crack a smile at the boyish pout on his face. The silken hair falling over his forehead now partly covers his right eye. "Maybe you'll agree to a dance instead?"

And I think it again: *Where the heck is Peter?* He's supposed to save me from an ambush like this.

My heart clips at an unhealthy rate as Hook slowly moves me backward into the middle of the dancing crowd. Both my hands in his, he brings them up to his neck. His warm skin, so tempting to touch, works like glue on fingers.

Caught in the spell of his deep blue eyes, my thought

of escape loses priority.

He's not wearing the black hoodie tonight. To my total astonishment, white suits him even better than black. The button up shirt he wears hangs over his dark pants and makes him almost blend in with the casual wear of the majority of the male crowd. The only thing he's missing is a tie loosely wrapped around his neck. With his wild, predatory look? Yeah, I can't see that happening.

Do you know those moments when you look at someone and, within seconds, everything around you fades? When the upbeat music you heard only seconds ago miraculously turns into something soft and sweet? When your knees buckle and your heart wants to give out for no obvious reason? Well, this is what happens to me right now. Only there's no chance of me falling with James Hook's arms enveloping me like my personal safety lines.

He starts to sway me to the music. "Someone's tense. Do I make you nervous?"

That would be the understatement of the century.

"Why are you scared of me, Angel?" he whispers, his face closer to mine now.

"Because you're a pirate."

"Says the boy who almost killed me last night when he shoved me off your balcony?"

"Says Peter Pan."

That makes Hook chuckle, only I can't tell if it's irritated or amused. "So am I to assume he told you everything else about Neverland, too? And you believe it now?"

Steeling my nerves with renewed determination, I challenge him with a look. "He told me that you're after me to get to him."

"Oh, he's right. I'm definitely after you, Angel." Hook dips his head just a little and nuzzles the side of my face.

Jeez, how can something so wrong feel so right?

"But why would I want to get to him?" Hook asks with just a bit of confusion in his voice that makes me pull back and search his face.

"Because he has a treasure that you obviously want," I snap. As if he really needs that bit of information.

A second ticks away before he speaks again. This time with leashed annoyance. "Is that so?"

I don't know what to make of it. "Are you telling me it was a lie?" Not that I would believe him if he said so.

"Aye."

Like I said, I don't believe him. That doesn't stop me from asking, "Why are you really here then?"

The hard muscles in his jaw soften and he strokes the backs of his fingers down my cheek. "I already told you last night. I'm here because of you."

"What am I to you, that you felt the need to leave Neverland for me?" Gosh, am I really having this conversation? Somehow I get the feeling I've read this book one too many times to my sisters. It must have gotten to my head. Then I remember how Peter carried me over London in his arms the previous night, and all doubt is blown away.

"You're everything to me," Hook answers. His tender voice dares me to believe him.

I can't. He's the mean guy. The pirate everyone fears. So why don't I? No way in hell should I be dancing with him and enjoying his touch so much.

"Come outside with me, Angel, and I will tell you everything you need to know."

What did he just say?

He wants to seduce you onto his ship. So he can steal you back to Neverland. Peter's words ring in my ears. As if under shock therapy, my common sense awakens. I yank myself free from Hook's embrace. "You're a pirate. *You* are the liar, not Peter," I hiss. "I'll go nowhere with you. Forget it! And now you better leave or I'll scream bloody murder and point a finger at you."

For an immeasurable moment, he just stares at me as though he's gauging how much of it I really mean. Then one of his eyebrows arches up in a challenging way. Just when I'm sure I lost this battle and really have to scream, he takes my hand and lifts it to his lips, breathing a kiss onto the back. "Until we meet again, Angel."

Then he turns and leaves the dance.

I take a minute to catch my breath. And when that

isn't enough, I take another. Finally feeling steady enough to carry my own weight, however ungracefully, I stumble back to the table my friends occupy. My hands find solid support on the backrest of Peter's vacated chair.

"Angel, what's the matter with you?" Carla Norris asks, shooting a worried glance my way. "You look like you've seen a ghost."

"Make that a pirate," I mumble, knowing no one can hear. "I'm coming down with a migraine." Lame excuse, all right, but what better thing was there to say? "Do you guys know where Peter went?"

"Said he saw a few friends of his and that he'll be gone for a while," Sebastian explains.

Great. Just great. "I think I'll call my dad and ask him to pick me up. When Peter comes back, can you tell him I went home?"

"Sure. But there's no way you're calling your dad out for a ride home," says Shawn Chennings, standing up and raking a hand though his straight brown hair. "I can take you."

Shawn has been hitting on me for the past couple years. Since he lives just down the street and I've known him my entire life, I just can't see us being anything other than friends. He knows it, and that's the only reason I'm giving in to his offer now. Well, that and the fact that I want to get home as fast as possible without running into James Hook again. He's a totally different case in the

ANNA KATMORE

matter of rejecting a kiss.

In Shawn's car, rubbing my forehead at my pretend headache saves me from any conversation. He just concentrates on the road. Then again, not all of the migraine is pretended. He lets me out in front of my house and says, "See you at school on Monday."

I nod, secretly thinking, *only if I happen to keep out of Hook's way until then.* Inwardly, I kick myself for that thought, because it adds a shiver to the chill that the night is already giving me. My gaze is all over the place as I head up to our door. Damn, if meeting a fairy tale figure comes with these creepy feelings, I take back all the times I wished myself into the story of Snow White or even to Middle Earth.

Luckily, nothing happens on the way through our front garden. Pushing out an audible sigh of relief, I let myself in. The house is silent. Mom and Dad must have gone to bed early. They surely didn't expect me back until thirty seconds before curfew, which would have been at two o'clock in the morning on weekends. According to the grandfather clock in our living room it's barely midnight.

I hit the shower, dress in my comfy short black sweats and a white tank top, and head to my room, turning on the light. There's no need to worry. I'm safe inside, I tell myself. And once Peter hears that I've gone home, he'll come here and protect me like he promised.

As if on cue, there's a tap on the French door. My

bed can wait for another short while. I need to talk to Peter first. I rush to the French door and pull it open. But Peter isn't outside. In fact, no one is. There's just a single gold coin lying on the ground.

The moment I pick it up, another coin is tossed onto my balcony. They look weird, heavy and not smoothly round. There's an island on one side of the coin, and the number one on the other. The word *doubloon* is imprinted in a circle along the edge.

"Peter?" I whisper, scanning the back of the garden where the second piece of gold came flying from. "Is that you?"

"Come out," he hisses back. "We need to talk."

Scratching my head, I wonder why he doesn't just fly over here so we can talk inside. Then it dawns on me that it has something to do with what happened at the dance. Maybe he feels bad for leaving me alone and is now too shy to come up here.

Silent as a mouse, I tiptoe downstairs and slip out through the back door. The grass is still warm after a sunny day. Keeping close to the house for safety, I whisper Peter's name again into the darkness. This time he doesn't reply, but from above another gold coin lands in front of my bare feet. I pick it up, and another one drops a few feet ahead. And then another ahead of that one. It's almost like he's leading me away from the house with those coins. What kind of game is he playing?

ANNA KATMORE

Then again, with Peter out here, I should be safe enough, so I take a deep breath before I follow the trail of coins.

With a small heap of treasure in my hands, I reach the back of our garden, standing inside a triangle of aged oaks, and lift my gaze to the sky. Everything is silent for a minute. I think even the wind holds its breath. Then suddenly, a gentle rain of gold falls.

Coin after coin drops from above and lands in the long grass that caresses my feet. Every time one lands on top of the other, a quiet chime sounds. More and more of the treasure rains down on me, turning into a romantic melody of gold clinking against gold.

I cannot describe the beauty that I find myself in the center of. With my hands raised up and my face tilted skyward, I smile as I dance in the mysterious rain. Whether it comes from the sky, the clouds, or from the tops of the trees—I can't tell. Soon the ground fills up with gold shining in the moonlight.

If this is Peter's way of making up for leaving me at the dance, he sure just broke back into my heart. All the way...

At a rustle in the treetops, I shift my gaze then turn around. Anticipation washes over me like the drizzle of gold did before. "Come down, Peter," I whisper. "You're forgiven."

In front of me, he drops from what seems to be the

highest branch of the tree and lands in a crouch, bracing his hands on the gold-covered ground. The first thing I notice is his fair hair—not brown. Then the white shirt. And when Hook finally lifts his chin to look into my eyes, I freeze.

ANNA KATMORE

Chapter 9

AT THE SHOCK in Angel's eyes, she obviously didn't expect me here, and there's only so much a girl can take, I guess. She's a hairbreadth away from screaming her head off. I decide to take it slow with her this time.

"Hook." The name is a whisper on her lips—an insult. I hate that she doesn't call me Jamie tonight. Peter has taken that last bit of happiness away from me too. All I want to do is skewer him for it, but now is not the time to plot his death.

I rise from the ground. There's no way I'll let Angel out of my sight and I think that's the one thing that keeps her from shrieking.

I don't know if it's safe to walk toward her...safe for her and for me, too, because as my eyes roam the length of her body, the ravenous pirate inside me struggles to get free. She's barely wearing anything, short pants and a strange top unsuitable for a young woman. These are for sure the most alluring clothes I've seen her in yet.

"What are you doing here?" Angel hisses at me, her body rigid.

That's better than screaming for help I guess and lift my shoulders in a helpless shrug. "I was hoping we could talk."

Her beautiful ebony hair falls forward as she lowers her chin and forces a frown on me. "Did *you* do this?" she snaps and, with her arms, she weakly gestures around her. "The gold, the treasure? Did you throw all that down on me?"

It escapes me how she does this all the time—look at me in a certain way or say something to totally send the pirate in me running. "You looked happier about it a couple of minutes ago," I answer in a small voice.

"That was because I thought Peter did it. You tricked me out here. Why?"

My tiny step forward scares her back a couple of big ones, so I stop again and take a deep breath, placating her with my hands lifted. "To prove something to you." It's obvious that all the lies Peter told her about me have taken hold. She's lost the trust in me that I'd worked so hard to earn when she'd been with me on the Jolly Roger. "Peter told you I wanted to use you to get to him and, thus, to the treasure. Right?" At least that's what she accused me of at the dance earlier.

She chews my words over for a moment, obviously

not understanding where I want to go with this.

"Well, here it is," I say and swipe my arms sideways, pointing out that we're standing right in the middle of my treasure. "Or part of it. The rest is still on my ship. I thought it'd be enough to convince you there's no need for me to use you for anything. I have my gold." After a pause, my voice drops a notch. "What I don't have is you, Angel. And it's been killing me ever since you left me."

"I left *you*?" When Angel laughs, it sounds more outraged than amused. "How could I have left you? When I was in Neverland I was"—her brows knit together and there's uncertainty in her voice now—"with Peter?"

"Is that what he told you? That you were together, like a couple?"

A reluctant nod from her gives me hope that she's at least considering what I'm going to tell her next. "Peter was a boy when you were in Neverland. About three years younger than you are now." The gold clings under my feet as I dare to take another small step toward her. "Does falling in love with him really make sense to you?"

The doubt in her eyes now is genuine. She shakes her head. "None of this makes sense to me. And Peter isn't a boy. He must be at least twenty or older, not fifteen like you say."

"He looks twenty now." I let go of a sigh that's rather painful. "And that's my fault. Peter Pan was the boy who wouldn't grow up. I was trying to catch him for a hundred years and then some, because he stole my treasure. I probably would have killed him too, if I'd gotten the chance." Abandoning the new edge to my voice, I continue, "Then you came to Neverland and weird things happened. To him, to me...to *us*." At the last word, I tilt my head and give her what I hope is a convincing and maybe seductive look as I point to the space between us. "Spending time with you was the best thing that happened to me in a long time." A really long time. Now I wonder how I could've lived all these years and not have gone insane. "Nevertheless, in the end we had to find a way to bring you back to London. So you could be with your family again. It was the first time Peter and I worked on something together. And it was"—I grimace—"nice."

Angel is silent for a long moment. Damn, I hate it when I don't know what's going on in that pretty head of hers. Finally, she shifts her mouth to one side. "Last night, you said you were brothers?"

Blow me down! There it is, that typical sweet lift of her chin when her true spirit comes out to play. A shiver of joy zaps through me. I can barely hold back a smirk. "Aye."

"And you buried the hatchet?"

"We did. For your sake. You did that for us."

The shimmer of trust that was on the rise disappears completely now. "Why are you lying to me, Hook? Peter hates you with all his heart. Why else would he warn me to stay away from you?" Her breath freezes in her lungs as though she's only now realizing something terrible. Her voice is cold next, and very low. "Where is he? What did you do to him at the dance?"

"Peter is all right. My men took care of him."

"Did you hurt him?"

I hate to see the fear for my brother in her eyes when she obviously doesn't remember who I was to her at all. "No. I'm just making sure he's keeping his nose out of this so you and I can have this conversation alone. It wasn't nice of him to interrupt us last night." That came out in an irritated growl, unfortunately. No chance to take it back, but I don't want to scare her. This time I take two steps toward her, which she immediately mirrors in the opposite direction. What she doesn't know is that only one more step and she'll bump into the tree behind her. My chance. She'll be trapped.

I walk on, ignoring her gasp when she hits the dead end. "You're right," I tell her and keep my voice soft as I lift my hand to her face and stroke my knuckles down her cheek. "He hates me now. In order to get to you, I had to force him to do something that changed him. I made him break the spell."

"What spell?"

"Hmm?" I know she said something, but I completely missed it because I'm sucked into the beauty of her eyes and stunned by the fact that she lets me touch her. *Blow me down*, she didn't even flinch.

"You said he broke the spell. *What* spell?"

"The spell that stopped time in Neverland," I answer absently. It's suddenly so hard to concentrate. She's too beautiful. Does she even know? The wisp of her hair I rub between my fingers feels soft like the rainbow essence the fairy extracted from my clothes. I hook the strand behind her ear, dipping my head just a little to breathe in the amazing scent that intoxicated me the first time I carried her in my arms.

Her soft hands come up to rest on my chest. If she wants to push me away, she's not trying very hard. "If you have everything, why did you come for me?"

Encouraged by her lack of resistance, I run the tip of my nose from the bridge of hers down to the tip. So close, her warm, hitched breath feathers against my skin, and I like it. Then I realize she's not pushing me away at all. She's actually feeling me up. I take her face between both my hands and tilt her head up, just a little, so she's looking me straight in the eyes when I tell her, "Because you're the reason that made thinking of eternity bearable for me."

It's the truth in my voice, I think, that she hears and that makes her gasp as she realizes I don't want to cause her any harm. All I want is to crush my mouth to hers. And she certainly sees that coming too. Her fingers claw slightly against my chest, digging into my shirt. Gentler

ANNA KATMORE

than should be possible for anyone in my very position, I touch my lips to hers.

Angel doesn't bite me, hiss, or spit at me. Neither does she scream *bloody murder* like she threatened earlier tonight. She just lets me kiss her and I know I'm one step closer, even if, most likely, she still has no clue who I am. Our lips mold together. Tender. In a slow, soft rhythm of their own. Heck, she feels so good, tastes so good, I want to eat her up.

But there's still some hesitance in her kissing me back. *Surrender*, I want to yell at her. How can I make her trust me completely? How can I get through to the girl that slept in my arms at Mermaid Lagoon? I don't know. I only know that I won't let her go now...for anything in the world.

I deepen the kiss. My tongue sweeps through her mouth and tangles with hers. Oh, the glory of kissing Angel again! And she so easily relents. Every last doubt is blown from my mind—she really is giving everything right now. No matter what she thinks of me, no matter how scared she might be, she wants this as much as I want it. My hands drop to her shoulders, and I run my fingers down her arms until they come to rest on her waist. She actually shivers.

When she inches back but let's me rest my forehead against hers, she whispers against my lips, "Who *are* you?"

The truth is I no longer know the answer myself. I've

been a pirate for such a long time, but when I'm with this girl there's always only one person present. "I'm Jamie," I tell her on the same whisper and kiss her again.

This time, she gives in to me completely. It's not my tongue that tries to catch hers anymore, but hers that starts to explore my mouth. As if finally feeling the gravity that's been between us from the start, she clings to me as if there's no other man in the world she ever wants to kiss again. My arms react of their own accord and wrap tightly around her, pulling her harder against me. I love that little moan of hers that I catch with my mouth, I love her trembling hands that roam up my chest and get a grip in my hair at the back of my head. Frankly—I love *her*. She's been mine to hold from the beginning, and I'll find ways to convince her of it time and time again, if needed.

As I ease back and gaze down at her face, her breaths take a few seconds to cool down. A sweet, soft blush sneaks to her cheeks, making her all the more adorable. Although she tries to pull back from me and her fingers loosen the death grip in my hair, I don't let her go. With my hands firmly where they were for the past couple of minutes, she should be able to figure out that she can't pull off a kiss like that and then just put that annoying distance between us again. No freakin' way.

I take a moment to catch my own breath. Then a smirk comes out to play. "You like it, don't you?"

"Listen." There's no volume in her voice just yet, so

ANNA KATMORE

she forcefully clears her throat and tries again. "I don't know what just happened here, but it's certainly not right to kiss a savage pirate after midnight."

"That shouldn't be a problem. We can change the after-midnight part to whenever you want."

She gives me a hard glare. "It's certainly not the after-midnight part that concerns me."

I know that, and still I couldn't resist teasing her. When she places her hands over mine behind her back, however, and pries my arms away from her, my easy smile goes into hiding. "What? You're still scared of me?" She holds my gaze for a moment then lowers hers to her toes, and it dawns on me. "No, you aren't. The kiss awakened *something*, didn't it?"

"Will you leave me alone if I say no?"

"No."

Her eyes shoot up to mine. She gasps. "But you promised. Last night—"

"Love, I'm a pirate. I make promises all day long only to forget them a minute later." Strangely enough, it's the promises to *her* that I tend to keep. "You might have stood a chance of getting rid of me if you really felt nothing. What happened between you and me just now, though, was definitely *not* nothing. So, I'm afraid this time you won't get your way with me."

"What do you mean?"

What I mean? That I have rainbow dust left for one

more night. If I go back to Neverland without her then, I might not see her ever again. If I take her with me on the other hand, there's enough dust left to bring her back in a little while. Heck, I'm definitely not leaving alone. All the fighting for Angel, all the shit I put up with and put Peter through to finally get to her—that sure wasn't for just a dance and one helluva kiss.

When Angel sees the determination in my eyes, her body tenses. In a brave dash to the left, she tries to escape. I'm faster than her and have my fingers wrapped around her wrist the instant she moves. "Sorry, I can't let you do that."

Spinning her around, I press her back flush to my chest and whistle, using two fingers of my free hand.

"What are you doing? Let me go!" The girl actually stomps on my foot. Not as bad as the blow to my chest she gave me the first time we met, but still quite impressive. I wince.

"See, I only have one more night in your world," I growl into her ear, "and chances are, you won't let me see you again tomorrow. I can't have this. We're going back to Neverland, now. You and I."

"Are you crazy?"

Maybe a little bit, but that, as well, is her fault.

"What about Peter?" she hisses.

Why the hell does she always have to care about him more than me? "Peter will stay behind. I'm not going to hurt him. He is, after all, my brother." When my men abducted him from the dance and tied him up to the highest branch of a birch tree in the park not far from here, I just couldn't bring myself to slice his throat, however much he'd deserved it. "It doesn't mean I'll let him interfere with this again."

The tighter I hold Angel the harder she struggles in my arms. It doesn't matter, she can fight me all she wants. In the end, she'll be happy I did this. Hopefully.

On my signal, Smee dropped one end of a rope that now dangles in front of us. Wrapping it around our bodies, I press one hand over Angel's mouth to kill the scream she just barely got started and shout, "Get us up, Smee!"

A steady pull begins. We're lifted into the air, out of her garden, through the shielding magic clouds, and onto the Jolly Roger. I hate to frighten Angel like that, but as it is, I don't see any other way at the moment. "Set sail!" I bark to the crew as soon as we stand firmly on deck. Well, I stand and Angel still squeals in my arms. "We're going home!"

Smee gives me the lightest of frowns. He knows better than to question me right now.

"All hands on deck, ye scabby dogs!" he yells out to the others and busies them with getting the Jolly Roger ready for departure.

Since I still have my hand over Angel's mouth,

there's no sound coming from her. Yet by the way her chest doesn't move for a minute, it's easy to see how much it surprises her to find herself on a ship with actual pirates. Just like the first time I took her aboard. What are sweet memories to me might not be so nice to her. Then again, she doesn't remember anything, so we're good on that front, I guess.

It's probably not a good idea to release Angel just yet. A silent place to talk and explain everything seems to be the way to go about this. I lift her from the floor and sort of drag-carry her into my quarters. Heck, that girl puts up a hell of a fight. It makes me smirk—but not put her back down.

Once in my quarters, I kick the door closed and stop in front of my bed. "I'm going to let you go now. Just don't freak out or run away. There's a reason why I brought you up to my ship. So can you please just promise to stay here and we'll talk about this?"

The hoped-for nod never comes. At least she's breathing again, if way too fast through her nose. Not only can I feel her chest lift and fall under my embrace, her warm breaths also dampen my hand over her mouth in quick intervals. I decide to take that hand away first.

"You bloody freaking pirate! Take your goddamn hands off me! You dirty liar! You kidnapped me!"

That was quite enough for round one. I cover her mouth again. "I meant *I* was doing the talking and you the *listening*," I say in her ear, slightly irritated with her swell of curses. Am I really that bad?

Angel thrashes about but, let's face it, she's a fragile girl and I'm—well, I'm a pirate. I know how to handle stubborn people. Too fast for her to see it coming, I push her flush against the wall and trap her, using the weight of my body behind hers. Both her hands now in mine, I lift them over her head and pin them to the wall too. Her head is turned sideways. It can't be comfortable how her cheek rubs against the rough wall as she let's go of round two of curses.

This time I don't interrupt her. Only when she becomes aware of me nuzzling her neck and the side of her head all this time, she falls silent.

"Feeling better now that it's all out?" I tease her.

"Go to hell," is her answer to that.

"Give me a chance here, Angel. Please. Let me tell you what really happened the last time you fell into my world."

She snorts. I get the feeling that she's at least ready to listen. Whether or not that's true, I have to try. "Peter saved you while dropping from the skies. He wouldn't help you find your home, though. That's when we met. I took you aboard, admittedly, with the worst intentions, but you stole my heart so easily—and I like to believe that I stole yours too. In the end, you left me no choice. I had to help you get back to your world, because your longing for your sisters killed you, and your pain killed me."

"And you got me back how?" she snaps after a moment.

As always, her sassy spirit provokes my smile, even though I make sure to hide it from her right now. "Peter figured out that you had to actually *fall* to get back. And we managed that. But when you were gone from my life, nothing felt right for me anymore. I needed you. In the end, I guess, I'd rather have died than face a life completely without you." There's no need to tell her all about the drop into the volcano and the morning after with the fairies. There'll be time for that later.

"So you did something to make Peter age and both of you came to see me in London." From her flat voice, I can't tell whether she believes that part or is just reiterating what we both told her before of our own versions.

"I didn't mean to make him age so fast. Actually, I had no idea it would happen, but yes, that's pretty much how it all went. Of course he got mad." And strangely enough, I can totally understand. "That's why he came after you first. See, he kept coming back and telling me how he was about to steal you from me. He even left a picture in my quarters the other night."

Angel turns her head just a little more my way and her gaze finds me over her shoulder. "What picture?"

"The one where he's carrying you." I can't help the

growl that comes with that memory. "I couldn't believe how happy you looked in his arms."

"He surprised me when he picked me up so quickly," she snaps. Then her frown intensifies. "Why am I even defending myself?" She turns her head as far away from me as possible with the wall at the other side.

It might make her mad at herself, but it sure raises a stupid swell of joy in my gut. "Because somewhere deep down here"—capturing both her wrists in one of my hands now, I place my other on her stomach—"you feel that I'm telling the truth. You might not remember what happened with us, but you do still care for me." I nuzzle her hair and revel in the wonderful scent of it. "Don't you?"

She doesn't reply with round three of cursing me, which could mean that she's starting to let me in. It feels safe to ease my grip on her. When I let go, she doesn't make a dash for freedom. Instead she keeps standing in this very spot, staring at the broken door in confusion for just another second, then she turns around with a scoff and stalks off toward the deck. Of course I follow on her heels. However, with this first little success of breaking through to her, I restrain from grabbing her arm to hold her back. Where can she run to? We're in the middle of a canopy of stars, after all.

Or so I think, until I step outside. The velvety blue of the skies around us has disappeared. In its place the warm sun rises over Neverland. The Jolly Roger is descending, and it only takes another minute until she touches the familiar waters a little offshore. Damn, how long have we been in my cabin? It didn't feel half as long as we obviously were.

With a gasp, Angel stops in the middle of the main deck and spins on the spot. "Where the heck are we?"

Sidling up to her, I put a gentle hand on her shoulder. "This is Neverland. My home."

"How did we get here?" Instead of letting me answer, she rubs her temples, shakes her head and mumbles, "No, don't tell me. I don't even want to know."

"Angel—"

Her gaze shoots up to meet mine. "No, don't! And don't touch me. I don't care if all you said is true or not. I want—no, I *demand* you take me back home this minute!"

"I will take you home."

"When?"

"Eventually."

"No. You take me back to London *now*!"

"Really, I can't do that." Feeling sorry for her and at a total loss, I grimace. "Just give me a little more time to help you understand."

Folding her arms over her chest, she starts to tap her foot. *"Now."*

Damn, that growl turns me on, but I can't give her that. I shake my head. Which might well have been a

ANNA KATMORE

mistake. I can see the decision in her eyes even before she actually makes it, so this time I'm prepared when she whirls about and dashes across the deck. Rushing after her, I grab her around the waist right before she can jump off the railing. "Oh no, you don't!"

And here round three of Angel's cursing finally comes. A show that obviously each and every member of my crew enjoys to the bone. The mangy dogs laugh their heads off at me.

I don't care. For now I'm at my limits with Angel and her stubbornness. Damn, I didn't have such a hard time convincing her of my love the first time, and that was right after I almost got the lass killed in the jungle.

I bend and toss her over my shoulder, ignoring her drumming fists on my back as I carry her to the cabin she once owned on this ship. The bilge rat who had to move out for her sake never moved back in.

Dropping Angel on the bed, I stalk back out, making sure I pull the key from the inside and lock the door once I've left. Her angry voice drifts through the walls. I can't even say round four of her cursing began, because round three actually never really stopped.

After a deep sigh and raking my hands through my hair, I cut a helpless glance to the sky. Then I stride into my quarters, intending to give Angel a couple of hours to cool off. Maybe we can start from scratch then.

Peter Pan

PETER! FREAKIN' HELL, how could you age so fast?
Hook's horrid voice still rings in my ears.

Struggling hard against the ropes that keep my wrists tied at my back and my body attached to this goddamned tree, I call him every foul name I can think of under my breath. It doesn't matter how resentful he looked when he whispered an apology. It doesn't matter how his sword in his hand lowered as if he couldn't bring himself to end my life tonight. And it sure doesn't matter that he called me *brother*.

I'm going to kill him for what he did to me.

And if he so much as harms a hair on Angel's head, I'll be exceptionally slow with my skewering him, too.

Dammit, what's gotten into me? I shake my head and snort. Hook would never hurt Angel. He loves her. My own lies must have gotten to me in the end. That doesn't change a thing, though. He's as good as dead.

Shark bait, as soon as I get free. If only I could loosen these bloody ropes. They cut deeper into my flesh the more I strain against them.

Helpless and frustrated to the core, I clamp down on my teeth. My glance skates over the silent and dark park beneath me. In a couple of hours, the first visitors will come. I can shout down to them and ask for help then. They'll find a way to free me from my prison up here. But morning is a long time coming.

Lifting my chin, I roar into the night, "Hook, you goddamned bastard! I'll get you for this! I'll smash you and spit on your wasting bones!"

Just when I hang my head and fight against the lump of anger in my throat, I feel one end of the rope ease off just a little.

Angelina

EVERYTHING FROM THE moment Hook kissed me under the tree in my garden is like freaking déjà vu. I'm perched on the bed where he dumped me and stare at the closed door. He actually had the nerve to lock me in this cabin. Is this what you do in Neverland after kissing someone? Imprison them?

Very subtle, Hook. I so believe your story now.

The thing is he almost had me believing him indeed. I've never been kissed like that before. Or maybe I have, because everything about it felt so amazingly familiar. His touch, his smell, even his taste—I rub my tongue against the roof of my mouth so I can savor it once more. And then there was this door in his room. I don't know where it's leading, but the sight of it broken sent shivers down my spine. Almost as if I was there when it happened, only there's no path in my mind leading to that information.

What's the purpose of bringing me here? He

ANNA KATMORE

kidnapped me, for Christ's sake. Does he really think that will make me trust him more? Oh boy, I should have listened to Peter and not be so stupid as to wander outside at night alone.

Massaging my temples in slow circles, I try to come up with a plan. How do I get back home and away from this ship, the scowling crew and their impossible captain? My parents will go insane with fear when they find out what happened in the morning. Then again, they won't be able to make any sense of it at all. Their daughter is gone and a small heap of gold sits in our garden. Jeez, they will think someone left the treasure to buy me!

I roll my eyes and would have kicked myself too for this stupid thought. Of course they'll know in an instant that I was kidnapped. They'll call the police.

And then what? I scold myself and cut a glance to the ceiling. *Send them after me to Neverland? Clever idea.*

Irritated to no end, I hug my knees to my chest and rest my forehead on them. Only when my thoughts shift to my little sisters and their broken hearts when they find out that I'll never come back, my anger at Hook turns into sadness. It's even more than that. It really frightens me to think of what will happen to me on board this ship. Never one to be scared easily, tears spring to my eyes. I refuse to let them take over.

I've cursed Hook in so many different ways and so loudly that my throat feels sore when I clear it now. I sniff, lift my chin and sweep the room with a glance. There must be a way to escape. Unfortunately, the window is sealed, so there's no chance of climbing out. Behind the dirty glass, the shore of what I believe is Neverland shrinks away. The Jolly Roger takes aim at the horizon.

"Where are you headed, Hook?" I mumble and let the purple satin band that ties one part of the curtains aside run through my easy grip. Suddenly a strange realization strikes and makes me spin around. This room, with the nice curtains, the purple carpet and the clean bed sheets isn't what one would exactly call the sleazy quarters of a pirate. Everything in here looks like it was chosen with caution. Chosen to suit a girl.

Me?

I gasp. Just like with the broken door, I feel like I've seen this cabin before. I've already been in here. The feeling is strong enough to make my chest tighten. Now, the question is, was I kept prisoner in this room before, or was I...a guest?

Sinking to my knees on the soft carpet in front of the simple bed in the corner, I pull at my hair and let go of a frustrated sigh. For some reason I have this feeling all would be good and I could go home if I only remembered what really happened the last time I was in Neverland. Both Peter's and Hook's stories have their similarities, but one of them is lying. I want to believe that it's Hook, except kissing him earlier felt right in so many ways. What if his story is closer to the truth than Peter's?

If only Peter was here now. There are so many questions I need answers to, and somehow I think I'll only find out what happened when I confront them both at the same time. And then Peter could fly me back to London, because from the determination in Hook's gaze since he brought me aboard, I dare say he's not going to do that anytime soon.

A rattle in the lock makes me snap up my head. Boy, maybe I was wrong and he already changed his mind?

It's a jolly old pirate with a red bandana on his head and a gold tooth who cracks the door open and shoves his head inside. "The cap'n says ye can move freely on the ship now. He also warns ye not to jump overboard, because there's sharks in the waters and he ain't not care about havin' to jump after ye."

The most dangerous of those sharks is the captain of this ship, I'm sure. When the pirate beams a bright smile at me that would send a horde of zombies running, an unexpected *thank you* slips over my lips. He closes the door before I can even question my sanity.

So Hook widened my leash. What's he playing at? Making me feel comfortable on his ship? Not gonna happen. I keep rooted to the spot on the floor, thinking hard on a solution for my problem for another hour. But the only chance I see of returning to my world after all this mulling is to leave this ship somehow. So with a grumble and limbs stiffer than twigs, I eventually rise from the floor and sneak to the door.

Just a crack to spy outside, that's enough for starters. Some merry singing in piratical language drifts to me together with laughing from a few men that are obviously playing a game that involves a lot of drinking. I open the door a little wider and peek around the corner. There are several smudgy men on the main deck, some working, some playing cards or with their daggers, and they all ignore me. Taking a wary step outside my cabin, my glance travels across the rest of the ship. Heaps of ropes thicker than my wrists lie everywhere. There's a stack of cargo boxes close to the railing, with folded, heavy white fabric on top, which are apparently sails not in use.

There's another deck above the main one. It's where Hook took me first. His quarters are located there, and above them is the bridge. Moving my explorative gaze up to that last tiny deck, I meet the captain's sharp blue eyes. With a gasp, I jump two steps back and hide in my cabin.

Gee, I should have known he was watching my door, even if he's obviously the only one on board who is. So why does that surprise me? In an attempt to steel my nerves, I square my shoulders and lift my chin, then step out once again. This time, when I seek out his gaze on purpose, I'm prepared and don't budge an inch. His answer to my staring him down is a slight twitch of his lips that grows into the faintest half-smile.

ANNA KATMORE

With the scowl still pasted on my face, I turn my head away, deliberately slow, and start exploring the ship. If he's still watching me, I don't care. The one pirate who sprang me from my prison is kneeling on the floor now, scrubbing the boards, a bucket with water standing next to him. As I pass him, he tilts his head up, almost shyly, then quickly looks back down. The same happens when I cautiously walk past the small group of men sitting around an upside-down barrel that serves as a table. There's a deck of cards on top, a bottle of rum, and a handful of coins. Playing poker? I can't tell. When I try to catch their eyes, they quickly lower their gazes back to the cards in their hands. It's almost like they all want to but were forbidden to talk to or even look at me. It makes me uncomfortable.

Did Hook give those orders? If so, why?

Since none of the crew pays me any obvious attention, I decide to take the chance and check out my options of getting off this ship. We're so far out on the sea now that there's no land in sight in either direction. Even if I jumped, I wouldn't know which way to swim to get back to the shore. And by the sight of many black fins in the water, I can tell there really are sharks. I shudder. Putting only a toe in there would be suicidal.

The captain's eyes follow me. I can feel them everywhere I go. It's like he's patiently waiting for a frightened little kitten to come out of its hiding spot and start eating from his hand. And you know what? I'm that stupid kitten. Except, I know perfectly well what he has in mind and will never give him that. He can stand there and watch me until hell freezes over. I'm going to find a way off the Jolly Roger in the meantime.

Ignoring Hook, I lean over the railing and find a rowboat tied to the ship's side. What if I loosen the ropes, let the boat drop to the sea, and jump into it? I could row myself away.

Casting a scrutinizing glance over my shoulder, I of course find Hook observing me with intrigue from his place on the bridge. When our gazes meet, he slowly shakes his head. He thinks to stop me with that gesture? Well, he's in for a surprise. I start working the first rope.

Heck, these knots are so tight, there's no chance I can loosen them even a little. The skin on my fingertips is sore after a couple of minutes and I'm not an inch closer to escaping.

A voice way too close beside me startles me out of the tedious task. "Need help with that?" My head snaps up and I face a guy dressed in black from head to toe, with shaggy ginger hair and a scar parting one of his tilted brows. He was with the card players.

"No thanks," I growl. "I can manage."

"I can see that." He really has the nerve to chuckle at me. Then he puts his calloused hands over mine, moving them out of the way. With one quick pull, the knot comes open and the boat dips down at one side. As he walks to the other side, he throws me an inquisitive look. "May I ask where you intend to go once you're in that dinghy, lass?"

Too stunned to really register what he just said, I switch my gaze back and forth between him and Hook, who watches us with strange amusement. "Aren't you scared your captain will whip you for helping me escape?"

"There's no whipping aboard this ship, angel."

Although he could only mean the last word as a derogative endearment, it somehow sounded like he called me by my name. The one only my sisters ever called me...and everyone in this fairy tale, as it is.

"Besides," pirate Scar Brow continues, "James Hook is a boneheaded fool. He should know better than trying to keep you trapped on the Jolly Roger. In the end you'll talk him into whatever you want again. There's no way around that."

Even though this guy is obviously eager to help me, I sense he's holding something back. He's two-faced. Every cell in my body screams caution.

"So, you plan on rowing back to London?" He makes it sound casual, yet I notice how he's fumbling with the second knot with great reluctance. "Because it sure is a long way there."

"I don't care how long I have to row," I snap. And it's the truth.

Startled by my tone, or maybe just acting like he is,

he placates me with his palms up, then fumbles some more with the rope. "All right, all right. I was just wondering if maybe you should take some water with you and food too, so you won't die after a day out there."

Concerned about my life? I eye him sideways.

Scar Brow lets a smirk slip. "It certainly would put the cap'n in a worse mood than before, and he was already insufferable the past few weeks."

"Insufferable?" I huff a laugh. "I can see where that comes from. With me gone and no way to press matters with Peter Pan for his lost treasure, he would surely let his anger out on the crew."

The man's eyes are trained on me as the rope suddenly slides with a swooshing sound through the iron ring, nearly startling me out of my skin. A second later there's a tremendous splash as the small boat lands on the water.

I glance down and back at the man who's acting so out of character for a pirate.

"So?" His mouth curves into a friendly smile. "Shall we go fetch some traveling fare for you now?" At my hesitation, he dares me with a trustworthy look. "Let me show you to the galley and maybe give you a quick tour through the ship too. I promise the boat will still be waiting down there for you when we get back." The most unbelievable thing happens then. He holds out his arm for me to hang on to.

Maybe it's the surprise switching off my reason, but my arm actually loops around his without me giving it intentional orders to do so. The guy seems even less surprised about my giving in than me. It sure makes him happy. "I'm Jack, by the way. Jack Smee." Somewhere under that layer of coppery stubble on his cheek appears a dimple.

"Angel," I murmur as he drags me away, back in the direction I came from.

His chuckle then sounds highly amused. "Yeah, I know."

Confused about what's actually happening here, I throw a look over my shoulder up to Captain Hook, who's still standing at the sterncastle, arms folded over his chest, his focus on me. All this chitchat and help from one of his men must have confused him too, because he arches one perfect brow at me, definitely more than just a little intrigued.

Jack Smee didn't lie about the food or the tour he promised me, because our first stop is in the ship's galley where he tells the tall, slim man who stands with his back to us that he should throw together some packed lunches for the captain's girl. When the man turns around with a disturbingly delighted face and calls out my name, I duck behind Smee to hide from being crushed in a bear hug.

"So it's true then, ye don't remember us," he states with obvious disappointment. The only word I have in my mind when looking at him is *potato*, but that can't mean anything and it must just be lingering, because he was peeling a pile of those when we came to disrupt him.

Loaded with a new charge of enthusiasm, he straightens his back like a true British gentleman that he surely is not and holds out his hand. "Me name's Ralph."

See? It's Ralph. Not Potato.

Coming out of my hiding, I shake his hand. "Ye gonna go on a journey or why the packed lunch?" Ralph wants to know.

Smee answers for me. "The lass wants to take the dinghy and row herself back to London."

So slow that it's almost funny, Ralph turns his head to Smee and questions him with a quirky look. The pirate in black next to me only lifts his shoulders and lets them fall again, making helpless, big eyes. He pulls me on then and tells the cook over his shoulder, "Fill her a bottle with water too. We'll pick it up in ten minutes."

I'm tempted to ask Jack Smee what's behind all his friendliness, but I don't get a chance, because where he leads me next is totally out of a picture book.

"Oh my freaking goodness!" words burst out of my mouth as we stop at the edge of a gallery, looking down at hills and hills of gold and silver. A ladder leads down to that part of the ship—unnecessarily, because I only have to take one step forward and I'd be standing on the highest pile of coins already. This is one hundred times the amount that landed in my garden before Hook cornered and kidnapped me.

"Where did all this gold come from?" I cry out. "I thought—"

"That Peter Pan had it?" Smee cuts me off. "He did. We found it a few weeks ago and of course reclaimed it."

I fully turn my skeptical scowl on the pirate Jack Smee now. "Why are you showing me this?"

"I think this speaks in the cap'n's favor, no? You said something up on deck that had me wondering." A shrug rolls off his shoulders. "Or maybe just because of the beauty of it, I don't know."

He does know, all right. So that was his plan from the beginning. To help his captain earn some brownie points with me. And heck, he almost managed it. Okay, who am I trying to fool here, he *did* manage it. Hook was right when he told me he had his treasure and didn't need me to find it. How much more of what he told me was true? I really start to wonder.

"Come on, lass. I'm sure Potato Ralph has your traveling fare ready."

Smee's words drag me back to the here and now. I shoot around, staring at him with two pizza-plate-sized eyes and a gaping mouth. "What did you just say?"

Seriously confused about my reaction for the first time since he approached me, he frowns down at me. "Come on?"

"No." *No!* That wasn't what I meant. "You said Potato Ralph."

"Because that's the man's name." The V between his eyes deepens even more. "Anything wrong?"

Wrong...right...I don't know which. That I knew the cook's name, or part of it, before anybody told me is not really comforting. It's just further proof of what I'm struggling to believe here. Jeez, my head is starting to hurt again.

Kneading my temples, I cut a wary glance at Smee. "All the pirates know me, don't they?"

"We sure do."

"And I knew you too?"

He nods.

"So you all remember me, but I don't remember you. Why is that?"

Losing only so much of his confidence, he shrugs casually. "I guess there's always something playing with your mind when you come here. See, last time you started to forget your own world, and once you were back home, who knows"—he grimaces—"maybe you started to forget Neverland."

"How long was I here last time?"

"Five nights."

"What?" I gasp. "I've never been gone from my world that long. If it really all happened the night I fell off my balcony, then it couldn't have been more than a few

ANNA KATMORE

minutes!" That was the time I'd been knocked out cold anyway. "I could have dreamed up a lot of stuff during that time, but *five nights in Neverland*? I beg you!"

Smee scrutinizes me like this bit of information is as valuable to him as it is confusing to me. "So maybe time works different in our two worlds?"

Time must definitely work differently. And suddenly, in all my anger and fear of being trapped on a pirate ship, I let out the first breath of tiny relief. If five nights here were no more than a couple of minutes there, my family might not worry I'd gone missing. I could be back before they even notice.

And I *will* be back, because I certainly don't intend to give this idiot captain what he wants and *surrender*. No way. However, a little more time might come in handy. I mean, come on, I'm in Neverland. The land of the infamous Peter Pan. Who in my place wouldn't want to know what's going on? And with all those freaking déjà vu things happening around me, I might be on to something here. Something big. Some *only-once-in-your-life* thing. Okay, apparently it's twice for me, but still.

A little later, we're back outside, Jack Smee carrying my food and water for the journey. As we reach the place where I have to climb down into the rowboat, I hesitate.

"What is it?" he demands innocently enough. I'm pretty sure I'm reacting totally according to his plan.

"Can you make sure none of the pirates eat my

lunch?" I ask him. "I want to check something before I go. Only a few minutes."

Smee presses his lips together, not very subtly trying to hold back another smirk. "Of course."

Casting a wary glance up to the bridge to see if the captain of this ship is still in his former position, I'm not disappointed. He stands with his back to me, talking to someone. As if he can feel my gaze on him, he glances over his shoulder then turns halfway to me. His look intensifies as does mine and he tilts his head.

It's really like we're communicating across the distance, even though there are no answers given to the silent questions we both throw at each other. The only thing it does to me is quicken my heartbeat. Then again, that's happened pretty much every time I've looked at him since the moment he slipped the little note into my hand in the street in front of my house.

I slowly walk away from Smee. But instead of going back to my quarters, I'm headed for Hook's.

Chapter 10

ANGEL IS WALKING my way. There's so much determination in her eyes that I wonder if she'll come up to the sterncastle and confront me with whatever is on her mind. Am I finally in for round five of her cursing me?

The ugly feeling when my chest tightens with uncertainty of what to expect turns into something totally different the moment she stops on the quarter deck, slides one last shy look up to me and then disappears in my quarters. *My. Freakin'. Quarters.*

And what was that look? Was she challenging me to follow her? Well, I sure will—after talking to Smee. I need to find out what the two of them spoke about during the past goddamned half hour.

There's no chance my first mate misses the tick in my jaw when he catches my eyes. He shrugs it off with a grin as he comes to seek me out by the helm. He has the gall to mock me with an innocent expression. "Cap'n?"

"Don't you *cap'n* me, Smee. What were you and Angel talking about? Why did you take her under deck? And why the hell were you helping her unfasten the dinghy?"

"Calm down, James." He laughs. "I was doing you a favor."

"By helping her escape from the ship? She wouldn't row the boat two miles before she'd slump over, beaten and drained of strength."

"Yeah, that's why we got her some lunch too." He lifts a small leather bag that smells of roast pork and cheese.

"Are you shittin' me?"

"Absolutely not. But your temper with the lass before wasn't quite helpful, now was it?" He frowns at me. "And having the crew backing off when she starts to remember isn't your best bet either."

My eyes widen. "She remembers them?"

A casual shrug rolls of his shoulders. "Can't tell for sure. She might have recognized Potato Ralph. Or maybe just his name, I don't know. She certainly reacted to it in surprise."

My heart stutters, which is always a bad sign because, from past experience, it proves that I can't think straight when I'm getting excited...especially about something that Angel did or said. "So what are we going to do now?"

"We," Smee says and emphasizes the word overly

dramatic, "are doing nothing. *You*, on the other hand, should go down to your quarters now and fast. Because the girl you're crazy about is in there for whatever harebrained reason and you'll never get a better chance to talk to her."

He's right. What am I waiting for? With a curt nod, I dump the command of the ship in his hands and climb down the stairs to the quarterdeck.

The door to my bedroom stands open. It might be an invitation. Or it could also be Angel's way of making sure she has a fast escape route if need be. When I catch the first glimpse of her, my heart comes to a total standstill. She's kneeling on the floor by my bed, staring at the door that, after all this time, is still out of its hinges.

It's impossible to say what she sees there, but she looks lost in yet another world. I approach with caution. Reluctance overcomes me in the doorway and I stop, leaning one shoulder against the frame.

Angel doesn't pay me any notice, so I just stand there and watch her. The nostalgia that comes with the memories of her in my room constricts my chest. I want to close the door behind me and lock the both of us in here forever. Of course, this isn't an option.

Now that she's back in Neverland, I really don't know what to do with her. She must hate me. She must want to go back home. And eventually I'll have to give in to that. As for now I'm just happy I can look at her.

After some time, she heaves a sigh, and I knock gently against the wooden frame. Her gaze flickers briefly to me, then back to where it lingered for the past few minutes. Her silence is driving me insane.

"Why are you in my cabin?" I ask in a soft voice.

There's a tick in her jaw that makes me wonder if she's angry or just trying to close off from me. When she speaks, she only sounds as lost as she looked before. "I was hoping I could put a puzzle together."

"Any success with that?" When she shakes her head, I offer, "Maybe I can help."

She slowly blinks her eyes. That's the only answer I get.

"Mind if I come in?"

"It's your room," she says no louder than I had.

I accept the invitation that probably wasn't really one and step into my quarters. Instead of walking all the way to her, I stop after a couple of steps and lower to my knees, sitting on my haunches, facing her. Avoiding my gaze, she falls back into maddening silence. It makes me want to grab her shoulders and shake the words right out of her mouth.

Patience has never been my strength. Since time seems to be the one thing Angel needs right now, though, I do my best. And she certainly exploits it. After some minutes, I start to grind my teeth to keep myself from saying whatever shit is forming in my mind.

"What's with that door?" Her tender voice shocks me out of my struggle.

I hesitate a second with my answer and try to keep my tone equally soft when I tell her, "I broke it."

"I know you did." She slowly turns her head my way. "And I was here when it happened. Wasn't I?"

Her last question settles like a pile of glowing coals in my chest. So insecure yet at the same time full of hope. It's almost like she *wants* me to say yes.

I smile and nod.

"I thought so." She nods too, as if she needs the gesture to assure herself before her gaze drifts back to the broken door. "I just can't recall it all."

Luckily, the memory is still as vivid in my mind as if all the fighting and shouting happened only this morning. With my head tilted and my hands braced on my thighs, I wait for her to look at me again. "We had a fight. You came after me with a dagger that I'd carelessly left in this room. When you pointed it at my throat I wanted to kiss you so bad it hurt."

The need in my voice surprises the both of us. Dammit, maybe it helps to show her just how serious I am about this. "Later that morning, when we had another argument and you were wrenching the word *sorry* from me, you slammed the door closed on my face. I got mad and kicked it open. I thought you'd locked it." I grimace. "You hadn't."

Angel takes a deep breath. Her gaze doesn't waver from mine. I can see how much the words that want to come out next trouble her. Hands clasped in her lap, she swallows then asks with a small voice, "When did we kiss for the first time?"

Stunned, I stare so hard at her that a beguiling blush creeps to her cheeks.

She can't hold my gaze very long and lowers her head, obviously feeling the need to explain. "Evidently the kiss down in my garden wasn't our first. I could tell by the way you went on about it." Her blush deepens as she cuts a quick glance back at me. Her voice is barely a whisper now. "So intimate."

Her shyness makes me smile, while my heart knocks in a triumphant flourish. "You're right. I kissed you before, on that very day of our argument. It was late at night and we were pretty much the only ones on deck." When the memory of Smee interrupting the best moment of my life returns, I huff, "With a few disturbances, that is."

Angel takes a couple of minutes to process this new bit of information. She falls so still that I want to help her breathe. Suddenly she croaks, "You took something from me. Something small." Closing her eyes, she obviously struggles to remember. "It looks like a piece of paper."

"The travelcard," I tell her and laugh. If she remembers that little thing, we can't be far from discovering the rest for her. Pumped with joy, I crawl toward her on the floor. She instantly backs away like a spider. I stop, trying to hide my disappointment. "Sorry, I didn't—don't want to scare you. It's just...you do remember, right?"

Angel looks only half convinced. "It's all so vague. Almost like I was a witness at this scene but can only see it through a haze now. It doesn't feel like I was really there, only the pictures are in my mind." Her shoulders sink and she tilts her head, looking forlorn and puzzled. "How can this be?"

There are about six feet separating us. Far too much distance. I want to reach out and pull her into my lap, hold her and whisper everything into her ear until she remembers exactly who I am. Except this is hardly the right way to make her trust me. It would ruin everything, and we've already come so far.

"Why don't we try to get to your memory from a different angle?" I suggest. "Maybe it will help if you tell me everything you can see in those pictures in your mind, and I can explain where they come from."

She sighs. It's not one of those sounds that make you feel frustrated, it's a sigh full of surrender. A wonderful sound. And then she starts to talk. "I see you and me, only you look different." Her gaze drops to the foreign pants I'm wearing on the fairy's advice then shifts back up to my face. "The only thing I can see clearly is your eyes. I remember their vibrant blue. The rest is...covered?" She makes such a hopeful face that it's hard for me to stay where I am and not touch her. "Sorry, I know it doesn't really make sense."

"Oh, it might make more sense than you'd believe. I used to wear a hat back then. You actually didn't like it."

"How do you know I didn't?"

I chuckle, rubbing the back of my neck. "You told me so on a couple occasions."

She stares at me for a long moment. Then her eyes narrow. "You scared me," she breathes.

My stomach drops. Why, of all things, does she have to remember this first? I let go of a long sigh. "Yes, I did. I wasn't very nice to you at the beginning. That's why you came after me with the dagger, actually."

Her gaze bores into mine. Suddenly a small smile plays on her lips. "And you brushed it off like it was nothing."

The air freezes in my lungs. "What did you just say?"

Angelina

I DON'T KNOW what it was exactly that managed to lift the fog in my mind, but once I start to remember, it all comes back like an avalanche. Though it's my feelings for James Hook that come back rather than the memories of entire situations.

"We were sitting on the wooden boxes on deck when you kissed me first, weren't we? And I was wearing your cape."

His face lights up as he nods.

"I *wanted* you to kiss me, right?"

"I've never forced myself on a woman," he growls through a smirk.

That's something I can easily believe. Ever since the first moment our eyes met in the street in front of my house I've wanted him to kiss me. I even let him shortly before he kidnapped me. And nothing ever felt so right before. But there's so much more to discover. So many things still don't make sense. Most of all the fact that I remember Peter as a boy and not the man that he is now. "How much time has passed since I left Neverland last time?"

"About three months."

That's exactly the time that has passed since my fall from the balcony. So if back then, five days in Neverland equaled five minutes in London, something must have changed. My theory about getting back to my world at the moment I left starts to crumble.

"It still hasn't fully returned, has it?"

"Hm?" Hook's question startles me out of my musing as much as the fact that he suddenly kneels in front of me, far closer than before. "What do you mean?"

"Your memory. You're struggling with something. And I know that look of yours." He smiles and lifts my chin with his finger. "I lost you."

A sigh escapes me. "Being in Neverland—again—doesn't make sense on either end." I wonder if it ever will. "There are flashes of you, pirates on deck, strange women." My brows knit together at the image of a girl with long dark hair and a fishtail. "Did I ever talk to a mermaid?"

When he chuckles, I cross my arms over my chest and glare at him. "I guess my confusion amuses you? Well, I'd rather get some answers."

The chuckle turns into a laugh. I like that sound. As

he rises from the floor, my gaze follows him until he towers over me and holds out one hand. "Come on, Miss London. You're in for a story."

Reluctantly, I slide my hand into his and he gently closes his fingers around mine. Then he pulls me to my feet.

Way too close, I'm suddenly standing flush to his body. His hand placed at the small of my back, he makes sure there's no space between us. I shape my palms to his firm chest, because the nearness startles me, but it's not uncomfortable. And then his forehead dips to mine.

"I've been dreaming of this for so many nights," he whispers. "You don't know what you did to me when you left."

Being in the arms of James Hook feels more than just right. It feels perfect. Even though the shiver his touch sends along my spine makes me aware that I know nothing about him yet. "You promised me a story," I tease in a shy voice.

He strokes my hair away from the side of my face and brushes it behind my ear. His fingers there make my skin tingle. Everything points at him going to ignore my weak protest, but a few heartbeats later, one corner of his mouth tilts up in a lovely, taunting way. "And a story you shall get."

Not letting go of my hand, he sits down on the edge of his bed and pulls me closer. I don't know what to do, because for a moment the urge to lower onto his lap overcomes me. Of course, that would be too awkward, even if there might have been a time when I did this and liked it.

"It all started with an apple. I sort of stole it from you." James Hook tilts his head and, with a sheepish look, starts to stroke his thumb back and forth over my knuckles. "Under the pretense of helping you find your way back home, I later lured you on board this ship."

For a while, I just stand in front of him and listen to each detail of the cruel beginnings of our supposed friendship. This guy clearly has a ruthless streak. But when he explains how he saved me from the deathly trap in the jungle and how later on he gradually fell in love with me, and apparently I with him, my grimness toward him starts to crack.

While James Hook keeps talking, I wander about in his room and try to hunt for objects in here that might help me remember more of the *us* thing. Nothing really stands out, so I sneak a glance into the room behind the broken door.

There's a huge desk by the window wall. Ambling toward it, I notice a black hat with an impressive feather waiting to be picked up. I don't dare touch it, but it stirs awake another blurred memory—images of James slumped forward in his chair and sleeping like an exhausted child with his arms folded on the desktop. The hat lay at the exact same place back then. Tracing my finger along the edge of the desk, I slowly skirt it then sit in the captain's chair for a moment.

"Apart from Smee, no one was ever allowed in this room."

I look up and find James leaning against the doorframe, arms casually crossed over his chest. He watches me like I'm his favorite TV show. One side of his mouth tilts up. "As soon as you came aboard my ship, you developed a habit of storming in an out of my quarters as if you owned them."

"I'm sorry." I grimace and stand, though I don't know if this was even the right thing to say. "Would you rather I didn't come in here again?"

James pushes himself away from the doorframe and crosses the room to me. He leans back against the desk, gripping the edge with both hands. The sun shining through the windows and falling on his face makes him look so much younger. "On the contrary, I'd rather you never again left my quarters," he tells me in a soft voice.

I can feel how part of me once wanted that too. Exploring that part is easy when it starts to rise and tries to take over. I'm not willing to give in to this need. "You know that's impossible, Captain. You have to take me back at some point."

"Do I?" A shiver races over my body at the mischievous tilt of one of his eyebrows. His hand sneaks up to my waist and, with a gentle pull, he makes me stand between his spread legs. He lowers his chin with a small smile so he's staring directly into my eyes. "I thought, maybe if somehow I found a way to keep you happy, you'd agree to stay this time."

The nearness should startle me or maybe make me feel uncomfortable. Instead I enjoy the way he stakes his claim on me. I know it's a pirate we're talking about, and if one can believe Disney, the meanest that has ever sailed the seas too. There's just one strange thing about it: When I look at his taunting, hopeful face, I feel perfectly safe with him. "Stay with you and leave my former life behind?" I ask, not bothering to keep a playful hint of skepticism out of my voice. "My family, my home, my everything?"

Both his hands wander to the small of my back where he laces his fingers. "Neverland has some qualities of its own."

"I'm not a pirate. You can't expect me to spend the rest of my life on a ship."

"I'll build you a house in the forest."

"I'd be pretty lost without my memories here."

"I don't care. I'm going to make new ones with you."

I give him a sidelong look. "Are you trying to seduce me, Captain Hook?"

"Possibly." He cracks a smile. "Is it working?"

Succumbing a little more to the part of me that still

ANNA KATMORE

knows James Hook in a way that *I* don't, I rest my forearms on his shoulders and loosely clasp my fingers behind his neck. "No. Way."

He bites then licks his bottom lip. "What if I let you wear my hat and cape again and you can be captain of the ship for a while?"

The hopeful glimmer in his eyes coaxes a resentful sigh from me. I free myself from his hold and walk to the window, turning my back to him. "This isn't my home. You know I have to go back, Jamie." In spite of the undeniable attraction I feel for this man and the vague memories I have recovered, staying in Neverland isn't an option at all.

I gasp when his hands slide over mine from behind and he intertwines our fingers. He brings our hands in front of my stomach and hugs me against his chest. I only let him because, just like before, being in his arms gives me a feeling of safety and comfort. Frankly, it does feel familiar. If only there was a chance for me to pull the rest of my memories out. I want to know what we had...he and I. I want to know it so bad that I close my eyes and dip my head backward to rest on his shoulder.

"I always loved it when you called me Jamie," he whispers into my ear and nuzzles my temple.

Laughing, I counter, "Apart from the one time when you threatened to cut my throat for it."

"Maybe I shouldn't have told you that." The warm

breath of his chuckle feathers against my skin.

I turn my head to look at his face. His long, fair lashes brush the skin underneath his eyes at each of his blinks. No matter what he does, how he looks or what he says, there's always a layer of dominance that overrides the warmth in his gaze. His moves are slow and deliberate, his words always sound considered. James Hook knows exactly what he wants.

And right now he wants...me.

Leaving one hand placed on my stomach, he lifts the other to my face and skims his fingertips feather-lightly across my cheek. Guided by his touch when he strokes his thumb over my bottom lip, I tilt my head a little more to him.

He leans in so close that I can feel the softest brush of his lips against mine when he whispers, "What do you think? Can you bear to spend one day with me before we ship you back to your world?"

Ten heartbeats pass.

In that time, I'm transfixed by his gaze while in my mind I play out all the possible scenarios my parents might go through when they wake up in the morning and find me missing. Hysterics. Police. Crying. Searching. Hoping. Calling friends. Soothing my sisters. Not once in my life have I run away from home. I'm quite aware of the sorrow I put them through with each passing hour I stay here.

ANNA KATMORE

On the other hand, this is Neverland. The land of the boy who wouldn't grow up. The land of fairies, treasures, pixie dust, and heck yeah, it's also the land of pirates and Captain Hook. Would anyone go back without taking the chance at seeing a mermaid, just once in their life?

Would I?

As I turn around in Jamie's arms, I draw in a deep breath and take his face between my hands. "One day," I say with determination and stand on my tiptoes. "And you have to show me a mermaid."

His attempt to suppress a joyful grin is ineffective. "I promise," he purrs then leans in to kiss me.

I let the part of me that feels most comfortable with Jamie take over and mold my lips to his. Have you ever been kissed by a pirate? I know I have more often than I remember, yet it still amazes me how an alleged scoundrel like Hook can turn into the gentlest lover. He leans back against the edge of the table like before and pulls me so close a sheet of paper wouldn't fit between us. One of his hands roams up my back, my shoulder, my neck, and disappears in my hair. The tenderness of his touch makes my skin tingle. Every square inch of it.

His tongue sweeps through my mouth, once, twice. The hunger in his kiss grows. With his hand at the back of my neck, he holds me tightly in place as if scared to lose me any second. Well, I don't intend to back away. My hands sink to his shoulders and lower down over his firm chest and hard stomach. Burying my fingers in the soft linen of his shirt, I release a fervid sigh that doesn't quite make it out of my mouth. The half-moan must have fueled his passion even more—I can feel it in the kiss that just turned a notch harder.

Jamie grabs my hips and, without me doing anything, we swap positions. He lifts me and sets me down on the desk in front of him. I take that moment to catch my breath. When he leans closer again, I lean back and lock gazes with him. How could I have ever doubted his intentions toward me? It's all there, so obvious in his eyes.

Startled by my pulling back for a moment, Jamie cocks his head. He seems to find pleasure in this game that really wasn't one and takes on the unspoken challenge. He leans so far in that I have to recline even more, bracing myself on my hands and soon on my elbows.

The left side of his mouth twitches to an adorable crooked smile as he takes my hands and forces me to lie down on my back, my feet still dangling. With our fingers intertwined, he spreads my arms sideways on the desk and slowly moves them up over my head, like he's drawing a snow angel. Propping himself on his elbows then, he braces his weight as he lowers on top of me. His body is so close above mine that I can feel him each time I take in a breath.

ANNA KATMORE

We're eye to eye, my favorite position with the captain as I find out, because I can so easily lose myself in the deep sea-blue of his irises. The smirk is still pasted on his lips, and his soft, golden blond hair tickles my brow as it falls forward.

"Trapped," he drawls. "What are you going to do about it?"

"Scream my way out?" I tease back and crack a smile. Then I add, "Later." Right now I have no intention of getting away from him. Quite the opposite, in fact. I sling my bare legs around his waist to anchor myself to him. His contented purr is my reward for that. It makes me shudder and at the same time wonder how someone so young and gentle can command a ship of honorless men.

There's no time for finding an answer. Jamie comes down the last couple of inches and kisses my bottom lip, wiping my mind blank in a heartbeat. I like how he starts to play with it, sucking and nibbling, before he traces the bow of my upper lip with his tongue. I do the same to him and would have never thought that something so simple could be so sensuous. He gives me another moment to savor him fully, then he trails downy kisses along my jaw and down the side of my neck. I heat up like a torch when he softly grates his teeth across my collarbone. With his nose he nudges my chin up to give him access to the base of my throat where he places another tender kiss.

I know I said I wanted to see the mermaids at some

point. Right now I'd be happy to spend the entire day with Jamie in his study, though. I don't even care if we stay on the desk the entire time. In fact, I'd like that.

A rap on the door explodes my beautiful dream.

As every muscle in my body tenses with alarm, my legs tighten around Jamie's waist, pushing out a startled breath from him. More than that happens. It's like the shock popped a cork from the storage of my memories. It's all back in an instant, leaving me with a thudding heart.

Jamie doesn't look half as appalled as me when he straightens just in time for the door to open. I don't see who's coming in, because I'm facing Jamie and the windows, but I recognize Smee's voice at his first sheepish cough.

"Sorry to—um..." The pirate cuts himself off.

At that moment, Jamie looks down at my face and I know what a horrible red flush he sees there. The man has no decency, I swear. He gives me an amused smile then skims his fingers over the outside of my naked thigh. What the hell, does he have to fondle me in front of his first mate? I gasp, until I realize he might only be trying to make me aware of my legs still anchored around him.

Oh God!

I unhook my heels and lower my legs, covering my face with my hands. That coaxes a chuckle from Jamie. He grabs his hat from next to me and drops it on my face.

In the meantime, Jack Smee clears his throat once

more. "The pixie is outside and wants to talk to you, Cap'n. She keeps fluttering above the ship and refuses to come down."

"The pixie? I wonder what she wants," Jamie replies. "Tell her to meet me at Mermaid Lagoon in an hour. I promised Angel a tour anyway."

The door clicks closed. A moment later, the hat is being lifted from my face and Jamie peeks underneath. "You good there?"

"Argh, James Hook, you have to teach the crew not to walk into your quarters uninvited!" I rant as I prop myself up on my elbows. "It's starting to get on my nerves, being interrupted every time we kiss!"

His jaw drops and his eyes grow wider and wider. "Angel?" he tests carefully.

"Now don't look so shocked. You knew my memory would come back eventually." I crack a smile because, hands down, the expression on his face is adorable.

He quirks his brows. "You. Remember?"

"Yes."

"You mean, you remember *everything*?"

"That's what I said, Jamie. Now let me get off this desk and—" I don't get to finish because he grabs my hands and pulls me up so fast that I fall against his chest. His arms encase me, cutting off the steady stream of air in and out of my lungs. We cling to each other and his face buries in my hair. No kissing this time, which I regret a little, then again it's good to be crushed for a moment.

"I missed you so much," he croaks.

Unfortunately, I can't say the same, because until very recently, I didn't even know of his existence. However, the swell of joy flooding me right now is hard to contain. "It's good to be back."

Drowning in his beguiling scent of seawater and tangerine, I close my eyes and, for the first time since he found me again, relive all the happy moments we had together not long ago.

Chapter 11

I HAVE HER back. Not only physically but in mind as well. Happiness fills my heart. She's here in Neverland with me. Finally. I squeeze Angel so hard that she begs me to give her some air to breathe. Reluctantly, I ease the embrace.

"Now that I remember it all, I can hardly believe how I survived those three months without you. But"—Angel steps away from me with her hands on her hips, giving me one of those spirited, scolding looks that I missed the most about her—"really, James Hook, you kidnapped me—again?"

I laugh and brush her ruffled hair behind her ears. "It was the only way. And you should be happy I did it."

Her mouth curls into a smile of surrender. "I am. More than happy, actually."

"Good. Does that mean our earlier deal is off and you're going to stay longer?"

"No. The deal is still on." She grimaces and then purses her lips, the gesture tempting me to kiss her. "But I'm thinking, maybe we should go see the fairies in the forest. They knew what to do last time when I got stranded in Neverland. Perhaps they have a solution to this problem too."

I'm glad she mentions the fairies, because that's exactly what I planned on doing with her later today. She didn't really think I'd agree to just one bloody day? "You mean find a way to help us see each other more often?"

Angel nods, her face displaying the hope that moved into my chest the moment I saw her again.

"All right. Let's do that. Do you still want to see a mermaid first?" I tease her.

"It would be great to meet Melody, though chances are slim, I guess. Didn't you tell Smee you were going to meet Tami at Mermaid Lagoon in an hour? If you don't mind, I'll come with you. I'd love to see *her* again."

With narrowed eyes, I cock my head. "Of course I'm going to take you." Whatever made her think I wouldn't? No one can tell how long I really get to have Angel around me this time. I'm not going to waste one goddamned minute.

"Great!" She claps her hands like an excited little girl and bounces on the balls of her feet. "Let's go!"

She really has no idea how sweet she can be even without her trying. I wrap my arm around her shoulders and tuck her to my side as I maneuver her around the desk and into my bedroom. "We're in the middle of the ocean, lass. No one goes *anywhere* right now."

Her face falls for a brief moment. Then she loops both her arms around my waist, presses her chin to my chest and grins up at me as we go. "Then you can let me steer the ship again."

"That you can do. And I have something for you, too." I release her and cross to my wardrobe where I've kept Angel's blue dress all this time.

When she sees it an infectious smile tugs on her lips. It's replaced, however fast, with a pout of mock defiance. "What? You don't like what I'm wearing now?"

Hooking one finger into the waistband of her shorts, I pull it away from her stomach a little. "You always wear the strangest things," I taunt her and keep the truth—that I didn't like how the crew ogled her naked legs before—to myself. "Anyway, if you don't like the dress, I can have Smee give it to some girl in town later."

"Don't you dare, Captain!" She snags the dress from my arm and hugs it to her chest, laughing. "You're not going to give this away."

I arch one brow. "Too many memories clinging to that dress?"

"Way too many." Her chiding gaze turns soft as she lifts the dress to behold it with great affection. "I can't believe you really kept it."

Remembering the first hard days without her brings back an oppressive tightness to my throat. "What else should I have done? It was the only thing I had left from you."

Angel must have heard the crack in my voice, because she tosses the dress on my bed and comes closer, enveloping me in a monster hug of her own. I love her tender body pressed so hard against mine. Only her pity makes me feel uncomfortable. Grabbing her by her shoulders, I move her a few inches away from me and stare into those warm, hazel eyes. "I'm good." *Now.* All the waiting, the suffering and the struggling with the rainbows was totally worth it, only because I can hold her again. "Put on the dress and come outside when you're done. I'll wait at the sterncastle for you."

"Save me a spot by the wheel," she mocks and turns around to change her clothes. A deep sigh works its hard way out of my chest. Even if I'd rather stay and watch Angel, not missing a single second, it's just like back in those old days with her. She makes me want to be a nice guy around her, so I give her some privacy and leave my quarters.

Jack already set the course to Mermaid Lagoon and, with the wind stroking the sails, the Jolly Roger picks up speed. "So the chat went well?" he asks with humor in his voice as I take over the helm.

While I don't mind being caught in an intimate

position, I know how embarrassed Angel was, so I cut Smee off with a hard glare. "As long as the girl is aboard, I suggest we conduct our conversations *outside* my quarters."

"Fine with me." He laughs and placates me with his hands up. "I suppose we're back to *Jamie* status now, so what's the plan?"

I arch both my eyebrows. "Jamie status?"

"Something Skyler came up with a while ago." Cocking his head, Smee makes a thoughtful face. Of course, it's all show. "Actually on the day that you threatened to cut his throat if he ever touched Angel again."

I remember that moment. Angel tried to bribe my crew into mutiny. It backfired on her and Yarrin' Brant Skyler got too close to her for my liking. Clenching my teeth at the thought, I grip the handles of the helm a little harder.

A soft hand slides over one of mine. "Hey, what's bothering you, big guy?" Angel's sweet voice blows most of the anger out of my mind in an instant. Seeing her in that blue dress again does the rest. To my great astonishment, she brought my hat and puts it on my head. Even out of sync with the funny pants and shoes Bre gave me for Angel's world, it certainly makes me feel a little more like captain of this ship again.

I cast her a wicked smile and push her between me

and the wheel, so she can take over. Blow me down, her beautiful scent bewitches me as it sneaks up my nostrils. On a deep breath, I savor as much of that smell as possible. Then I lean down to kiss the sensitive spot beneath her ear. "You look enchanting, Miss London."

Angel shudders, I can feel it. And it's getting to my head. Doing my best not to eat her up out in the open with a crew of sixteen men to watch, I let her steer the ship back to shore where we anchor at Mermaid Lagoon. Angel and I are the only ones going on land. She clings to my hand with girlish strength as we walk over the gangplank together, me leading the way.

"What do you think it is that Tami wants from you?" she asks as we stand a little away from the Jolly Roger, tossing stones into the sea and waiting for the little bug to show up.

I shrug. "Maybe there's more trouble with Peter and she wants our help."

"More trouble?"

"As in...she's worried about him aging so fast." I find a flat stone close to the tip of my shoe. Picking it up, I aim it across the water and let it jump multiple times on the surface. "But I really have no idea. I only hope she'll come soon, because I want to talk to the fairies before it gets too late."

Angel agrees to that with a nod. For a while she's silent, then she says, "So, you finally got Peter to destroy

258   ANNA KATMORE

the watch."

"M-hm."

Her gaze lifts to mine. "How did you do it?"

I sigh. Thinking back to the break in my brother's and my relationship makes me hesitate with an answer. Of course, there's no sense in keeping the truth from her, so eventually I tell her everything, starting with the night that Jack, Peter and I went to town to get the bathwater.

When Angel hears that I used a gun on Peter Pan the next day, her chin drops to her chest. "I wouldn't have shot him," I state with what I hope is truth ringing in my voice. At least I've been trying to convince myself of that every day since. Last night, when I couldn't bring myself to kill or even hurt Peter with my sword, no matter what shit he pulled off with Angel, I finally got the proof I needed to be sure.

After a long pause in which Angel has enough time to contemplate, the hard lines of her face soften. I guess she believed me a lot faster than I was able to believe myself.

"After the spell was undone, did the rest of the people in Neverland age as fast as Peter? Because you and Jack and the rest of the crew obviously didn't."

"Nobody aged as fast as him. At least that's what I observed." I throw another stone with more force than necessary and it shoots far out before it dives into the waves. "There was a young woman in town. She was pregnant for so long."

"Because that's how she was when Peter decided to never grow up, right?"

"Exactly. There was never a change visible in her, all these years. Then, the few times I've gone to town lately, I've noticed how her belly keeps swelling. Unless I'm very much mistaken, she should have finally given birth to that child."

"Well, that's nice." From the corner of my eye, I see how Angel looks hopefully at me. "So apart from Peter, Neverland is back to normal."

"I started to shave again," I answer. "I didn't have to do that for over a hundred years. Things have changed, yes."

With the backs of her fingers, she strokes over the stubble on my cheek and smirks. "I like it the way it is now. If Peter ever restarts the curse, make sure you're not clean-shaven."

I wrap one arm around her waist and pull her into me, chuckling. "God forbid that should happen again!" The moment I place a kiss on her forehead, cool seawater douses us. "What the hell—"

"Hi, Angel!" someone calls from the ocean.

Angel twists in my arm, her body tensing with excitement. "Melody?" She squirms out of my arm and hurries to the rocky edge of the low cliff we're standing on.

ANNA KATMORE

"I thought I heard your voice," the amber-haired fish girl says excitedly as the upper third of her body sticks out of the water and bobs gently on the waves. "When did you get back to Neverland? And how?"

"Jamie came to my home and"—she hesitates a heartbeat—"brought me here. I've only been back for a few hours."

Yeah, I'm glad she didn't use the word *kidnap* again. When the mermaid nods her head in greeting in my direction, I lift my hand in a feeble response of my own and grin. Last time I saw her, I had her deliver a message to Peter for Angel and me.

"Wait here for a moment!" she then calls to Angel. "I've got something for you." She dives into the blue sea, her fishtail coming up before she completely disappears underwater. Angel turns a puzzled face to me. I shrug. Heck, I have no idea what she's up to. Melody doesn't take long to reappear. And in her hand, she holds something black. Swimming close to the shore, she tosses the wet bundle up and I catch it for Angel.

I wring the water from the fabric and unfold it. The astonished look on Angels face is priceless. "That's my sweater!" she cries out and swipes the thing from my hands. "Where did you get that from?"

"Found it underwater a while ago. I remembered you wearing something like that the first day we met, so I took it home with me."

"And all this time, I was wondering why I never found it in the tree when my sisters claimed it got snagged in the branches." Angel beams down at the mermaid. "Thank you!" The garment that resembles a pirate flag is wetting the front of her dress. She hugs it to her chest anyway.

"You're welcome." Melody sends her a warm smile, then she looks over her shoulder as a pack of other fish girls shout her name and beckon from a safe distance away. "Sorry, I have to go," she says with a sheepish look. "It's my father's birthday. My sisters always get so pushy when I'm late for something."

"You go and have fun," Angel tells her. "And thank you so much again for getting this back to me."

The mermaid nods and, with a backward somersault into the ocean, swims away to her family.

I step up to Angel and enclose her in my arms, because I want to savor each minute we have to us. Unfortunately, we're not alone for long. The distinct smell of blackberries and honey creeps up my nose. I know exactly when I smelled that last. "Hello, pixie," I say and turn around.

The little thing with a head full of golden locks and a dress made of ivy stands a little offside and nervously clasps her hands. Until she sees Angel stepping around from behind me. Her eyes light up and both girls squeal as they head toward each other, Angel shoving the wet sweater into my arms before she runs off. Tameeka pushes up to hover a couple of feet above the ground, making her able to fling her arms around Angel's neck. They hug like old friends, though Angel takes every caution not to crush the pixie's fluttering silhouette wings.

When they let go of each other after an endless time, I walk up to them and put one caring arm around Angel, hoping the gesture draws more trust from the tiny girl than offering a handshake would do. Though she doesn't look intimidated by me, she prefers to talk to Angel only. "I didn't know you were back with Captain Hook. You look happy, though, so I guess nothing bad has happened to you."

"Bad? What do you mean?" Angel asks. I can feel the uneasy tension creeping over her body.

"Peter." The pixie's face turns red with childish anger. "I was afraid he did something to you. He was so furious the last time I saw him."

"Well, he tried to warn me away from Jamie, that was all. He didn't hurt me or anything. I'm sure he would never do that."

I'm not so sure about that myself. However, it's not the right time to interrupt the girls.

"No, you're right. He likes you. He wouldn't harm you. But Peter was talking about getting back at Hook for what he did to him." Tami throws a dirty look my way. "He was in so much pain and, ever since, he's aged so fast."

Gritting my teeth, *I'm* the one choosing not to talk to *her* now.

"Even though he sent me away, I kept an eye on him and you, Angel. When both of you were gone after last night, I feared—"

"Wait," Angel cuts her off with narrowed eyes. Absently, she takes my hand from her shoulders and slides her fingers through mine, squeezing anxiously. "He sent you away?"

"Yes. When he spoke about his plan to use you for revenge on Hook, the Lost Boys and I told him he was crazy and confused and that we wouldn't help him with it. He was so angry, Angel. And blinded by it, too. I'm sure he felt like everyone betrayed him in the end."

Breathing with a tight chest is an ugly feeling. The bad conscience taking over makes it hard for me to return Angel's understanding squeeze. I ease the grip and her hand slips away from mine.

"I saw the two of you heading out of your house last night," the pixie continues. "Then only you returned. Since Hook already came to your world, the boys and I thought talking to Peter again was worth a try. I went looking for Peter, but I couldn't find him in the house where he's been living or anywhere else. And then you were gone too."

I take a deep breath. "You couldn't find him, because

my men and I tied him up in a tree quite a bit away from Angel's house."

"You. Did. *What?*" both girls shout at me at the same time.

"What? I had to keep him out of the way or he would have ruined everything again. You heard the pixie," I defend myself to Angel. "He wanted to use you for revenge."

"Because he was hurt," she counters with way more affection than he deserves and places both her hands on my forearm. "Think of the shock he must have been in when he found himself grown up one morning. Together, we can certainly talk sense into him. We must go back and release him. Now!"

"No way! I only have magic stuff left for one last trip back to your world. I'm not wasting that on Peter Pan." I pause and clench my teeth then mumble, "The ropes weren't tied too tightly anyway. I'm sure the bastard could've freed himself by now. For all you know, he could already be back in Neverland."

And that's the exact reason why I want to take Angel to the fairies as soon as possible. His plan to steal my girl from me failed once. Who can say what he'll come up with next to get back at me. I need to talk to him alone and sort things out between us. But finding a way to keep Angel with me is of greater importance right now. I'm not giving her up. Not now. Or ever.

Angelina

JAMIE'S STUBBORNNESS SURPRISES me. I know he and Peter had issues in the past, but the last time I saw them together in Neverland, they made a great team. What will it take to make them each see in the other again what they saw when they helped me go back to London?

As if he can read my thoughts, Jamie says, "It's no use, Angel. Too many things have happened since you were gone."

"Fine. Be that way," I mutter. If he thinks for a moment I'll give up trying, he's in for a surprise. And then I see them. A set of blue eyes staring at us from behind a line of bushes. My heart starts pounding like elephant feet, because I surely know those eyes. I've seen them all morning, while gazing at Jamie. Did I ever notice how much alike the brothers really look?

Neither of the others has noticed Peter watching us yet. On the other hand, he's certainly heard every word

ANNA KATMORE

we've spoken. So, what if he's here to put things right with everyone? He hurt Tami when he sent her away, and from all I know about the two of them, they were inseparable for many years. He must miss her like she obviously misses him.

And Jamie? Now that I'm here, I just *know* that I can make the two of them talk things out. They don't hate each other. No matter how much they might think they do, this feeling deep inside me tells me otherwise.

I almost blurt out Peter's hiding spot and point a finger. Just in time, I hold back. He's hurt and—by God, I know how stubborn he can be. It must run in their family.

When Tami takes over convincing Jamie that they must find Peter fast, before anything bad happens, I seize the chance and grab my still-wet sweater from Jamie. He throws me a questioning look, which I try to return with a reassuring one of my own. "I'm going to hang this over some twigs so it can dry in the sun."

He strokes my cheek, certainly glad that I'm no longer angry with him, and lets me go.

Like I expected, Peter ducks the moment I walk over to the bushes. Since he doesn't fly away, though, I believe he's ready to talk. Busying myself with the sweater, I keep my chin low and whisper, "Peter, I know you're here. Look, everyone is ready to t—"

I don't get to finish, because Peter grips my wrist hard and pulls me into the bushes, one hand clapped over my mouth. The sweater drops to the ground. "I'm sorry, Angel, but you didn't leave me a choice," he hisses in my ear, wrapping his arm around me and shooting up into the sky.

We've zoomed up a couple hundred feet before Tami and Jamie even realize what happened. Both cry out our names. I can't see them below, because Peter is going way too fast. Everything is just one massive blur.

While Jamie's voice fades, Tami's follows us for a few seconds from an ever-growing distance. She can fly, just not nearly as fast as Peter. Soon we shake her off. The thought to fight Peter and wrestle myself free crosses my mind for a minute. Then again if he drops me from this height, there's no chance I'll survive, which renders me stiff in his arms. Only when he takes his hand off my mouth, I give an ear-piercing shriek. "Jamie! Tami! Help me, I'm here!"

"You can stop that. They won't hear you. No one will." The ice in Peter's voice scares me.

The way he holds me with my back against his chest, I can see the jungle racing by below. We pass the volcano to our right and fly farther east until we reach a formation of three mountains in a triangle. In one of them, right beneath the peak, is a cave. Peter chooses to land there and sets me down.

I spin around and slap his face hard the moment he takes his arms away. At the smack, his head jerks to the side.

"Dammit, Peter! What do you think you're doing?" Then I gasp with shock. At Mermaid Lagoon, I only saw his eyes when he was hiding in the bushes. Now that he's standing in front of me, my lips start to tremble. Wrinkles are etched around his eyes and streaks of gray flash in his light brown hair. Peter has aged again. At least fifteen years from the last time I saw him.

He clenches his teeth and gives me a mean scowl. "You better not do that again, or I'll rethink my plan for you and shove you off that cliff right now."

"What?" My voice cracks on the one word.

"You're a bloody betrayer. You act like we're friends." He gives me a tight, hurt, and sinister smile. "But look whose side you're on again. You always end up with Hook."

I take a step back as he spits the words at me. There's so much hurt in his eyes that it squeezes my chest. But when he comes forward, forcing me to back farther off against the wall, and braces himself on the rock face at either side of my head, all I feel is fear.

The smell of his leather jacket creeps up my nose, as he glares down at me. "I thought you liked me, when in fact all you've ever done is destroy my life. From the moment you fell to Neverland, everything changed. You changed it. He did it all because of *you*!"

"Peter, I'm so sorry. I didn't mean for this—"

"Shut up!" His yell echoes off the walls inside the cave and makes me cringe.

Suddenly his eyes glaze over. He strokes his fingers down my cheek and dips his forehead to mine. "Forgive me, Angel. I just—" Pushing himself away from the wall he paces to the middle of the ten-by-ten-foot place that's all gray rock. Clawed fingers shove through his hair. "It's so hard to be inside this head. This is not my body. And not my mind!" He jerks around, glaring at me, broken and lost.

I'm still trying to catch my breath from the panic he unleashed in me. Pressing against the wall, I swallow hard. "Come back to Jamie and Tami with me. We can figure out how to help you."

"No!" He rushes toward me once more. "Don't you dare trick me again. I'm not going to see my brother." He pauses then speaks through a sneer. "Not on his terms anyway."

"What do you mean?"

His mad grin widens as he nods his head toward the back corner of the cave. A rope lies on the ground, together with a slingshot and a sword. Whatever he intends to do with that, it can't be anything nice. My panic resurfaces. As we flew here, I saw the way leading down from the cave. Although it's steep and certainly dangerous, I could climb down there. Except Peter would catch me a thousand times before I even made it ten steps.

Well aware of how my eyes have wandered to the only way of escape, Peter grabs my arm and pulls me farther to the back. He's too strong. All my screaming and fighting is in vain when he ties the rope around my wrists.

"And now what?" I shout at him. "What's your brilliant plan, Peter Pan? Are you going to keep me prisoner up here? Is that how you think you can take revenge on me?"

"Oh, not on you, dear Angel. I'm taking vengeance on my brother. You'll only help me with that." Pulling hard on the rope, he makes me follow him to the edge of the cave, then he flies out and loops it over a tree that grows sideways out of the mountain, next to the cave's entrance. It takes him three seconds to stand in front of me again. We stare at each other for the length of five breaths. My eyes certainly grow wider with horror as his grin spreads wider with madness. "Guess what," he says.

The next instant, I'm ripped away from the ground, out of the cave and to the side. A terrified shriek escapes me as it all goes so fast. Peter only had to pull on the end of the rope in his hands to catapult me up. The momentum keeps me swaying madly for a few seconds. Panic and the pain in my wrists bring tears to my eyes.

"Oh God! Peter! Please, pull me inside again. *Please!* You don't have to do this!"

"Do have to." He ties the rope around a protruding rock.

I'm hanging from the tree to the left of the cave, with a two-hundred-meter abyss beneath me. He's left the rope long enough that I can't reach the tree. Struggling is the worst I can do, so I keep as still as I can and fight to breathe again.

Inside the cave's mouth, Peter sits down on the stone ground and pulls a small notebook and pen from the back pocket of his jeans. "Now, what to write to my dear brother?" Tapping the pen to his pursed lips, he finally lifts his gaze to mine.

There's a sudden change in his look. His mouth parts slightly, his eyes widen with understanding and shock. I'm assailed by hope. *Oh Lord*, he's going to free me, because he's realized what a terrible thing he's doing to me.

A moment later he rubs his brow vigorously like a child that had to think too hard for too long. The muscles in his jaw tick as he clamps his teeth together. "It's the only way," he mumbles to himself.

Streams of tears forge down my cheeks. "Please, Peter. Release me." I wrap my fingers around the rope above the tight knot and try to ease the painful pull on my wrists. "I didn't betray you. I'm your friend."

He stares at me and shakes his head. Then he lowers his gaze to the notebook placed on his thighs and starts to write. "If you want your girl alive, come and fight." He cuts me a quick glance. "How's that?"

As a message for Jamie? *No!* "You're cruel, Peter

Pan! It will never work!"

"You're right." His eyes narrow back on the notebook. He rips off the first page, scrunches it up and tosses it against the wall. Then he mumbles along as he writes a new line, "Your life for hers."

At this moment, we both jerk our heads in the same direction. Tami's worried voice drifts to us as she repeatedly calls out my name.

"Tameeka! I'm here!" I shout hoarsely.

Peter jumps to his feet. "Stupid little thing. How did she find us here so fast?" Striding to the back of the cave, he fetches the slingshot and loads it with a walnut-size stone that he picked up from the ground. He pulls the rubber band until it's dangerously taut and aims it in the direction of Tami's voice.

"No! No, Peter, don't do this!" I scream. "Don't shoot her. Tami's your friend!"

Peter hesitates, and so does Tami as she reaches us. Hovering in front of the cave, her face is full of horror and regret. Whatever Peter has done in the past, she surely never expected him to raise a weapon against her. It's breaking her heart. And mine breaks for hers.

"Peter," she whispers.

After an endless moment, he lowers the slingshot and turns, growling, "Go away, Tami. This is not your concern."

Tami lands behind him and lifts one hand to touch

his arm.

"I said go away!" he yells at her, pulling his arm out of her reach.

Even though she cringes at his harsh voice she ignores his demand and straightens, asking in the softest tone, "What's happening to you?"

"You know very well what's happening. I'm growing old. Look at me." He grabs her shoulders and shakes her once. "I'm aging faster and it's unstoppable."

I don't know when Tami saw him last or how old he looked then, but his face now scares her speechless. She realizes he's speaking the truth. We both do.

The boy who wouldn't grow up is going to die.

And I know this because his hair's grayer now than fifteen minutes before.

Silent tears start to trail down Tami's cheek. They are drops of sparkling silver. One drips off her jaw and as it leaves her skin, it turns into a small diamond that clanks away on the hard stone ground.

"Don't waste your tears on me," Peter says in a much softer voice than before. "I know it's going to happen soon. I can't stop it." Then the muscles in his face harden. "But I won't go down without destroying Hook first, I swear."

I sob, which no one hears.

"No, Peter. I don't want you to become this monster," Tameeka pleads with him.

He just pushes her away. "I don't care what you want! Leave me alone!"

Her entire body starts to shake. I've never seen a girl turn this pale before.

"And since you're going back to Hook anyway," Peter continues, shoving the note he wrote before into her small hand, "take this with you. Tell him where I am and to come alone."

Slowly, the pixie shakes her head. For once there's no rain of golden pixie dust. "I won't help you. You're mean and losing yourself. I don't want to be your friend anymore, Peter Pan." She wipes her nose with the back of her hand. "Not if you are like this."

"What? Old?"

"No. *Cruel.*"

What she said cuts him deep, but he tries to hide his hurt behind compressed lips.

"You can give Hook the note yourself," Tami tells him.

"So you can free Angel in the meantime? I don't think so." Peter's voice cracks. He pulls himself together quickly. "Take the note to Hook. And you better be fast. He has two hours. Then I'll cut the rope."

Horrorstruck, Tami's gaze traces the rope until we're looking at each other. She doesn't say another word before she wraps her fingers around the sheet of paper that Peter gave her and zooms off with fluttering wings.

"Why did you do that?" I ask Peter when we're alone again. The words are barely loud enough for him to hear. He glances over his shoulder to me. "Why did you have to hurt her so?" I ask again.

He lifts in the air so fast that I gasp when he's right in front of my face. "Because she's a traitor just like you are, and Hook, and the Lost Boys. I don't need her—or them."

He says that out loud, his eyes tell a different story, though. And then he abruptly sinks, like there's a gap in the air. If it wasn't for his reflex to grab the branch next to my head, he'd have fallen who knows how far.

"What is it?" I demand with more concern than he deserves.

"Nothing," he growls back and cuts a glance to the cave as he hangs helplessly next to me.

"It's not nothing. You can't *fly*! Why can't you fly anymore, Peter Pan?"

"Be still. Of course I can still fly." Yet he doesn't. He's as anxious as I am. After a moment to deliberate, he starts swinging back and forth on the branch. When he lets go, the momentum takes him in a gentle arc through the air. I shriek, because he misses the cave's entrance and can only grab the rock's edge with the tips of his fingers. It's enough, thank God, to keep him from falling. I let out a breath of relief as he hoists himself onto the platform.

When he gives me a sideways look through narrowed

eyes, adjusting the collar of his black leather jacket, I can feel how he once again blames me for what just happened. But what did I do?

And then the truth smacks me hard in the face.

"Oh my God, it was *her*. It takes a happy thought to fly, and you've lost yours." I swallow hard at the way I'm suddenly aching for Peter. "Tami was your happy thought."

Chapter 12

WHERE THE HELL is the pixie? She said she'd find Angel and come back to tell me where Peter took her. What's keeping her away so long?

Pacing the length of the ship, I drag my hands through my hair and scan the sky for the hundredth time during the past half hour. There is no sign of the pixie. The urge to go find Angel on my own overcomes me, but I can't even set sail, because there's no way to tell the crew which direction to go. Hard as it is to bear, at the moment, the pixie is my best bet.

And then she shoots across the sky like a tiny green and golden cannonball right into my arms. The impact knocks us both backward. I barely manage to regain my balance and stand. "Where is she?" I demand as I put the pixie down.

Her cheeks are wet from crying and she dabs at her tears. "In a cave in the mountains at the other side of

ANNA KATMORE

Neverland. You have to leave immediately. Peter said you have two hours." She shoves a tiny piece of paper into my hands. "If you don't come to him in that time, he'll hurt Angel."

Reading Peter's note, my jaw hardens to a point where I might crush one of my molars. I scrunch up the note and throw it overboard. "Smee! Set sail to the east side!"

"James," Smee says and startles me, as he's standing right next to me. "It'll take us half a day to get around the island. The pixie said a couple of hours."

"And he wants you to come alone," the small girl adds.

"What am I supposed to do?" I bark, trying to contain the worry and wrath that consume me whole, then close my eyes and pinch the bridge of my nose. "There's no way to make it from one side of Neverland to the other in such a short time."

"There is a way." It's the pixie's small voice that makes me look down. "How fast can you run?"

"As fast as I'll have to, to save Angel."

She nods. "You have to go through the jungle."

"Are you kidding?" Smee shouts. "He'll never make it even halfway through those trap-littered grounds."

"He will, if I show him the way." Tami's determination and honest concern for Angel has me convinced in an instant.

"All right. I'll go. You"—I turn to Smee—"follow with the Jolly Roger. If anything happens in the jungle, you have to save Angel for me." I don't wait for Jack to hurl any bullshit about it being too dangerous but dash down the gangplank and run up toward the forest, the pixie flying above my head.

The shoes I got from Bre are a great help right now. I don't think I'd be able to make it that fast wearing my boots.

When I reach the first trees of the jungle about thirty minutes later, I'm drenched in sweat and quite out of breath. Bracing myself with my hands on my knees, I rest for a moment.

"Come on, Captain." Tami pulls on my shirt, fluttering her wings anxiously. "We don't have a minute to lose."

I want to brush her off with my arm, but she's right. Sucking in one last deep breath, I straighten and jog after her through the thickening jungle. She flies in a zigzag course, telling me where and when to watch out, jump, or duck. Or stop until she can trigger yet another trap, before a heavy trunk swinging down knocks me off my feet.

Time is ticking away, and we haven't made it very far. I start to wonder if going through the jungle was the best choice after all. At this pace, it'll probably save me a quarter of an hour, no more.

"Wait here!" the pixie suddenly cries out to me then

and bats her wings harder to reach the top of a high tree. She cups her hands around her mouth and shouts into the twigs, "Lost Boys, come out! I need your help!"

An hour ago, she told me to go to Peter alone, and now she calls for support? I quirk my brows as she silently sinks back to my side. The boys won't be happy to see me here. I only hope they still care for Angel as much as they did a few months ago.

Moments later, the top of a stump flaps open and two guys climb out. One looks like a man-sized squirrel with huge ears and teeth inclined like those of a troll. The other wears a hat with fox ears. I don't remember this one's name, the first one's called Skippy, though. When they see me, they look just as appalled as I imagined and pull out the knives they carry in their belts.

Placating them with my hands out, I say in a calm voice, "I'm not here to fight. I just need to find—"

"Peter kidnapped Angel," Tami cuts me off, flying in front of me, shielding me from the boys. "He has changed so much. I don't think he knows what he's doing. He's threatened to kill Angel if Hook doesn't get there within the next hour."

"Wait!" I yell and spin her around. "Kill? You said he might hurt her. You never said he would go as far as to kill her!"

"Let her go!" the Lost Boys immediately growl at me, one pointing his knife at the base of my throat. "You already did enough harm to Peter. We won't let you hurt Tami, too."

I ease my grip on the pixie's shoulders and step back. Drawing my sword and engaging Fox Hat in a fight wouldn't help Angel right now. And I sure didn't intend to hurt the little girl. Or my brother for that matter...

"Stop it, boys!" Tami warns us all. "We have to take Hook to the mountains. Fast. He must save Angel. Cart him through the jungle."

Whatever does she mean by that? What could these boys do to get me to Peter faster than I can run?

The two boys glare at me. Finally they seem to grasp the urgency of the moment. Angel needs help. Skippy puts two fingers in his mouth and whistles as he leads us over to the hole in the stump that's obviously the entrance to their hideout. "Get out here, boys!" he shouts then.

Three more Lost Boys join us and Tami explains everything that happened in one breath. My heart stops as I hear about Angel being tied up and left hanging from the cliff. I might not have wanted to hurt Peter Pan before. Now it's all changed. I want him dead.

The guy with black hair, which he has tied into a ponytail, and three-quarter-length buffalo-leather pants, seems to be their new leader since Pan has left them. He calls everyone—except me—to a small circle to explain whatever he thinks needs to be done. When all the boys nod their agreement, he grabs a fistful of my shirt and

ANNA KATMORE

pulls me along through the jungle after his friends.

Not far from their den, they make me climb a tree. At this point, I don't ask, just follow orders, trusting them to do whatever they can to help me save my girl. There's a shaky wooden platform on top where we all gather. Hanging from ropes above this platform are three tiny boats that sit two people each. Little Bear pushes me into one of them. The construction sways a little, and I really start to wonder what the hell this is. He climbs in after me and takes the front seat.

I'm surprised he's the one teaming up with me. After all, I threatened to cut his throat if Peter didn't save Angel from a deathly trap the night after I met her.

"Are you ready?" the leader calls to my companion, who's still in that furry vest he's always wearing when I see him.

"Get it going, Toby!" Little Bear calls back, then he slides a glance at me over his shoulder. "Hold on tight."

A queasy feeling makes my stomach roll. I grip the edge of the boat. Toby, who's still standing on the platform, pushes down a long branch that's obviously a switch and our boat starts to glide forward. First we go at a gentle pace, then after a few seconds, the rope tied from tree to tree which we hang on takes a sharp tilt downward and we reach a speed that knocks the air out of my lungs in a surprised gasp. The wind in my face makes my eyes water.

As we race through the jungle, twigs and leaves brush my shoulders and the sides of my head. Little Bear ducks forward. He knows best, so I follow suit and escape further cuts to my skin.

We move along the tree-suspended line for what feels like three to four minutes, then the boat starts to sink and a row of bushes slows us down. The end of the line is tied to another tree, far lower than at the start of our ride. On top of the tree is another platform. From there, one line leads in the direction we just came from, and another goes further on.

"We have to unhook the cart and carry it up there," my assigned Lost Boy tells me. The boat is made of water reed, so that's not a difficult thing to do. After we attach it to the new line, the second part of our journey through the jungle begins. This time, he reaches out and flips the switch himself.

Sink me, these guys have definitely made themselves comfortable in the jungle. Their creativity impresses me and I'm more than grateful for it right now. In less than ten minutes, we've covered a distance that would have taken me at least three hours if I were on my own.

When we finally step out of the boat after the second ride, I glimpse the mountains through the thinning treetops. We wait for the others. They arrive only minutes later, then all of them accompany me to the foot of the mountain.

Together we climb the smooth bottom until we're out of the jungle. Everyone turns their head skyward, up to the mouth of a cave. The air freezes in my lungs. Despite the distance, I can see Angel dangling helplessly from a tree that grows sideways out of the rock face. "Peter, you bloody bastard," I mumble, clenching my teeth. Then I face my followers. "Listen, the pixie said I was supposed to meet Peter alone. What you did was great, but from here I go unaccompanied."

The boys look uncomfortable. It impresses me how much they want to go up there with me to save Angel. Only at Tami's urging, they relent.

"We'll wait down here. If you need help, whistle," Toby tells me with insistence.

I nod and shake his hand. "Thanks."

Then I start climbing the steep mountainside. Peter must see me coming. Surely he's prepared and I wonder if I'm going to get hit by a rock before I even make it up to the cave. Nothing falls on my head, however. Maybe he's at the back and hasn't seen me yet.

Every now and then, I cast a glance down to the ground and up to the tree where Angel is hanging. Her eyes are closed, the pain obvious on her face. For the first time in my life, I really wish I was able to fly, so I could sweep up there and release her from her torture. Right now, however, I don't even dare shout her name.

I'm almost to the top when Angel looks down at me

for the first time. She gasps, her eyes filling with hope and fear at the same time. It's apparent that she's going to call to me. Before she can I shake my head. If Peter hasn't noticed me yet, I'd rather have the advantage of surprise on my side.

Angel nods slowly, readjusting her grip on the ropes above her tied hands. Knowing about her pain tortures me. I can't look at her any longer, because the cave is right above me now and I need to keep a clear head when I face Peter. I may only have one chance to save Angel and I can't screw it up.

Angelina

HE'S HERE! JAMIE came to free me. I don't know if I should be happy or terrified. Because Peter has been silent for so long, I'm afraid he's plotting something awful in his crazy, grown-up mind. And he has aged again. His hair is grayer now and deep furrows mar his forehead.

Sitting on the stone floor with his back leaning against the rocky wall, he started sharpening a piece of wood with his knife a while ago. He wouldn't talk to me, wouldn't answer my questions, only worked the blade on the stick in his hand with a vengeance.

I can see how sad he is about what happened between Tami and him. There's only so much a person can take, and Peter seems to have reached his limit. Growing older so fast must hurt, not only in his soul but also physically. And he's facing his death. After losing his brother and his best friends too, it's no wonder he's not coping.

Instead of hatred I feel sorry for Peter. He was my friend. I wish I could help him, I just don't know how. And letting me hang above this abyss isn't going to do anyone any good. Least of all me. My wrists burn like hellfire and my shoulders feel like my body suddenly weighs two hundred pounds. Why can't he just release me so we can try to find a way to save him together?

The look full of loathing he throws me every so often reminds me that he gave up on himself already. All he wants is to destroy his brother before he dies.

Jamie has almost reached the entrance to the cave when Peter stands up and walks to the back. When I turn my head to see what he's doing, my arm is in my way and I'm too weak to lean forward or twist to get a better view. Several times in the past couple of hours I've prayed that the pain in my arms and shoulders would let me pass out. Seems like now is the moment that my wish will come true.

I fight against the dizziness taking over and struggle to stay conscious. Jamie is here. He'll save me. It won't be long now.

Concentrating on my breathing, I tighten my fingers around the rope once more. A tortured whine escapes me and Jamie glances my way. The worry in his face turns to ice-cold hatred. There's murder on his mind when he grips the edge of the stone platform.

In one swift move, he hoists himself onto it. Standing

at the entrance to the cave, he draws his sword. Peter comes out of the shadows, a sword in his own hand. So that's what he was going to the get from the back. He must have heard Jamie coming after all.

At the aged appearance of Peter, shock crosses Jamie's face. He sucks in a sharp breath. Clearly, it's worse than he expected and he probably only now realizes the full extent of what *us* being together has cost Peter.

"So we meet again, dear brother," Peter Pan drawls with venom in his voice. "For the last time, I assume."

Jamie doesn't move an inch. "Let Angel go."

"I'm not taking orders from *you*, pirate!" Peter spits, and in the next moment the clanging of blades drifts to me.

It's not going to help anyone, still all I can do is shriek. Tears of fear for Jamie override the ones of pain.

The two of them thrust and parry hard blows at each other. As cuts appear on their arms and body, they continue fighting without so much as blinking. Peter runs Jamie up against the wall and aims a kick to his chest. Jamie evades him, so Peter's foot drives into the rock instead. It unbalances him for a second. Jamie takes the chance to kick him in the knee and bring him down to the ground. Before the blade of Jamie's sword can hit him square in the back, Peter Pan rolls to the side. He jumps to his feet and they cross blades again.

I've never seen someone fight with such

determination to destroy each other. My bones rattle with fear for both.

Peter slams Jamie against the wall, his forearm pressed hard against Jamie's throat in order to squash his windpipe. I yell out both their names, begging for them to stop. They simply ignore me. I don't think either of them even hear my screams.

Jamie throws a hard punch to Peter's jaw, making him stagger back. Fury etched in Jamie's face, he goes after Peter and lands another punch to his face. Peter stumbles backward again and falls against the rope he used to tie me up. I feel a hard jerk against my wrists. Another shriek escapes me. I seem to be the only one who notices how the rope loosens from the rock.

"Jamie! The rope!" I shout. "Help me! I'm going to fall!"

Both of them stiffen and turn to me, Jamie bleeding from his nose and a cut on his upper arm, Peter wiping blood from the corner of his mouth. He's the one nearer to the rope. In his eyes, I can read the shock—they almost killed me as they fought. Maybe he's finally coming to his senses.

"Free me, Peter! Please," I beg.

He just stares at me for another long moment.

"By Davie Jones' locker, take her down from there!" Jamie barks and rushes across the cave to my aid. He must think the same, that Peter is having a moment of clarity and understands what he's really doing me—to his friend.

But Peter startles us both as he whirls around and blocks Jamie's way. He throws a punch so hard at his brother's abdomen that Jamie drops to his knees, spitting blood.

"You'll never get to her," Peter hisses and cements his words with a kick to the side of Jamie's head.

I squeeze my eyes shut because I can't watch this any longer. It doesn't matter, the punches thrown echo in my ears. The men groan and shout as they keep fighting. Then the worst of all sounds makes me sick. A dull thud as someone is slammed against the wall. A body smacks on the ground.

I don't want to see Jamie hurt or... *Oh God, please don't be dead.*

There was already so much blood on his face and shirt. And then being thrown against the wall... It sounded like someone's skull breaking. Why is Peter so cruel? Why did he have to kill him?

Suddenly I drop two feet. A hoarse gasp escapes my throat and hurts like murder. My eyes shoot open. "What are you going to do with me?" I shout at Peter.

Only, it's not Peter Pan standing in the cave's opening with the rope wrapped around his hand. Jamie, bloodied and beaten, crashes against the wall for support. "Angel," he drawls, exhausted. "You need to swing on that rope. Swing over to me. I'll catch you."

What? He can't expect me to do that, when my life hangs on a brittle tree six hundred feet above the ground.

At the sheer terror on my face, Jamie takes a small step forward, the move visibly hurting him. He coughs and spits more blood as he wraps the rope a couple times around his hand. "Come on, love. It's not far. Swing."

Hanging above nothingness is the horror of my life, but swinging takes the word panic to a whole new level. "I can't!"

"Yes, you can! I'll catch you. Trust me." He stretches out his free arm, encouraging me to start moving in the air. "Come on. You have to swing now before Peter comes to. He won't be out for much longer."

My own panic is mirrored in his eyes, only he doesn't fear that I'll drop. He's scared of what will happen to me when Peter wakes up. Clenching my teeth, I summon all the bravery I can muster and start moving my legs back and forth in a slow rhythm. Every bone inside me screams in pain. I hold on to the rope so tight that my fingers get numb. In the end I'm swinging really far. Except, it's not far enough. Jamie can't reach me.

"Don't panic, now. I'm going to give you more rope." He unwinds the rope from his hand, giving me another couple feet of line. I swallow all my fear and keep swinging. "Just a little bit more, Angel," he urges.

Squinting my eyes shut, I put more of my weight into the next turn. A strong arm catches me around my

ANNA KATMORE

waist and stops my swinging abruptly. I'm pulled against a protective chest. "I have you, Angel. You're safe now."

It hurts like crazy when I lower my arms around Jamie's neck, and yet nothing ever felt so good.

He cuts my ties and gently rubs the burn marks on my wrists. Then he brushes my hair out of my face. Gazing into my eyes, he exhales a long, relieved breath. "Don't you ever run away from me like that again."

He almost makes me laugh, but I'm aching too much. A weak sob comes out instead. After he kisses me on my mouth, quick and hard, he hugs me to his chest. I bury my face in his shoulder, enjoying the brief moment of reunion.

When I look up again and catch a glimpse over his shoulder, I go rigid in his arms. Peter has gotten to his feet. Dead-set determination on his face, he tightens his grip on the knife in his hand and lunges at Jamie. Too many things happen at once.

I scream.

Jamie whirls about, shoves me to the side, and ducks.

Peter stabs the air instead of his brother.

He loses balance.

Jamie throws himself against Peter's legs and tosses him over his shoulder.

He doesn't know.

I scream again.

Far too close to the edge off the cliff, Peter hits the

stone ground with a groan and skitters on. He shoots out over the platform and falls. I dash forward, but there's nothing I can do. He's falling. And he's lost his happy thought.

"No! Jamie, no!" I grab his arm. "Peter can't fly. He'll die!"

After the brutal fight with his brother, one would have thought Jamie would take the news with joy. Instead, the horror on his face proves my suspicion. He never wanted his brother dead, or he would have killed him before he saved me.

Jamie stumbles to his knees beside me, gripping the edge of the rock. Peter flails with his arms and legs, to no avail. He can't lift himself in the air. My heart stops and I almost throw up.

Suddenly, a tiny spot shoots up from the depths of the abyss. Golden hair and a lush green dress. "Tami!" She beats her wings as fast as she can to reach Peter in time. When she gets a hold of his jacket's collar, she pulls hard upward, but he's too big and heavy for her. All she can do is slow his fall, a little. He's dragging her down with him. And then they disappear out of sight.

"We must get down to him!" I shout, rushing to my feet and starting to descend the steep slope of the mountain. Jamie is close behind me. The fact that he's so silent scares me the most. It can only mean one thing. He has the same fear as me—that Peter didn't survive the fall.

I'm barefoot and not anywhere near as used to the wilderness as Jamie. I know I'm only holding him up and he wants to go down and find his brother so desperately. After we've made it half the way together, I stop and let him get ahead of me. When he turns and casts me a look from a face so pale it can't be human, I push at his arm. "Go! I'll follow you!"

Jamie nods. I know he's grateful that I can watch after myself, but he still says nothing. I wish I could soothe him. I wish I could get down faster and find Peter alive. I wish I could change everything.

And for the briefest moment, I wish I had never fallen off my balcony.

At another push from me, Jamie eventually turns and half-runs, half-skates down the serpentine dirt path. When he reaches the upper level of the trees, I lose sight of him. It takes me an eternity to make my own way down the mountain. The nearer I get to the jungle, the louder the sobs of the Lost Boys and Tami's crying become.

Dear Lord, it can't be. Peter must be alive!

Tears stream down my cheeks as I send prayer after prayer to the heavens above. When I find the small group of boys and Jamie huddled above a figure lying on the ground, it almost breaks me. Slowing to an uncertain pace, I croak out Jamie's name. Everyone turns their head in my direction.

Jamie looks up and stares at me with a determined

expression, quietly mumbling along with the pumps as he gives Peter a cardiac massage. "Come. On. Come. On..." I wonder where he learned to do that. Then again, living on a ship he might have had to save some of his men from drowning over the years.

After a few more pumps, Peter's body jerks and he coughs. Everyone sucks in a gasp of relief. I fall forward on my knees and take his hand. He doesn't return my squeeze. His eyes flutter open for a second, unfocused, then they close again. At least, he's inhaling and exhaling in deep intervals now.

"We must get him out of here," Jamie says sternly, his voice so full of worry, it kills me.

"Where to?" Toby demands.

Jamie and I reply at the same time, "The fairies."

From the looks on the Lost Boys' faces I can tell how much the two women in the forest scare them. Yet they're Peter's only hope...if there's any at all. And they know it. Slowly, one after the other, they nod.

Stan, the tallest of the boys, and Jamie haul Peter to his feet, slipping their shoulders under his arms, supporting his weight. That Peter stumbles along with them is the best sign we have of him yet, even though his head is hanging.

Anxiously rubbing my upper arms, I follow with the rest of the boys. All of them are silent. It doesn't matter what Peter Pan did or said—to anyone. His family

ANNA KATMORE

surrounds him now, and everyone in this small group loves him like he's their real brother. That's what family is for, I think to myself, watching Jamie half-drag, half-carry Peter out of the jungle.

We wander across the meadows to the fairy forest ahead of us. A quiet sound follows me for a long while. It takes some time until it sinks in what that sound really is. I turn around and find Tami walking close behind me, sobbing.

Putting an arm around her shoulders, I pull her into my side. "It's all right. The fairies will know how to help him. They won't let him down." I wonder if I said this to soothe myself more than Tami. She nods briefly. There's not much confidence in that move. And then I realize what's really concerning her. It makes me stop and twist her to face me. "Peter didn't mean what he said up there. He wasn't himself, Tami."

The pixie sniffs and wipes the back of her small hand across her nose. "He hates me."

"No, he doesn't. He was just...confused." Gently, I stroke her golden locks away from her face. "When you were gone, he was so sad that he lost his happy thought. I know he wanted to take back all the mean things he said to you. And I know he didn't want to do all"—shrugging helplessly, I glance back at the mountain we left behind—"that."

"I don't want him to die, Angel," Tami pushes out

between sobs. "I don't want to be without him."

Hugging her to my chest, I caress her hair. "And you won't." Then I take her hand and tug her with me, so we don't lose the others. As we catch up with them, I ask Tami, "How did you and Peter meet?" I was always curious about it, even though right now it's more to distract Tami and myself from thoughts of doom.

She inhales deeply and wipes her tears away. "I wasn't born in Neverland, did you know?"

I shake my head.

"I don't know how to get back to the place where I was born, but it looks like an endless forest, far away from here. There are only pixies there and some animals that I've never seen here."

"It sounds like a beautiful place."

"It was. Only my folks weren't very friendly. They're a hard-working people, caring about nature, the four seasons, and the elements. Every pixie has a special ability to bring to our daily life. Everyone, except me." Her cheeks turn red with shame and she lowers her gaze to the glimmering nails of her tiny toes. "I should have learned to communicate with the wind, because that's what my line did. But I just couldn't. And instead of tending to the forest's needs, I always found myself distracted by simple things. I loved to tinker with things."

We fall a little behind again, and it makes me wonder if Tami doesn't want the boys to hear her story. "One day,

ANNA KATMORE

my folks made me cry again—like they did so often when they weren't pleased with my inability to fit in. I was so devastated that I wished myself away from that place and all the other pixies."

My eyes grow big. "And that worked?"

"The next thing I knew, I was hanging in a tree with my wings entangled in twigs, and Peter Pan freed me. I had no idea how to get back to the Pixie Forest. I didn't care about it either. Peter had already decided to never grow up at that point, and he was alone like me. He said if I stayed with him, he'd be my family from then on. He said he'd always take care of me and never make me cry."

"Did he keep his promise?" I ask in a soft voice.

"He did. Until today."

I force a smile. "So you really were the first Lost *Girl*."

"Peter is my family. He and the other Lost Boys. I've never been as happy as I was after Peter Pan took me in. He was a great big brother, not at all the mean man he has become lately."

Silently, I agree with her. Peter was a funny and lovely guy when I first met him. The man Jamie and Stan carry in front of us now has nothing in common with the person he once was. Growing up so fast did this to him. I feel unspeakably sorry for Peter Pan.

We walk the rest of the long way in silence. Toby and Loney take turns replacing Stan, but Jamie never let's go of his brother when asked. He carries him all the way to the fairies' house.

Bre'Shun is at the gate of their small garden and receives us with a concerned look on her pale face. No one pays attention to the beautiful white horse that's grazing at the back. When it takes a step forward and eyes us suspiciously, I see the elegant white horn glimmering in the sunlight. The unicorn inclines its head as if to greet me. I know I shouldn't be surprised about anything that's happening in this forest, so I respond with a tilt of my own and follow the others.

The boys lower Peter into the grass and we all kneel down around him, Tami and I each taking his hand.

"Why did you wait so long?" The fairy with the golden hair piled on her head narrows her turquoise eyes at Jamie. "I expected you way sooner."

Jamie catches his breath after the exhausting hike. "What do you mean?"

"Look at him. Did you really have to wait until his heart gave out to think of consulting me?"

I, like everyone else, gaze down at Peter. His hair is now white like snow. When my grandfather died of a heart attack at age seventy-eight, he didn't look as old as Peter. "Are we too late?" I whisper.

Bre'Shun lowers to her knees next to Jamie, her long, deep red dress fanning out around her. "Too late for the cure I could have provided," she answers with pain in her voice.

My heart sinks, my throat constricts, cutting off any air. I shake my head, slowly at first, then violently, as I hear the desperate cry of a young pixie next to me.

Chapter 13

I KILLED MY brother. The only family I had left. Peter's breaths become shallow and they let out for longer than they should every so often.

"This can't be it! You always know what to do!" I shout at the fairy. In despair, I grab her shoulders and shake her, growling through gritted teeth. "Do *something*. Now!"

Bre tilts her head. The look she gives me is disappointed yet somewhat hurtful. The skin where I'm touching her glazes over and turns into shockingly cold ice. My hands burn. I jerk them away, my palms red and marred with angry blisters.

Nostrils flaring, she breathes slowly through her nose. Her eyes turn a much darker shade of blue. I'm expecting a thunderstorm to come down on me any minute as we stare at each other, especially when Remona, who no doubt is having the time of her life as a unicorn, sidles up to her sister and snuffles in my face. But nothing happens. Bre's anger cools off quickly. Or rather, she warms over...

Her friendly smile returning, she lets go of a long sigh. "James Hook. Whatever shall I do with you?" She turns to Peter and strokes her cold hand over his forehead. First I think she's only showing her affection, until I notice how Peter's lips suddenly turn blue, his skin pales to whiter than chalk, and his chest is no longer lifting.

"Stop it!" I shout, reaching out for Bre'Shun, but Remona nudges my hand away with her horn. "She's freezing him," I argue with the insane horse. "He'll die."

"Peter Pan *will* die, if we do nothing to stop the ageing process," Bre answers to me in her gentle voice, her gaze still focused on Peter. His skin glazes over like Bre'Shun's did earlier when I grabbed her so harshly. He turns hard and stiff, his eyes freezing over, the lids at half-mast.

As the girls cry, I feel my throat tighten too. No matter how hard I swallow, the lump in there won't go away. "And now what?" I croak. "Let him vegetate as a giant icicle?" How is this any better than letting him die?

"Not forever, James Hook. Only until you make a decision."

"What?" What can *I* do? Finding Angel's eyes across my brother's cold body, I feel how my bones start to tremble. Which kind of decision could I make that would

save Peter?

Certainly reading my mind again, or maybe just the obvious question on my face, Bre tells me, "The decision of how much your brother really means to you."

I turn my head and silently scrutinize the fairy. Peter means a lot to me. More than I ever thought was possible. He's a part of Neverland. A part of my family...

"If you want to save your brother, things have to go back to how they were," Bre explains. "He must, once again, become the boy who wouldn't grow. And time will stand still again."

"I'm fine with that," I tell her through a clenched jaw.

She lifts her brows. "The gates to the other world will close."

"I understand."

"And Angel can't stay in Neverland."

No!

I squeeze my eyes shut. This is the only thing I can't agree to. I can't lose Angel again. She's my everything. I need her with me.

"Jamie, he's your brother," Angel whispers and gently takes my hand in hers. I wonder how much of my thoughts *she* can read.

Sliding my fingers through hers, I shake my head.

"Please, James, don't let Peter die," Skippy mumbles and all the other Lost Boys lift their pleading gazes to me.

ANNA KATMORE

The one looking like she's aching for Peter the most is the little pixie. The hope she puts in me constricts my chest.

With a feeling of having rocks tied to my limbs, I rise from the ground and pull Angel into my arms. I hug her so hard that I might crack her ribs. She pillows her cheek against my chest and wraps her arms around me with the same force. This is the place I want to stay for the rest of my life.

But I don't want my brother to die, and it means I have to let go of Angel. From what I could read in Bre's eyes, this time, there won't be a way to see her ever again. It's like the fairies have played a cruel joke on me. Teased me with the biggest adventure, as Bre put it once, and then ripped it from my arms with one snap of her fingers.

But Neverland wouldn't be the same without Peter Pan.

I have to choose. My brother. Or my love.

"You love your brother," Angel whispers in my ear as she slides her arms around my neck and stands on her tiptoes. "The same way I love my sisters. There really isn't a choice. Saving Peter is the only thing that counts."

I bury my face in her hair for a long moment and savor every second of the time I have to hold her. Her beautiful scent will be etched in my memory forever, as will the feeling of embracing her like this.

I know Angel is crying; her tears dampen the side of my face. For once, I'm glad I'm not looking at her. Or I wouldn't be able to hold it together.

Clearing my throat, I lift my gaze to the fairy and quietly ask her, "What does it take?"

Bre'Shun gets to her feet, smoothing her long dress. "Someone has to take his years."

"I will," Toby blurts out first, followed by Skippy's, "Me, too."

Each of the Lost Boys enthusiastically offer to take a share of Peter's years, so they will all be—what, twenty-five in the end? Also the pixie volunteers.

Bre'Shun shakes her head, her gaze filled with compassion. "No. There's only one who can do it," she says.

Me.

Her eyes find mine. With a nod, I agree.

"Peter gained eighty years, James Hook. Are you willing to take them all to save your brother?"

Angel stiffens in my arms and everyone on the ground sucks in an appalled gasp.

Sink me, eighty years.

I'm nineteen. This would mean my immediate death. Then again, remembering all the things I did to Peter— when he was a child, and later, after I made him break the spell—I know I deserve it. And living in Neverland without ever being able to see Angel again is not an option for me anyway.

With my hand in Angel's hair, I cuddle her to my

chest. She shouldn't have to see the ache for her in my face as I tell the fairy with a determined edge to my voice, "All right. I'll do it."

Angel's chest vibrates against mine. "No," she whispers.

I caress her hair and rest my cheek on the top of her head. The decision has been made. She was right, there was really no choice from the beginning.

Taking her face in my hands, I tilt her head up and kiss her on the lips. They tremble, wet from her tears. And yet she's never tasted this real to me before. I know I could have said many things then, like *I love you*, or *You'll always be in my heart*. What I really tell her is, "It's been a pleasure to meet you, Angelina McFarland."

Angel says nothing. She only lets me kiss her again. One last time to remember.

Eventually, my hands drop from her face. I stroke my palm down the side of her arm and slide my fingers through hers. Taking a deep breath, I then face the fairy. "Bring it on."

Bre gazes at us for a long moment. Something isn't right. I can feel it. But she, like Angel, remains silent. In the end, she kneels down beside Peter and beckons Remona with a wave of her hand. The other she extends to me. Taking it, I let her pull me down opposite her.

"Place your hand over Peter's heart," she tells me and guides my hand there. He's ice-cold. A shudder zooms through me. "Only the touch of a unicorn's horn can perform magic like this."

Now aren't we lucky we have one on hand? An ironic chuckle dies in my throat.

"Peter will wake up when the transfer has finished." Bre turns to look me straight in the eyes. "You don't have much time then. If you want to say goodbye to him, do it fast."

I nod.

Remona lowers her head, her long, silky white mane falling forward. Angel squeezes my other hand. I close my eyes.

"Wait!"

Startled by Angel's shout I jerk around.

"Don't do it. I have an idea."

Whatever does she mean? My brows furrowing to a line, I look from Bre to Angel and back. Even though the fairy's focus is still on Peter's face, a smirk sneaks to her mouth that makes me wonder if she's been waiting for this. If she's actually *pleased.*

The tip of Remona's horn hovers above my hand on Peter's heart. She doesn't move. Her dark eyes glimmer, and I can see all the Lost Boys' anxious faces reflected in them as they're gathered around their friend.

"Tell me about your idea, Angelina," Bre'Shun says, slowly tilting her head.

"I—I was thinking, maybe you could contain the

years for Jamie somewhere. Give him one at a time. So he will age like it's meant to be."

She's trying to save me. I love this girl with all my heart. But she isn't making it any easier for me. Living in Neverland, away from her, is not what I want. "That would be eighty years without you, Angel." My voice grows hoarse. "I can't bear that."

"And he cannot grow older while the rest of Neverland stands still," Bre explains with a smile. She seems too happy about how this conversation is going. What the hell—

"Then let him come with me," Angel argues.

"*With* you?" I blurt out.

"Yes, Jamie." On her knees, she scoots closer to me, her face glowing with new hope. "Come with me. To my world. We would have eighty years together."

The boys break out in excited mumbling. The pixie flutters her wings behind her back. I don't even know if that is possible, but growing older with Angel... *By the rainbows of Neverland*, this sounds wonderful. "Is that—I mean, can I—"

Now Bre's smirk expands to the happiest smile I've seen on her since the day we first met in this forest. "Oh yes, James Hook. You can." Then she turns to Angel and her smile fades to a warm expression. "But as always, there is a price to pay. If a resident of Neverland leaves, someone else has to take his place."

Who?

The two of them lock their gazes for an infinite moment, obviously communicating in their own way. Everyone holds their breath. Tami places a small hand on Angel's shoulder, biting her bottom lip. A bad feeling rises in my gut. The fairies' bargains are never easy to fulfill. I tighten my hold around Angel's hand and want to tell her to back out but, by the time I open my mouth, it's already too late.

"I agree," Angel says.

The calm determination in her voice shocks me. Bre'Shun nods. What in the world did they agree on? A cold shiver skitters down my back.

Gracefully, the fairy rises to her feet and holds out a hand to Angel. "No one is ever forced to stay in Neverland. The only thing *you* have to do is give your own approval when the time comes."

Angel smiles as she pushes to her feet, but it looks forced. "I understand."

"No!" I shout at her. "You know how tricky these bargains are. Don't do it. Not for me."

"It's okay, Jamie. Come with me and stay in my world." She caresses my cheek, and her smile takes on genuine warmth. "It will be all right, I know it will."

For some reason I can't explain, I feel it too at this moment. Maybe it's just wishful thinking or it's the fairies granting me glimpses of my future, I guess I'll never know. What I see is a warm house with Angel in the kitchen, me standing behind her, holding her with all the love I feel for her now. Laughter of children drifts from the garden. It's a place where I long to be.

"So be it," Bre says in a low voice. She tells the others to stay with Peter while she asks me to follow her to the back of the house. I don't like leaving my brother or Angel, but there seems to be some fairy magic to perform so I can go with the girl I love.

Bre and I walk through her amazing vegetable garden that is now in full bloom. As we pass the small square bed with the label *carrots of horror* and stroll farther to the back, I finally realize where we're headed. "The tree of wishes?"

She gives me a sideways glance, the corners of her mouth curving up. When we reach the spot where this young tree that I helped water not so long ago should be, there now stands a giant apple tree with lush green leaves and juicy fruits, casting a shadow over half the place. My breath catches in my throat. "Blow me down, what did you do to that tree?"

"Not me, James Hook. You."

I lift one eyebrow. "How? Because I spat into your soup back then?" When I think back to that strange morning in the fairy's garden, another realization suddenly sinks in. "You planned this. All of it."

"Of course I did."

"But why?"

With a sigh, Bre reaches up and plucks a shiny red apple. "Because you and Angel needed a happy ending."

"So you saw this coming?"

"Oh yes, I did." She rubs the fruit on the skirt of her dress then holds it out to me. "The only thing I don't get is why you'd grow apples on your personal tree of wishes. Would you care to explain that to me?"

"Why, don't they grow on everyone's tree?" I take the fruit from her and scrutinize it, not sure what to do with it.

"No. They usually carry nuts or, in some rare cases, cherries." Her forehead creases. "You're the first to ever have an apple tree."

A smile stretches my lips, because I think I know why apples. The pleasant memory of how I first met Angel comes up.

"Ah," the fairy drawls knowingly.

It really creeps me out every time she reads my mind. Since I obviously answered her question already, it's only fair that she answers one of mine now. I lean on the tree and cross my arms over my chest, one of my feet resting against the trunk. "After the curse was broken, why did Peter age so much faster than everyone else?"

Bre smirks. "Spells are a tricky thing. I told you, you had to get him to break the spell."

"And so I did."

"Did you really? Or did you actually force him to? Peter Pan himself never *wanted* to grow up."

"I had no choice. He would have never agreed."

"I know."

I don't understand the fairy's logic in this, or her amusement. "And yet you made me do it to get my own wishes fulfilled. You knew what would happen then. You knew all of it. Why did you let me destroy my brother's life?"

"My dear boy." Bre sighs and caresses my cheek with her cold hand. "You and Peter are both the children of Neverland. We love you. And you both deserve your happy endings. Peter already found his. He decided to stay a boy forever, and he was happy with it. You, on the other hand, needed your adventure."

There's only one real adventure in this world. Love. It's finding the one person who makes you want to be better than you are. The words ring with a fairy-light laugh in my mind.

"To give you both what you want, Remona and I had to create something a long time ago. Something that would move *you* in the right direction."

They created something? It can only be one thing. "A spell bound to a watch," I mumble, lifting my gaze from the ground to her face. "Peter never needed to destroy the watch to grow older, did he? He made the decision to stay a child, he can simply make a decision again."

"You're a smart young man, James Hook."

"You could have told me that before, you know."

"Yes," is all she says. And I realize if she *had* told me, nothing would have worked out for the ending we're all facing. Peter will be the boy who wouldn't grow up again. He will be happy with his friends and the pixie. And I will have Angel. That's all I want.

Adapting her expression to my confident one, Bre gently places her hands on my forearms. "Now, if you don't mind, Captain, take a bite of the apple but let me word your wish for you. We don't want anything bad to happen because of the wrong phrasing."

With a shake of my head, I agree and lift the apple to my lips. Keeping my gaze locked with hers, I take a cautious bite. An exotic, sweet-sour taste explodes in my mouth. I chew and swallow then take another bite. It's better than anything I've ever eaten.

All the time, Bre'Shun mumbles something unintelligible, spreading her hands slightly and lowering to her knees. When there's nothing left of the apple, she looks up at me and says, "Would you mind digging up this spot? There's something in the ground you'll need."

Digging? "With my hands?"

"You can take the spade."

"What sp—"

Cutting me off, Bre nods toward my feet. I look down and sure enough there's a small shovel leaning

ANNA KATMORE

against the tree. It definitely wasn't there when we came here. Of course, there's no need to start questioning the fairy. I just pick it up and start to dig a hole in the dirt. On the third delve of the spade, I hit something hard.

"Careful," she tells me. "You don't want to break this."

Using my hands instead of the shovel, I clear the rest of the dirt away and expose an ivory hourglass with golden sand inside that bears a striking similarity to pixie dust.

"Remona will put Peter's years into this. Once the sand starts running, nothing can stop it. Wait to turn it until you're in your new world."

Grateful for everything, I nod and lean in to kiss the fairy on her ice-cold cheek. She chuckles as we both rise from the ground. "Now come. Let's finish this story."

Walking around the house to the front with her, I rub the back of my neck. "How will Angel and I get to London?"

"With your ship, of course. I believe you still have rainbow powder left for one more journey?" The indication in her voice is unmistakable. She and her sister knew I'd be stealing Angel to Neverland before all the dust was used up. Maybe that's what Remona meant in the first place that day inside their house, when she told me to just be myself. It makes me laugh now. I'm a pirate after all.

As soon as we reach the front garden again, Angel jumps to her feet and flings her arms around me. "Is it done? You didn't change your mind, did you?"

If I had backed out of the deal, Angel's hopeful face would have broken my heart. "We're almost there," I tell her, smiling, and place a chaste kiss on her lips. Then I lift the hourglass to her eyes. "Remona only has to bottle my years."

"Remona?" Angel glances round the place until the unicorn lifts its head and whinnies joyfully. Realization dawns in Angel's eyes. "Is she—"

I nod and pull her along with me to put the hourglass in position over Peter's heart like Bre did with my hand before. The Lost Boys move aside to let the unicorn through. With a simple touch of the horn, the hourglass begins to glow. And the ice melts out of Peter's body.

Everyone gapes, their mouths dropped open, as Peter's aging process rewinds. The white is fading out of his thick brown hair, the bushy eyebrows thin back to tilted lines. All the wrinkles disappear from his face. He even shrinks the few inches he's had on me these past few weeks.

When all the clothes hang sloppily on him and his skin is smooth like the surface of a pearl again, he slowly opens his eyes. The collective exhale of relieved sighs makes me realize even I was holding my breath. I laugh. I'm the first to grab my brother and crush him to my chest in a hug that has been overdue for a long time.

ANNA KATMORE

"Hey, wait! What—"

I don't give him a chance for questions, because I'm clearly cutting the airflow off from his lungs. "Oh, you little bastard! You scared me witless!" Ruffling his hair, I squeeze him even harder. "Never do that again, do you hear me?"

When he has enough room to breathe again and leans away, he narrows his eyes at me. "I'm no longer an old man?"

"No, you aren't."

"And you did this? You made me younger again?"

"I guess, somehow I did. With the help of a few friends."

Puzzled as heck, Peter looks around, obviously confused to find all his friends here. Until his gaze lights on the pixie. She's the first he swoops up in his arms after I release him, making her squeak with surprise. "Sorry about all the things I said to you! I'm so sorry I made you cry," he tells her. "Please forgive me."

She nods her curly head and golden dust rains down on her shoulders. But she's not the only one he begs for forgiveness. Seemingly he has some making up to do with the Lost Boys too. And then of course with Angel. When he hears from the fairy about our deal, he takes Angel aside and embraces her with true sorrow and also gratitude. I catch the words *never wanted to hurt you* and *hope you'll always be happy* at some point. I don't want to stand in their way right now, so I turn to the fairies and say goodbye to them.

Stroking Remona's satiny mane, I glance over her head to Bre'Shun. She seems pleased with the way today turned out. I'll miss her and her crazy house. A sudden tightness moves into my throat.

"I sent Smee off with the ship to help me save Angel. Where do I find them?" I ask her to quench the awkward feeling.

"The Jolly Roger still berths at Mermaid Lagoon. For some reason, the men never got the anchor out of the sea." She winks one shiny turquoise eye at me.

Bracing myself for an ice-cold shock, I walk over to her and take her in my arms. "Thank you, fairy," I whisper in her ear.

She hugs me back then releases me before I turn into an icicle like Peter did. "You've played well in this game. Now go and enjoy the outcome."

Lacing my fingers with Angel's when she comes over, I walk out through the gate in the small white picket fence, following the others.

"James."

At Bre's gentle voice, I stop and turn around once more. "Hm?"

"The ship needs a captain."

We look at each other for a couple of seconds, both sporting a smirk now, and I nod. Then we leave the fairy forest—Angel and I for the last time.

With the jolly bunch of boys, the pixie, and a flying Peter Pan as company, the journey back to the ship, though it takes hours, seems far too short for me. I finally learn all their names and listen to their many stories. Neverland wouldn't be the same without any of them. Wondering if any of them think the same about me, I only have to look at each of their faces when we arrive at the Jolly Roger and it's time to say goodbye. So many hugs, so many wishes—heck yeah, I know they'll be bored to death without me.

Even the pixie flutters up a couple of feet and throws her arms around my neck. "Thank you for saving my Peter!"

Her Peter? The sound of it makes me laugh. I guess now it's Peter's turn to be the big brother to someone. Hopefully he does a better job than I did. When the little thing releases me, I step up to him.

Saying goodbye to Peter is funny. We just stand there and grin at each other. There's really not much I can say to the bloody scamp.

Peter shoves his hands into his pockets and digs a hole in the dirt with his toe. "We did have some good times, right?"

"We sure did." I hold out my hand to him. When he takes it, I pull him into me and hug him quickly. "Take care, little brother."

"You too. Neverland will suck without you, you know." He grimaces then smirks. "Guess I'll have to put up with your first mate instead now."

Oh, Smee will love to hear that. Or maybe he won't. He doesn't even know I'm leaving yet.

When Peter and I step apart, Angel comes to say goodbye and holds on to Peter for the longest time. She has a hard time letting him go. After a few minutes, Peter wraps his arms tighter around her and flies her up onto the deck of the Jolly Roger. Her cheerful squeal echoes across the sea. I follow them over the gangplank.

Jack Smee greets me with an arched eyebrow. "What's this all about?"

After a heavy sigh, I tell him, "In a minute, Jack."

Ignoring the crew's curious stares for now, I walk to Angel and put my arms around her, kissing her forehead, then I lift my gaze to Peter, who still hovers above us and grins.

"Until we meet again, Hook!" he shouts down and laughs. Then he somersaults in the air and flies away, following the others.

Angel and I stand by the railing and gaze after the merry group long after they're out of sight.

"Cap'n?" Smee says next to me. Uncertainty has crept into his voice.

Clearing my throat, I face him. There's a lot to explain.

ANNA KATMORE

Chapter 14

WE REACH LONDON by night. Everything is dark and quiet. Angel's balcony door is still open and light burns in her room. It looks exactly the way it did when she came out to me after the dance.

"Do you think we came back the same night we left?" she asks me.

Tilting her chin up with my knuckle, I kiss her on the lips. "I guess we're going to find out."

On the journey from Neverland to London, I had enough time to fill Smee in on everything that happened after I left the ship to save Angel. It surprised me how little it surprised *him* that I was ready to settle down in Angel's world. The bilge rat even had the cheek to tell me he saw it coming from the day I started jumping off the ship's mast. Bloody bastard!

Well, I guess it's been a given all along.

After a final detour to the booty, where I picked a

last souvenir—a diamond the size of a pixie's tear—I walk out on deck and say goodbye to my crew. The pirates take off their hats and press their fists to their hearts. They are good men. We've had great times together. Hopefully, their new captain can handle them as well as I did.

That reminds me... Walking up to Jack Smee, I take off my hat with the big, black feather and put it on his head.

"What the hell—" he growls, quirking his brows in protest.

I shrug. "The Jolly Roger needs a captain. Take care of her."

His chest swelling with pride, Jack straightens, growing a couple of inches. "Consider her in good hands." He grins and we embrace quickly, smacking each other on the back for luck.

Angel must have said goodbye to everyone while I was under deck, because she's waiting by the railing where the men fastened the rope on which we're supposed to climb down into her garden. With a diamond in my pocket and the hourglass in my hand, I nod at them all then start sliding down the rope first.

There's still that small heap of my treasure in the grass, and the coins clink under my shoes when I jump down the last couple of meters. Moments later, Angel follows me. It's definitely something she hasn't done often. The way she clings to the rope for dear life makes me laugh. Until she loses her grip halfway and falls, shrieking. Dropping the hourglass, I catch her in my arms.

The air pushes out of Angel's lungs, then she smiles. "You look beautiful when you're happy," I tell her. That gives her cheeks an adorable rosy flush.

Setting her to her feet, I'm just about to kiss her when something black glides down from the sky, catching my attention. It's my hat, and it lands on the hive of gold.

"This ship will always have a captain!" Jack's voice drifts on the wind, followed by a hearty laugh.

Closing my eyes for a brief moment, I envision for the last time how the crew would draw anchor and set sail under my command. Being a pirate is all I've ever known. The thought of fitting into a strange new world fills me with more anxiety than I care to admit, but there's also a swell of anticipation taking over. I'll be in this world with the girl I love. Nothing can take that away from me.

With Angel's hand in mine, I walk over to pick up my hat, then I sit under a tree and pull her into my lap. Her legs tucked under the fine blue dress she's still wearing, she nestles against my chest, shapes her soft palm to my cheek, and mumbles, "I can't believe we're finally here."

Yeah, tell me about it. I nuzzle the side of her face and breathe a kiss to her brow. "Can I ask you something?" I whisper.

"Anything."

"What did you trade to the fairy for me?"

The way she stiffens and falls silent makes my uneasiness grow. "Angel?" I prompt her.

She sucks in a breath through her teeth, then exhales in a long blow. "When she told me there was a price to pay, the first thing that came to my mind was *the firstborn.*"

"What?" The thought was so absurd it made me laugh. We've been back together for only a few days, and this is clearly far too early to think about having children. But even if we do—one day—how could she trade off our baby?

"Calm down," she tells me and strokes her fingers along my arm. "Bre said someone has to take your place one day. I'm sure she's not stealing our child out of the cradle."

"How can you be so sure?"

"Because she made me see images in my mind. Pictures of a young woman. She will want to go to Neverland, Jamie. And all it needs is my approval, you heard that."

I hear Angel's voice, but the meaning doesn't sink in because my mind got stuck on one word. Finding her eyes with mine, I lick my bottom lip. A smile tugs on the corners of my mouth.

"What?" she demands, a little nervous now.

"We'll have a girl."

Angel takes a second to contemplate what I said, then she starts smiling too. "I guess that's right."

I don't know why this makes me so happy when the thought of having a family never occurred to me before. Maybe it's the certainty that I'm going to be a much better father than the one Peter and I had. At least I'll work hard at it.

Angel snuggles up to me and rests her head under my chin. After some time she heaves a sigh full of nostalgia. "It's really over, isn't it? Our adventure in Neverland, I mean."

My glance sweeps over the treasure and lands on the hourglass with the golden sand. It's standing upside down. When it slipped from my hand, time started running.

"Or," I whisper back, "it's the beginning of eighty fantastic years."

*

A twinkle of sunlight tickles my nose and I blink my eyes open. Neither of us wanted to go inside last night, so Angel and I just sat under that tree in her garden until we fell asleep in each other's arms. Not a bad place to spend the night.

With my thumb and forefinger, I rub my eyes. The hat fell off my head while I slept and is resting on Angel's bent knees now. I watch her happy face for a moment, her eyes still closed peacefully.

Last night we made plans for our future together.

Angel is set on telling her family who I really am, even though I don't think this is the best idea she ever had. Considering the hard time I had convincing *her* I'm real, what will her parents say?

Then again it's her world. She knows best. I'm just happy to be here with her.

Sighing into her soft hair, I brush a few stray wisps behind her ear. Angel stirs against me, but she doesn't wake yet. Even though my body is stiff from sitting against the tree all night, I decide to give her a few more minutes.

From the direction of the house, the sound of two excited voices drifts to us. Straining my neck, I try to catch a glimpse over my shoulder, around the tree, but I have to wait until they lope over and stop right in front of me. It's two little girls. They must be the notorious twins. When they find us sitting in an embrace on the ground, one sucks in her breath and claps her hands over her mouth. The other, wrapped in a purple dress, waves her wand at my face and pulls her brows to a tiny V.

"Who. Are. You?" she exclaims.

Angel's extra minutes are over. At the shocked voice of the dwarf that I assume is called Brittney Renae, she jerks awake and straightens in my lap. "Huh? What?"

"Angel! Why are you sleeping in the garden?" the other half of the twin couple demands, then she snickers. "Is this your boyfriend?"

"I—uh..." Angel rubs her eyes then her temples.

ANNA KATMORE

Now I'm dying to hear her answer. Smirking, I give her a sideways glance. "Tell your sister. Am I?"

She laughs and pokes me in the ribs. I guess that's a yes.

After shooting a volley of questions about why there's suddenly so much money in their garden and why Angel is wearing this funny dress, which Brittney Renae actually loves but Paulina not so much, the girls have to break for a breath and that's when I casually tell them, "Hi. I'm James Hook."

The name immediately rings a bell with them. Their eyes grow wide and their tiny mouths hang open. "No way!" says Paulina and pulls on the two pigtails framing her heart-shaped face. "You can't be him. He's from a fairy tale." She claims not to believe me, yet my name made both girls back away a tiny step. It's hilarious.

"Are you sure?" I tease them and put my hat on, remembering perfectly well what kind of reaction it provoked from Angel the first time. The twins don't disappoint. Full of wonder, they stare at me.

Then suddenly the one Angel kept calling the fairy bug in her stories runs at me and smacks me hard on the head with her star-tipped wand. "Let go of our sister, you thief! You will not take her away to your ship!"

Angel and I look at each other, then we both burst out laughing at the same time. So the convincing part is done. Now it's time to explain why I'm holding their sister in my arms.

We have them sit on the ground with us and Angel starts her tale with the night she fell off the balcony. The girls listen with awe-filled faces. There's not one moment when they doubt even a single word of what she tells them. And I enjoy hearing it all again.

We've almost made it to the end when a woman's gentle voice calls the three girls. Apparently, it's breakfast time in London. Angel smiles at me. "Are you ready to meet the rest of my family?"

I'm a pirate. I haven't been scared of many things in my life. But when Angel rises to her feet and holds out her hand to me, I hesitate.

"Come on, Jamie," she says. "They'll like you."

"You really think they'll let me move in with you once they know who I am?" Given that they'll believe me as easily as the twins, that is.

"Of course. They'll understand how important this is to me. And if not, well"—she bends down and picks up a handful of coins—"take three of these and you can buy any house you like."

The thought of having a house of my own where I can take Angel appeals to me far more than moving in with strange people. Well, at least this way we have a backup plan. I let her and the twins pull me to my feet. Brittney Renae skips excitedly ahead, while Paulina slips her tiny hand into mine and walks with me and Angel over to the big house at the other end of the garden.

My heart pounds a wild beat. It seems like the real adventure begins now.

Angelina

Ten years later...

I'M CHOPPING tomatoes and cucumbers for a salad. A delicious-smelling roast pork cooks in the oven, while a strawberry cream cake sits in the fridge, waiting to be cut later, after dinner. I like busying myself in the kitchen. It's the sunniest place in our house in Fairy Cross.

"When will Jamie be home?" Paulina asks me as she takes four plates from the cupboard and puts them together with some glasses and cutlery on a tray to carry outside into the garden.

After a quick glance at the clock above the wide archway that leads to the dining room, I tell her, "In about an hour. He said he'll try to be here no later than seven." And then I sigh—for the thirty-fifth time in the past forty minutes. I miss him and can't wait until he comes back from his biking tour with the guys. Three days away? That's just too long.

330   ANNA KATMORE

On the other hand, I'm more than glad that Jamie has made such good friends in our new hometown. The way he suffered the first few months after he'd left Neverland, the ship with his crew, and of course Peter behind, tugged on my heartstrings. That my parents never believed where he really came from and called him a kid with serious issues as he struggled so hard to cope with the change didn't make it any better.

Instead of moving in with us, Jamie bought the house in our street where Peter had made himself comfortable for a while, but not even there did he seem to be happy. It wasn't until three years later, when we made a trip to Southwest England, just the two of us, and found this beautiful house in a dreamy town called Fairy Cross, that he appeared to find his spark again. It didn't take him more than twenty seconds to convince me to buy the property and settle down here.

Not for a minute of my life did I regret that decision.

"Angel? Are you in Neverland again?"

I jerk around and stare at Paulina's questioning eyes. My cheeks warm over as I rub my hands on the back of my cut-off jeans. "Not in Neverland, no."

"You looked a little lost for a moment."

Unfortunately, that's one thing that happens to me quite often. Ever since I came back from Neverland, I keep having moments where my thoughts suck me into short time outs. It's okay for me. I just don't like it when others catch me lost in memories. "I'm fine." Taking a step toward Paulina, I shape my palm to her cheek. "Just thinking about how happy I am to have you girls here with us."

A brief glimmer of sadness crosses her face. It disappears fast enough and she smiles again. "Okay, I'll set the table and then read a little outside. Call me if you need me to help with anything."

I nod and watch her carry the tray out onto the terrace, her plaid skirt swaying around her bare knees. She's become a pretty young girl. Both twins have. Every time I look at them or run my fingers through their soft strawberry-blond hair, I'm reminded of my mother. They look so much like her, especially on the day I saw her and my father for the last time.

I was home for the weekend to watch my then nine-year-old sisters. Mom had straightened her curls with a flat iron and put on very little make-up that evening, which was quite unusual for her, but it made her look young and so very beautiful. Dad took her out to a candlelight dinner for their twenty-seventh anniversary.

They never came back.

A truck slammed their car off the road. There was no chance of survival for any of the passengers the policeman told me.

Jamie was wonderful at that time. Knowing what it means to lose family, he helped my sisters and me through the worst. We took the twins in with us and, since we both love them above all, we're raising them like our own children now.

Brittney Renae struggled with the loss the most, so one night Jamie and I had a long conversation about her. We found a way to drag her out of her depression. Two Neverland doubloons were enough to buy the three-hectare land adjoining our property. Jamie built a stable there and we got the fairy bug a young horse. She called it Becky, after the doll she got from our parents for her sixth birthday. Hardly a day goes by where she doesn't take the paint horse out for a ride—like she's doing right now. It's good to see her happy again.

Releasing another sigh, I push the sleeves of my white shirt up to my elbows and continue chopping the veggies.

If it wasn't for this dreamy place we've found for ourselves, with the coast not far and miles away from the city traffic, I think I would often wish myself back to Neverland. It's been ten years since that adventure ended for Jamie and me, but I can't think of a time in my life when I felt more like myself.

"I know where you are..."

At the sound of my favorite voice in the world, a tiny butterfly in my stomach quickly calls his friends out to play. I drop the knife and whirl about, beaming at Jamie, who's leaning with one shoulder against the wall in the arch. His hands clasped behind his back, the dark leather jacket parts at the front and reveals a firm chest beneath a white tee. He cracks a smile, because he surely notices my staring.

Leaning back against the counter and gripping the edge, I let my gaze skate over him, from his tousled blond hair to the toes of his motorcycle boots. He's a gorgeous eyeful. Ten years have passed, and he still looks the same. Adventurous with a whiff of danger. A perfect mix.

"You know me too well," I tease him.

"That's one of the pleasures of being your husband."

Naturally, I cast a glance at the ring on my finger and smile to myself. It bears a tiny diamond from Neverland. Jamie proposed to me with this ring. I never take it off, nor the necklace with the ruby heart. It'll always remind me of the unlikely brothers that found a happy ending after all.

When I look up again, Jamie is holding a shiny red apple. He tosses it across the island counter and I catch it with both hands. Apples have become dear to me, and warmth fills my chest at the small gesture that revives one of my favorite memories with Captain Hook.

"I missed you, Miss London," he drawls as he slowly walks toward me.

Putting the apple aside, I fling my arms around his neck and surrender when his tongue starts roaming my mouth. *By the rainbows of Neverland*, I'll never get enough of his taste. Standing on my tiptoes, my fingers in his hair, I enjoy the feeling of his hands sliding down my spine and over my backside. Thrilling shivers run over me.

But Jamie pulls back all too quickly, his eyebrows narrowed to a confused V. "Did you hear that?"

"No, what?" I gasp, trying to catch my breath, and tilt my head to listen.

He releases me and turns around to glance out the French doors to the terrace. "Is there someone in the garden?"

"Only Paulina. She's reading."

Suddenly, I hear it too. The voice of a boy. "...tried to shoot me with his cannon! I barely escaped."

I freeze on the spot.

Jamie's eyes grow wide and his breathing hitches. It takes me all of five seconds to find my own voice again. "It can't be—"

"It *must* be!" he cuts me off, grabs my hand and drags me outside with him. I've never seen him so fevered before, then again I haven't felt this surge of excitement in a long time myself.

Together we stumble into the garden, where Jamie pulls me to a halt. Paulina is sitting in the shade under a tree, flattening her book to her chest with both hands, and staring with an open mouth at the thick branch above her head.

On that very branch hunches a slim, teenage boy,

wearing a grass-green tee, his thick brown hair windblown, and with eyes as blue as the endless sea. When he notices us gaping and rooted to the ground, he cocks his head. A mischievous smirk plays on his lips. "Hello, James. Angel."

"Peter," I croak, feeling the tight squeeze of my stunned husband's hand. Now it's me who pulls him along until we stand right in front of the tree.

"You—came here, you bloody little bastard!" Jamie laughs, his surprise ringing in each syllable.

"How is that possible?" I blurt out.

Peter Pan wraps his fingers around the twigs above him and leans farther down from the branch. His eyes sparkle in the sun as he winks at Paulina, then his mouth curves into a full, wicked grin and he turns to us.

"With magic..."

THE END

To all my dear readers,

Thank you for bearing with me when the first book ended on such a mean hook. I still believe writing a sequel was the only way to solve all the riddles of Neverland...and give Angel and Jamie their deserved *Happily Ever After*.

On another note, even though Peter Pan made it out of Neverland, I'm not planning a third book at this point. If I should ever change my mind, you'll be the first to hear. ;-)

xoxo
Anna

Playlist

Sunrise Avenue — Lifesaver
(Three guys and bathwater)

Dexter Britain — Nothing to fear
(Shockwave)

One Direction — Story of my life
(The boy who wouldn't grow up)

Dexter Britain — On my way home
(Meeting Hook)

Ed Sheeran — Kiss me
(Let me kiss you)

Tunes of Fantasy — My world
(The Dance)

Edward Scissorhands — Icedance
(Bits of a treasure)

Christina Perri — Human
(There once was a love. Stealing Angel)

ANNA KATMORE

Martin Herzberg — Variations of Dragostea din tei
(Broken door)

One Direction — You & I
(You and I)

Ed Sheeran and Christina Grimmie — All of the stars
(I'll show you a mermaid)

Once Upon A Time Theme music
(Saving Angel)

Tunes of Fantasy — White Angel
(The bargain)

Casper Soundtracl — Casper's lullaby
(Until we meet again)

Jonatha Brooke — Second star to the right
(Ten years later...)

Dexter Britain — Conquering time
(With magic...)

Here's Anna Katmore's sweetly romantic recipe for falling in love with an angel!

He's annoyingly gorgeous, provocative, and fast becoming her best friend. But he also has a secret that makes the little hairs on her arms stand on end...

It wasn't nicking an expensive watch or diamond bracelet that landed streetwise Jona Montiniere in the clutches of the police. It was a darn sweater. A judge decides that she has to return to her terminally ill mother, who dumped her in an orphanage more than twelve years ago. Worse, for the coming six weeks, she has to do charity work on an estranged aunt's vineyards in France.

Yeah, right.

Jona is determined to sneak off at the first chance she gets. But then she meets Julian, her mother's caretaker. Playful, understanding, and sinfully sexy, he's everything she dreams of—but she'd be damned if she let him know.

So when the first week in her new home is over, Jona is asking herself two things. One, how could it happen that she ended up in Julian's arms after only three days? And two, how the hell did he just awaken her mother from the dead...?

The sweet, hot and funny
Grover Beach Team series!
By Anna Katmore

*

Play With Me

Ryan Hunter

T Is For...

Kiss With Cherry Flavor

Special thanks
to my wonderful Street Team!

Jessa Markert, Silje Victoria Kirketeig, Krystle Lynn
Thomas, Felisha Miller, Connie Nguyen, Tiffany Williams,
Stevie Morell, Norma Salazar, Nikisha Evans McKinney,
Cassi Haley-Munday, Shannon R Miller Hodges, Diana
Terrado, Jennifer Herondale, Alesia Jean Farnham,
Ashlynd Kyle, and Crystal Scott

ABOUT THE AUTHOR

ANNA KATMORE prefers blue to green, spring to winter, and writing to almost everything else. It helps her escape from a boring world to something with actual adventure and romance, she says. Even when she's not crafting a new story, you'll see her lounging with a book in some quiet spot. She was 17 when she left Vienna to live in the tranquil countryside of Austria, and from there she loves to plan trips with her family to anywhere in the world. Two of her favorite places? Disneyland and the deep dungeons of her creative mind.

For more information, please visit her website at www.annakatmore.com

17543556R00208

Made in the USA
San Bernardino, CA
13 December 2014